HORSE THIEF

The kidnap of Sir Gert, the famous racehorse, and the disappear-ance of Rory and his old mare Shera become intertwined in this thrilling adventure story.

When Da sets off to find Rory – and the three English girls – Sam, Nina and Jenny – discover not one but two horses on their new farm, a train of events is unleashed which involves the police, the gang of ruthless horse thieves, the Concerned Parents, the kids - and a few others! – all tracking each other through the dense woods.

The plot twists and turns with ever-increasing tension, and ends with a surprise!

About *Bike Hunt*, Hugh Galt's first book, winner of the IRISH BOOK AWARDS Young People's Books medal:

'At last a teenage novel set convincingly in an urban setting. The plot is fast-moving, keeping the reader turning the pages right to the very end'
CONSUMER CHOICE

'This is a real thriller for kids ... I think everyone would like this book, girls and boys ... brilliant.'
RTE GUIDE

'A must for 9-13s ... a thrilling story ... the book is extremely exciting and moves quickly. It is full of new ideas.'
THE SUNDAY PRESS

'Extremely good ... well worth reading.'
IN DUBLIN

HUGH GALT

Horse Thief is Hugh's second book. His first, *Bike Hunt*, also an exciting adventure story set in contemporary Dublin, has sold very successfully in many parts of the world and has been translated into German, French, Italian, Dutch and Danish.

Born in West Scotland and educated in Edinburgh, Hugh went to London to train as a journalist. After working for a few years in journalism in Edinburgh, he set off for Mexico, but somehow ended up in Ireland! He worked in the West of Ireland for several years – as a disc jockey, then in fishing, and he and a friend salvaged a sunken trawler which they rebuilt completely.

For many years he has lived near Dublin and worked as senior sub-editor at the *Irish Independent* newspaper.

HORSE THIEF

◆

HUGH GALT

THE O'BRIEN PRESS
DUBLIN

First published 1992 by The O'Brien Press Ltd.,
20 Victoria Road, Dublin 6, Ireland.

British Library Cataloguing-in-publication Data
Galt, Hugh
Horse Thief
I. Title
823.914 [J]

ISBN 0-86278-278-3

10 9 8 7 6 5 4 3 2 1

Typesetting and layout: The O'Brien Press
Cover illustration: Cathy Henderson
Separations: The City Office, Dublin
Printing: Cox and Wyman Ltd.

Prologue

THE NIGHT AIR was dank and sweaty after a day of lashing rain. On top of a low tower on a grand country house somewhere in the Irish midlands, a large clock showed it was almost one a.m.

A figure emerged from the shadows at the rear of the house, and hopped its way across puddles and squelchy stuff towards several neat rows of low, white-painted buildings nearby. It was a youth of about eighteen, very small and slight for his age, dressed in old riding boots and a long hunting jacket. He looked like an off-duty jockey, and indeed a jockey was exactly what he wanted to be in years to come. Right now, he was a stable boy at one of the top horse stud farms in the country, and he was on his way to make a last check on all the retired famous racehorses in his charge, before he could finally fall into bed.

He glanced up into the blackness for any sign of a renewed downpour, then yawned as he hurried towards the stables. He'd started watching a late-night movie while he waited for the rain to stop, and hadn't realised it was so late. Should've been fast asleep an hour-and-a-half ago, he told himself. Have to be up at seven to exercise the horses.

He yawned again as he turned the corner to the first row of stables. But what he saw there made the yawn freeze into a gape of astonishment.

Standing in front of the stall that held Sir Gert, the most famous of all the famous horses in the stables, were four black-clothed figures with black balaclavas over their heads.

The stable boy stood stock still, staring in shock. The four figures had turned sharply at the sound of his step, and seemed just as startled by his presence as he was by theirs.

They stood like this, staring at each other, for what seemed like an age, though it was in fact only two or three seconds. Then the stable boy muttered 'Jeez!' and took a step backwards, then a second.

He never took the third. A black-gloved hand appeared suddenly from behind him and pressed a thick pad over his mouth and nose. Sickly fumes flooded into his throat and lungs. He tried to cry out, but before he could make even a token struggle, his mind went blank and he sagged into oblivion.

The black figures immediately unfroze into silent action. Two of them leapt forward to help the fifth man drag the drugged stableboy to an empty stall, where they dumped him unceremoniously on the straw. The other two meantime opened a small black bag from which they took a big hypodermic syringe, the kind vets use on large animals, and proceeded to fill it from a plastic bottle.

When it was full, one of them held it up and gave it a squirt to test it.

The others came back, and all five exchanged a tense, silent look before they swung open the top door of the stall. In the warm steamy darkness of the stable, a horse snorted, almost as if in annoyance at being disturbed at this hour. The men stood either side of the door, waiting. Then the curious stallion's head appeared. Large, chestnut brown, and perfectly formed, the dark eyes glinting with mute intelligence. Sir Gert.

Instantly, the black figures jumped forward and grabbed the halter. The horse jerked back in surprise, but before he could pull himself free, the hypodermic needle had been jammed into his neck and the plunger pushed home. With a sharp whinny of pain and protest, Sir Gert wrenched free of their grasp and disappeared back into the darkness.

The men stood waiting tensely, one of them counting seconds on his watch. Then he nodded to the others, and they warily opened both doors of the stall. Two of them entered, and after a few moments, re-emerged leading the now drugged and docile stallion by a rope. They led him off in the direction of the main gates, while the others closed up the stall and listened for any sound of activity in the big house, before they too disappeared into the damp night.

The rain began again, filling the night with the faint hiss of falling water. Somewhere beyond the main gates, a heavy engine started up.

Moments later, the faint outline of an articulated lorry pulling a box trailer passed across the main gate, and was swallowed up in the dark downpour.

In their stalls, the other horses in the stable pawed the straw restlessly and made low huffing noises, as if they knew what had just happened. Sir Gert had been kidnapped.

1

The Inheritance

IN THE LARGE, UNTIDY GARDEN of a Victorian stone cottage in the English midlands, two girls dragged large cardboard boxes of rubbish towards a roaring bonfire.

'Don't get too close to the flames this time, Jenny!' the elder ordered the younger. 'You've nearly set yourself on fire twice already.'

'Oh, shut up, Sam!' Jenny snapped back. 'I'm nearly eleven – I know how to look after myself!'

It was obvious they were sisters. Both had fair hair and blue eyes, and the same strong-limbed, square-shouldered bodies. But overlaid on their facial resemblance were expressions that bespoke totally different personalities.

Sam – real name Samantha – was nearly fourteen, and beginning to change shape. Her eyes had a faintly distant, in-turned look about them, as if she was constantly mulling over things that nobody else could possibly understand. She seemed to observe the world from the outside, and her normal reaction to what she saw was either cool disdain or snappy irritation. And it was the irritation that was best known to Jenny.

For Jenny, by contrast, was just the type to drive a dreamer like Sam up the wall. Impulsive, noisy, scatterbrained, cheeky, and innocently thoughtless about other people's private space and things. Living with her was like living with an untrained chimpanzee, Sam frequently moaned. The two sisters feuded constantly.

Once they got close enough to the leaping flames, Jenny immediately began pulling rubbish from her box and throwing it onto the fire. Her eyes glinted gleefully as the blaze crackled, and the ash of incinerated cardboard whirled upwards in the smoky heat haze.

'Don't put too much on at once!' Sam warned her.

'Quit bossing me, will you!' Jenny snapped back without looking at her. 'I don't want the fire to go out.'

Defiantly, she threw on another armful of rubbish, and grinned as the flames roared ever higher.

'That's enough!' Sam ordered, stepping back from the heat. 'I'll tell Garry if you don't stop it!'

The bonfire was at the far end of the long garden, which was virtually all laid out with vegetable and soft fruit patches. These had been lovingly tended till quite recently, but now only a few neglected plants still stood in the beds, surrounded by invading weeds. Down one side was a high green hedge, and along the other were some old low fruit trees, just casting their early summer bloom. Between the trees stood Garry, the girls' father, an athletic-looking man with an untidy beard and hair of burnt gold, going thin on top. He had his back to the fire as he stared grimfaced over a sagging fence into what had once been the grounds of a large house. The house itself was now a pile of rubble which a mechanical excavator was noisily piling into an enormous truck. Another excavator was growling aggressively nearby as it pushed over stately old trees. A gang of site workers attacked the thick trunks with chainsaws as soon as they fell, slicing them into segments destined to be sold off as firewood.

Garry's eyes were narrow and his lips tight, and his shoulders rose and fell as he let out a faint snort of frustrated anger. He reached out to touch the bark of the apple tree nearest him for a moment, then abruptly turned and marched back to the girls at the fire.

The argument over the rubbish had by now turned physical. Sam was trying to pull Jenny's box away from her, and Jenny was resisting with the tight-jawed determination of a young bulldog.

'That's enough!' Garry yelled at them.

But it was too late. The box tore asunder, and both girls fell backwards into the ashy churned-up soil.

'You little monster!' Sam hissed as she pulled her caked hands from the mud and looked down at her muck-covered bottom. 'That's my best pair of Levi's!'

'Good! Serves you right!' Jenny spat impishly at her. She scrambled to her feet and prepared to run from her furious sister, but Garry arrived in time to prevent any real violence.

'I warned you to be careful around the fire!' he barked at them, but he seemed distracted and the words had no real force.

He pulled Sam up from the mud. 'Look at the pair of you now! We've enough on our plate without adding a pile of filthy laundry to it.'

'It was her fault!' Jenny announced innocently.

'No it wasn't!' Sam retorted. 'You started it by being stupid!'

'Sam,' Garry said wearily. 'You're old enough now to know better than to get involved in these childish squabbles.'

From behind Garry's back, Jenny pulled a face and made a rude gesture at Sam. Sam flushed red and opened her mouth to protest, but her words were cut short by the sound of a car. An elderly red Renault 4 rattled along the driveway at the side of the cottage and came to a halt beside the large white rust-spotted van that belonged to Garry.

Garry's face changed instantly. 'Ah. They've arrived.'

Two figures got out of the car as he marched back down the garden towards it. One was a slim pale-faced woman with long curly dark hair and very bright brown eyes. She wore a black top and jeans, market-stall jewellery, and an Arab-style scarf round her neck. The impression she made was vaguely hippy-ish.

The second person was a girl somewhere between the ages of Sam and Jenny. Her face, hair and build were so like the woman's it was obvious they were mother and daughter. She was dressed in a black miniskirt, Doc Martens, and a cheap imitation of a biker's leather jacket. She didn't look too happy about being here.

'Hi there!' Garry greeted them, his mood completely changed. He went straight up to the woman and lifted her off the ground in an affectionate bearhug. 'Monica, you look terrific!'

'You too!' Monica told him, and kissed him on the lips. 'Now quit squeezing me. I'm too full after my lunch!'

Garry put her down and stood looking into her eyes, a big grin all over his face. Monica prodded him playfully in the belly. 'You've been overeating again, haven't you?'

'Junk food,' he agreed. 'Nobody's looking after me.'

'Maybe you should ask somebody.'

'Maybe I should. How's London?'

'Hell. I hate the place. But where else can you go to earn a living these days? If you can call it a living.'

At the bonfire, Sam and Jenny stood motionless, watching all this, feud forgotten. The new girl, hands in pockets, sent them a long nonchalant stare. Sam and Jenny turned their heads just enough to exchange a glance of solidarity.

'Hey, you two!' Garry waved a muscular arm at them. 'Come down here and say hello to Monica and Nina!'

The two girls trudged unenthusiastically down the garden together. 'Hi,' they said in flat unison.

'Well, don't we get a hug? A handshake even?' Monica demanded cheerfully.

Sam and Jenny showed their hands. 'We got a bit mucky,' Sam explained.

'Oh. Making mudpies?' Nina asked with the vaguest hint of a sneer. 'That must be fun.'

'Nina!' Monica said in a warning voice, as Sam and Jenny glared back. But a crescendo from the roaring machinery beyond the trees made Monica turn away.

'So they've started,' she frowned. 'How long before they move in to knock this place down?'

'We've got three weeks to get out,' Garry told her. His face had hardened again. 'In six months' time, right here where we're standing, there'll be a motorway.'

They all turned to watch as the top of a high tree leaned slowly sideways and then crashed out of sight behind the patchy apple blossom.

'If Birmingham goes on expanding like this,' Garry muttered, 'there won't be any countryside left at all.'

'What are you going to do?' Monica asked him. 'Have you found another place to rent yet?'

'Ah. Well, that's what I wanted to talk to you about.' His face changed again. A determined glint came into his eyes.

'You're being very mysterious,' Monica frowned. 'What's going on that you couldn't tell me on the phone?'

Garry didn't reply. He turned to the three girls, stuck a hand in his pocket, and produced a fiver.

'Listen, Monica and I have got something important to discuss. Why don't you three go down to the shop and get yourselves some crisps and chocolate and things?'

Sam stared at the proffered note in surprise, but Jenny turned longingly to the bonfire.

'But Dad!' she objected, 'we've got lots more stuff to burn!'

'Jenny,' Garry said sternly. 'Don't argue.'

Sam snatched the fiver and herded Jenny off towards the drive. Monica flicked her head at Nina in a silent instruction to follow them. Nina gave her a rebellious glare, but turned to follow the others, shoulders slumped.

Garry and Monica watched as Sam and Jenny quickly rinsed the muck off their hands under a tap on the side of the cottage, already into a new argument about who was going to buy what. Then they disappeared along the driveway onto the road, Nina plodding along behind them with heavy steps.

Garry shook his head. 'They get worse instead of better as they get older.'

Monica put an arm through his. 'Ah, come on. They're fine kids. You've done a great job bringing them up over the last three years, since their mother died.'

A brief cloud passed over Garry's face, then disappeared. 'You've done pretty well as a single parent yourself.'

Monica kissed him quickly. 'See? We're brilliant, the two of us. Now what's this big mystery you want to talk to me about?'

Jenny and Sam had already made their purchases and were wolfing down potato crisps when Nina eventually sauntered up to the shop.

Sam held out a fistful of hot coins at her. 'We didn't know what you'd like, so you can buy your own.'

Nina coolly took the money and stuck it in a pocket. 'Thanks. But I never touch that kind of muck. We're vegetarian.'

Jenny pulled an exaggerated face of distaste. 'Vegetarian? Ooooh, scum!'

Nina shrugged her eyebrows superciliously, and turned her head to watch some boys playing football on a patch of grass on the other side of the road.

Sam nudged Jenny, then addressed Nina. 'What's it like living in London then, Nina?'

'Cool,' Nina replied without turning around. 'Lot more buzz than this deadsville, anyway.'

Sam nudged Jenny again as they munched their crisps. 'We might be going to live in London too, y'know,' she went on.

Nina turned back. 'Yeah? Your dad got a job there, has he?'

Sam and Jenny exchanged a knowing grin.

'Na. He won't have to bother about jobs any more,' Jenny informed her cockily.

'And if we go to London, WE won't be living in bedsits or flats, will we?' Sam jumped in. 'We'll probably buy our own house. Somewhere nice. Chelsea, maybe.'

Nina gave them a sceptical look. 'You won the pools?'

Sam and Jenny exchanged another grinning glance. They were enjoying this. But while Sam was thinking how to spin out the tease, Jenny gave the game away.

'Our dad's inherited a farm!'

'A farm?' Nina echoed. 'You're winding me up.'

'No, serious!' Jenny insisted, spraying bits of half-chewed crisps onto Nina's boots. 'A real farm! With a farmhouse and fields and all! Soon as he sells it, we'll be rich!'

Nina wavered, still unsure whether this was a joke or not. 'Where is this farm, then?'

'In Ireland,' said Sam.

'Ireland?' Nina repeated, incredulous.

Monica was having the same reaction at that very moment. 'It's true, I swear,' Garry assured her, his face alight with enthusiasm as he emptied the last of the rubbish onto the bonfire.

'But who in Ireland would want to leave a farm to you? You've never even been there, have you?' Monica protested.

Garry shook his head in agreement. 'I couldn't believe it myself when I got the letter. It belonged to some old bachelor uncle of my mother's. Her family came from over there – her maiden name was O'Dwyer. Anyway, this old guy had no surviving close relatives except my mother. He didn't want the government over there to get the proceeds of selling the place if he died without an heir, so he made a will in her favour. Then about a year ago, he got seriously ill and tried to get in touch with Ma to tell her what was coming to her. When he discovered she was already dead, he changed the will to my name, even though he didn't even know me. He just wanted somebody, anybody, to have it rather than the government. Apparently he was trying to trace me when he popped off. His solicitors tracked me down – don't ask me how. Look, here's the letter.'

He pulled some crumpled folded-up sheets of paper from his shirt pocket and handed them to Monica. She opened them out and skimmed her eyes over the words, looking a bit dazed.

'Eighteen acres,' she read out. 'Is that big?'

'Not really,' said Garry. 'It's a small family farm.'

'And there's a house?'

Garry produced some small photographs. 'They sent me these snaps of it.'

Monica looked. The photos, badly taken from a distance, showed a small two-storey building, nestling amid greenery.

'Looks nice. How much do you think you'll get for it when you sell it?'

Garry stood beside her to look at the photos. 'I'm not going to sell it,' he announced quietly but firmly.

'You're not? What are you going to do with it, then?'

'Live in it.'

Monica stared at him. 'You're not serious!' she said finally.

'I am,' he assured her. 'The way I look at it is this. I've no job and not much hope of getting one while this recession lasts. I'm about to be thrown out of my home, and I'd have a helluva job finding another one without any money. Then out of the blue, somebody leaves me this place. It's like a gift from the gods. Somebody up there is telling me to go and live in Ireland.'

Monica was amazed. 'You mean, you're going to be a farmer?'

'Not quite,' he grinned. 'An organic vegetable grower. Just like I was doing in this garden, only on a much bigger scale. Commercially. I read in the paper the government over there gives grants to anyone who wants to go into the business. And the climate is ideal for it. Mild winters and plenty of rain.'

Monica stared at him for a moment, shaking her head. 'And what do the girls think of this?'

'I haven't told them yet. I wanted to talk to you first.'

'Me?'

'Yes, you.' He took a deep breath. 'Monica. I want you and Nina to come with us.'

Monica's mouth fell open. 'Garry ...'

'Listen, Monica,' he went on intensely. 'You and I have been having this on-off relationship for two years now. It's make or break time now. The crunch. I know you hate having to live in London to get work. And you're always talking about how you'd love to live in the country. Well, here's our opportunity to solve everything at once.'

Concern came into Monica's eyes. 'Garry, what are you talking about? Getting married?'

He looked at his feet then back into her eyes. 'Sure. If you want. I don't mind. Well actually ... I'd really like that.'

Monica put her hand to her forehead. 'This is too much! Garry, I tried marriage before and look how that turned out. I swore I'd never put myself through that hell again.'

'But we're both older and wiser than we used to be. It doesn't have to be the same. But if you'd rather we just lived together, well, that's okay by me too.'

'Hang on a minute!' Monica laughed dizzily. 'You're jumping from A to Z. I need time to take all this in. Think about it!'

Garry smiled and nodded. 'Right. I'll go and make some coffee. You've got five minutes.'

Monica gaped after him as he strode down the garden towards the cottage.

Back at the shop, the girls sat on a low wall while Jenny enthusiastically reeled off a long list of fantasies about all the things she would buy with the farm money. But Sam and Nina were only half-listening. Their attention kept sneaking away to the footballers on the other side of the road.

The boys too had become aware of the spectators, and their shouts had grown louder and their sporting antics more theatrical. The furious game edged closer and closer to the road.

'What are you two peeping at over there?' Jenny finally demanded.

'Nothing,' Sam snapped at her. 'I was just thinking about something.'

Nina looked at the outsize watch on her wrist. 'Suppose we can head back now. Half-hour's nearly up.'

'I wonder what they wanted to talk about in private?' Jenny asked, her mouth full of yet more chocolate.

'Probably wanted to tell her about the farm,' said Sam.

They started to walk back up the road. The boys saw them going, and slowed the frantic pace of their athletic efforts.

'Hey, Sam!' one of them shouted as a pass intended for him sailed past onto the road. He was taller and a bit older than the others, with stylishly cut blond hair. 'Fancy comin' down the canal for a bit? We got a bottle of cider!'

Sam pretended not to hear, and walked on stiffly.

'Do you know him?' Nina asked, glancing back furtively.

'Only to see,' Sam replied dismissively. 'He goes to the same school.'

'And he picks his nose and wipes it on the school bus seats,' Jenny announced with contempt. 'I saw him.'

'I suppose you've got boyfriends in London?' Sam asked Nina without looking around.

'Boyfriends?' Nina snorted. 'I'd rather have a headache. They're dipsticks the lot of them.'

'Yeah. Right,' Sam agreed. But they both caught each other darting a look back at the footballers.

'Hurry up, you two!' Jenny shouted as she ran ahead. 'We don't want the fire to go out!'

Garry and Monica were sitting on the bench behind the cottage when the girls arrived back. At their feet were two half-empty cups of coffee and an open wine bottle. They each had one arm round the other as they gulped wine from large glasses. Garry was talking excitedly while Monica listened and shook her head in a giggly daze.

'There you are, girls!' Garry called out when he spotted them. 'We were beginning to think you'd got lost!'

'But you told us not to come back for half an hour!' Sam protested, indignant and puzzled.

'Never mind that,' he told her. 'Come over here, we've got something to tell you. Does Nina know about the farm yet?'

The girls nodded. Garry glanced at Monica before he went on.

'Well then. How would you three fancy it if we all went to live there?'

The girls froze for a moment. Then Jenny threw herself on him, making him spill his wine. 'That's a brilliant idea, Dad! I want to, I want to, I want to! Can I have a horse? Please?!'

'D'you mean, go and live in Ireland? On a farm? All five of us?' Sam said slowly. Garry nodded, grinning expectantly.

'But Ireland's full of nothing but bogs and terrorists!'

Garry laughed. 'The terrorists are all in Belfast. We'll be in County Cavan, a long way away. It might have a few bogs here and there, but it's got beautiful lakes and woods and hills. Here. Look at the map.'

He handed Sam a map that was lying on the bench. Jenny jumped up to look at the spot he had marked on it.

Nina stared at Monica, confused. 'What's this got to do with us, Mom?'

Monica looked awkward for a moment. 'Well. Garry and I have decided we'd like to be together, Nina.'

'You mean, married?'

'Well, kind of,' Gary intervened, a bit awkward. 'We're just going to be together at first. Till we see how things work out.'

'But I don't want to live in sodding Ireland!' Nina burst out. 'I want to live in London. I want to be near cinemas and gear shops and things. There's nothing like that in County what's-its-name!'

'Cavan,' Garry prompted. 'But it's only a couple of hours' drive from Dublin. It's not the Australian outback.'

Sam handed the map back, frowning. 'I don't fancy the sound of it either. I thought we were going to buy a house in some nice place around here?'

Garry and Monica exchanged an exasperated look.

'Honest, kids, it'll be great. An adventure. A big holiday. We'll go over there for six months to see how it works out. Come Christmas, if it hasn't turned out okay, and the majority of us wants to quit, well, then we can sell up and come back. That's democratic now. Is it a deal?'

Nina scowled, Sam looked dubious, but Jenny was jumping up and down. 'I want a horse! I want a horse!'

Garry looked at Monica and shrugged. 'We'll leave you to talk it over between yourselves for a bit,' he told the girls, and motioned Monica to follow him indoors. 'Once you've got over the shock, I bet you'll get really excited about the idea.'

'I hope that's true for me too!' said Monica.

Monica and Garry went inside and closed the kitchen door. Jenny grabbed both Sam and Nina by an arm and tried to drag them into a dance of joy.

'We're going to have a horse, we're going to have a horse!' she kept chanting.

'I don't want a horse!' said Nina, and tried to free herself from Jenny's grip. 'I'd rather have a motorbike.'

Jenny stopped jumping as something suddenly struck her. She looked from one to other. 'I just realised. If Garry and Monica are going to be together, that means all three of us are going to be sisters! Isn't that terrific!'

She started jigging up and down again. Across the top of her bobbing head, Nina and Sam exchanged cold stares.

2
A Boy and His Horse

ACROSS A BARREN STRETCH of wasteground in a tatty suburb of Dublin's northside, Rory Brennan, thirteen, ran for all he was worth.

His square chest heaved with exertion, and his face was contorted with anxiety and rage. At a distance behind him followed his friend Hoppy, a smaller boy with a pale face and blond hair, stumbling and hopping along as fast as his bad leg would allow him.

Ahead of them, on the far side of the rubbish-littered ground, was a group of young skinheads wearing tight jeans, teeshirts, braces and combat boots. They stood in a wide circle, laughing and jeering and whooping as they watched another of their gang riding around and around bareback on a scruffy little piebald mare.

The unfortunate horse looked totally exhausted. Its muddy flanks heaved, and flecks of white foam blew from its black lips with every gasping breath. But the rider, a skinhead with a squashed, aggressive-looking face, goaded the animal on without mercy. He lashed its sides with the free end of the rope reins, and kicked its soft belly with his big boots to force it to keep up the gruelling pace.

'Get off my horse! Get off my horse!' Rory tried to roar at them as he drew near. But he was just as out of breath as the horse, and his voice was drowned out by harsh rock music blaring from a ghettoblaster standing on an old oil drum nearby.

He reached the circle of skinheads just as horse and rider were coming around again. Before any of them had a chance to realise what was happening, he charged through them and grabbed the horse's rope halter. The horse slithered to a halt as he hung all his weight on her neck to pull her up. The rider, startled, almost fell off.

'Get off!' Rory snarled up at him, almost in tears. 'Get off my horse!'

A look of vicious anger squashed the rider's face even more.

'What d'ya mean your horse!' he spat down at Rory. 'This nag's ours. We found it, didn't we, lads? Now let go of that before I flay yer ears off!'

He whipped Rory around the head with the rope rein and kicked the horse's flanks at the same time. The frightened, sweating mare tried to set off again, dragging Rory with it. The onlooking skinheads laughed and roared obscenities as horse, rider and Rory staggered clumsily round.

Unnoticed, Rory's friend Hoppy hobbled up behind them, panting. He stopped to watch for a moment, then bent down to pick up a stone. He took careful aim, then lobbed it through the air across the heads of the roaring skinheads. It came down right on top of the rider's skull. A perfect shot.

'Ayah!'

The rider's head contracted into his shoulders as he clutched his shaven scalp. His eyes screwed up in pain. Seeing his chance, Rory grabbed a black boot, heaved with all his strength, and sent the skinhead toppling off into the churned-up earth.

The other skinheads tittered for a moment, then went silent. Rory tried to calm the nervous mare, holding it tight to stop it running off in a panic. On the ground, the rider rolled over and looked around for a moment, before getting slowly to his feet. His face was white with vicious anger. Hoppy began to back slowly away.

'Grab that little brat there!' the rider ordered the other skinheads, pointing to Hoppy. 'I'm gonna break his other leg after I've dealt with this one!'

Hoppy turned quickly to hobble off, but only managed one-and-a-half steps before they grabbed him. Holding him roughly, the skinheads turned to watch their leader advance on Rory and the horse. A thin trickle of blood ran from his stubbly head and onto his forehead.

'You can't treat Shera like that!' Rory shouted at him, anger making him fearless. 'She's too old. It'll kill her!'

'It's you that's gonna get killed!' the rider hissed back.

He jumped forward and grabbed Rory by his dark red hair. But before he could raise his fist, the sound of a lorry braking to a halt, horn honking, made them all look around.

On the road bordering the waste ground, a battered flatbacked lorry had pulled up. A hydraulic lifting arm stuck up behind the cab, and the back of the lorry was piled with scrap – old washing machines, prams, other tangles of unrecognisable metal. The door of the cab instantly flew open, and a rough thickset man, wearing cheap brown-rimmed spectacles, jumped out and started running towards the group.

'Da!' Rory shouted gratefully.

The rider held onto Rory's hair, but the other skinheads dropped Hoppy in a heap and started backing away.

'It's The Scrapper!' one of them warned the rider. 'Better move, Brazzer. He's a headcase.'

Brazzer, the rider, watched for a moment as Rory's father broke into a trot and began bearing ominously down on them. Then he let go of Rory's hair, leapt to snatch up the ghettoblaster, and sprinted off after his fast-retreating friends.

Rory's father, The Scrapper Brennan, lumbered up to Rory and the mare as Hoppy got unsteadily to his feet.

'You all right?' Scrapper asked his son. He was breathing heavily, and his eyebrows were bunched tight behind his spectacles, one leg of which was bound together with sticking plaster.

'Okay,' Rory assured him, his attention still on the distressed mare. 'They were riding Shera into the ground.'

Scrapper glared across the horse's bare back at the band of skinheads, who had regrouped at a safe distance.

'Bleedin' scum!' Scrapper muttered. 'How'd they get hold of her anyway?'

'They broke her out of the yard,' Hoppy volunteered from behind. 'I saw them and warned Rory.' He had a pixie-like face but the dark twinkling eyes of a cunning old man. Apart from his leg – damaged in a car accident when he was much younger – his body was lean and well-shaped, and radiated animal energy. Something in his manner suggested he was desperate to be liked and accepted, but only by the chosen few he admired. The rest of the world he regarded with contempt, and gleefully carried on guerilla warfare against it whenever he got the chance.

Scrapper went around the horse, and stood, legs apart, pointing threateningly at the skinheads.

'I'll get a hold of you someday, Quinlan,' he roared. 'And I'll break your bleedin' arms when I do!'

The leader of the skinheads gave him the fingers, face contorted in a sneer.

'My oul' fellah'll break yer legs!' he yelled back.

Scrapper snorted. 'Your oul' fellah? Will you go on out of that! I threw bigger men than him at dogs when stones were scarce!'

'Yaah! You're past it, Scrapper,' the skinhead leader jeered back.

Scrapper suddenly made a little sprint in the direction of the skinheads. They turned in panic and fled down various side streets. Scrapper turned back, his mouth a white line of anger.

'Come on. Let's go home,' he told Rory. 'You go ahead with the horse and Hoppy can come with me.'

Rory turned Shera towards the road and coaxed her gently away, while Scrapper took Hoppy by one arm and helped him to hop over to the lorry.

Scrapper was silent at first as the lorry grumbled along behind Rory and Shera. Hoppy could see by the way his work-battered fists gripped the steering wheel that he was still fighting mad. Rory's Da was a legend in the area for the battles he had fought with other local hard men in his youth. He was older and quieter now. But 'past it'? Hoppy didn't fancy the chances of anyone who tried to prove that.

'Why's Rory so mad about that old carthorse, anyway?' Hoppy wondered out loud eventually. 'She's too old and slow.'

'Ah, he's always been more friendly with animals than people, ever since he was small,' Scrapper grumbled. 'But I'm sorry now I bought the nag for him. Nothin' but trouble, she is. And you should hear the missus go on about the smell off his clothes. Mind you, she was always too hard on him, whatever he did. Maybe that's the problem with him.'

They both looked out at Rory leading Shera along the road in front of them.

'When I get old enough, I'm gonna get me some real transport,' Hoppy announced. 'Kawasaki 1000cc. Vroom, vroom!' He held his arms out and mimed riding a motorcycle.

'Hey!' he went on. 'Did you hear any more about that racehorse that got kidnapped last night?'

Scrapper's mood changed. 'Sir Gert? Na, it was all over the papers this morning, but I didn't get a chance to look at them. Too bleedin' busy.' He looked at his watch, then reached for the radio switch. 'It's probably on the news.'

He switched on just in time to catch the lunchtime bulletin. First came the introductory fanfare, then the announcer's voice.

'Today's main news story,' said the voice, 'is the dramatic kidnapping from a County Kildare stud of Sir Gert, one of the greatest and most valuable racehorses of all time. Earlier today it was reported that the owners, a group of international businessmen, have received a ransom demand for one million pounds for the horse's safe return. However, the special police team set up to investigate were unable to confirm or deny this, and so far, no group has claimed responsibility.'

'A million?' Hoppy whistled.

'Sure!' said Scrapper. 'Sir Gert must be worth at least ten times that. He's won every big race worth running.'

The news announcer had already moved on: 'Sir Gert was taken from his stable a few miles from Kildare town last night by a gang who drugged a stable boy. They are believed to have made their getaway several hours before the alarm was raised. Here now with the details is our security correspondent, Tom McCaughren.'

Scrapper reached out to lower the volume, as outside Rory and Shera turned down a rutted laneway between terraces of small houses.

'Bet it was the Provos!' said Hoppy, almost happily.

Scrapper manoeuvred the lorry into the bumpy lane. 'Well, whoever they are they must be well away by now. I just hope they don't do the animal any harm. I won a good few bets on Sir Gert before he retired, so I've a bit of a soft spot for him. Here we go.'

At the end of the lane, Rory had pulled open the rickety wooden gates of Scrapper's yard, which was filled to overflowing with scrap and junk. Rory led Shera across the yard to a low shed, while Scrapper eased the lorry in, turned off the engine, and helped Hoppy to jump down.

'They got in over there,' Hoppy told Scrapper, and pointed to the wall above the shed.

Rory was filling a battered metal baby bath with horse feed for Shera, but he looked around when he heard Hoppy's words.

'Can we put up some barbed wire there, Da?' he asked. He had the same thick shoulders as Scrapper, only smaller, and his mouth made the same white line in anger.

'They won't come back,' Scrapper assured him. 'They wouldn't dare. Come on now – we're way late for the dinner. Ma will be raging again.'

He turned and walked back out to the lane. Rory beckoned Hoppy into the shed. 'Keep an eye on her till I get back, right?'

Hoppy nodded, and watched Rory hurry off after his father. Hoppy had always felt drawn to Rory by a kind of fellow-feeling of misfits. Rory was an oddball, but dead straight. Not like most of the other messers in the area, whose idea of a great time was plaguing the life out of anybody who couldn't get back at them. All the same, Hoppy had to admit to himself, there was something annoying about Rory. You could only get so far with him, and then zip! he was gone. Almost as if he couldn't handle being friendly.

Rory and Scrapper reached the end of the lane and turned out of sight. Hoppy snorted, and looked at Shera.

'What've you got that I don't?' he asked her.

Shera kept her muzzle in the battered bath and ate gratefully while Hoppy leaned back against the wall of the shed and watched her.

'Well, one thing,' he said to her twitching ears. 'There's not much chance of you being held to ransom, sweetheart. You can't be worth ten quid at this stage, never mind a million.'

Rory's house was a drab two-storey terraced house exactly like all the hundreds of others in the district. He caught up with Scrapper at the front door and they went in together, warily and quietly. But no sooner had they gently closed the door behind them than the kitchen door at the far end of the narrow hall jerked open. Ma appeared, glaring at both of them with narrowed lips.

'So there ye are!' she greeted them. She was a thin, almost scrawny woman, untidily dressed in old clothes. She might have been good-looking in her youth, but time and habitual ill-temper had given her face an unattractive pinched look.

'What kept ye?' she went on. 'The dinner's on the table half an hour. Don't go complaining to me now if it's cold!'

Scrapper meekly hung up his jacket. Despite the fighting-man legend, he was quite evidently not the boss within these walls. He moved sheepishly towards the kitchen door, and Rory followed, taking shelter behind his father's broad shape.

'Sorry,' Scrapper told Ma with a forced little smile. 'We were delayed. Some skinheads went joyriding on Rory's horse.'

Ma let out a disgusted snort. 'That horse again!'

She turned around and Scrapper and Rory followed her in.

The kitchen was small and cramped, and in need of redecoration. At the table in the middle sat Rory's brother Anto, an adolescent smoothie of about fifteen, busily wolfing up the last forkfuls of his dinner. His modishly cut hair was shiny with gel, and he wore a cowboy-style string necktie at the collar of his baggy white shirt. His black jeans were new and spotless.

Bleedin' poser, Rory thought to himself. He had a deep burning contempt for Anto on account of his two-faced way of always being Ma's golden boy. She was forever holding him up to Rory as a glowing example of the Good Son who could do no wrong. But Rory knew otherwise. There was a long list of unsettled scores beween them that went back years, mainly to do with Rory getting the blame for things Anto had done, and denied.

Anto looked up and gave Rory a darting look, almost as if he had heard the silent insult. Rory sat down opposite him while Scrapper went to the sink, pulled out several unwashed pots, and began washing his mucky hands. Anto watched him from the corner of his eye, like a dog watching an unpredictable master. Rory looked down to hide a little smile. Scrapper hadn't much time for Anto, the mammy's boy.

Rory took up his knife and fork and prepared to devour the meat, potatoes and carrots on his plate. Ma started to open a can on top of a cupboard, but sudddenly stopped and sniffed. Her nose wrinkled and her brow furrowed. She turned around.

'What's that smell?' She sprang forward and grabbed Rory's leg under the table. 'Look at that on your jeans!'

Rory looked. There was a dull green stain along the bottom part of his leg. Horse manure.

'Will you get out of here and get them disgusting things off you!' Ma ordered. 'Go on!'

She pulled him off the chair and propelled him to the door. Anto looked up and smirked at Rory as he scuttled out.

'And wash yer hands while you're at it!' Ma called out as the door closed. She went back to the half-opened can, muttering. 'Sick of the stink of horses in this place, so I am. Sick of it!'

Scrapper was drying his hands. 'I don't know why you have to be so hard on him all the time.'

''Cause he never does what he's told!' she replied without looking at him. 'That's why!'

'He's just a kid,' Scrapper said quietly, and threw the towel aside.

'He's thirteen years old,' Ma objected irritably. 'Anto was twice as sensible at that age.'

'Oh yeah,' said Scrapper with a slight sneer. 'Anto. I forgot.'

Anto meanwhile had taken the opportunity, unnoticed, to steal one of the pieces of meat from Rory's plate. When Scrapper sat down beside him, he was chewing innocently on it.

'Any more spuds, Ma?' Anto inquired in a pleasant voice.

Ma finished pouring the contents of the can into a bowl, then brought over a pot. She was spooning more potatoes onto Anto's plate when the door opened and Rory reappeared, dressed in a pair of garish Bermuda shorts.

'I couldn't find anything else,' he explained uncomfortably as they all stared at him.

'I give up!' Ma muttered and took the pot back to the cooker.

Scrapper started eating while Rory sat down and looked at his plate.

'Hey! Somebody's taken my –'

'Shut up and eat!' Ma barked at him. Rory obeyed, glaring at Anto, who smiled innocently back as he chewed the stolen meat.

'That's some gas about that racehorse getting kidnapped, eh, Da?' Anto ventured. 'You gotta hand it to them for cheek.'

'Well, that's something you'd know all about,' Scrapper said drily, before shovelling a heap of food into his mouth.

Anto sagged sullenly. But the subject had reminded Rory of Shera and the skinheads.

'Da,' he said, 'maybe we should get a guard dog for the yard. Just in case.'

Scrapper looked at him with sympathetic patience.

'Look, son. I have to go down the country for a day or two, but I'll put some wire up on the wall as soon as I get the chance.' He reached one of his big battered paws to pat Rory reassuringly on the hand. 'Quit worrying, will you. They won't do it again.'

Down at the yard, Hoppy had grown bored watching Shera eat, and had wandered off to investigate the piles of junk. Machinery of any kind fascinated him. He'd learned a lot from poking around the corpses of dead cars, washing machines, fridges and all the other stuff heaped around Scrapper's yard. And then again, there was always the chance of finding a stash of stolen loot hidden in the boot of a wrecked getaway car ...

Sometimes Scrapper would give him some tools and let him try to take an engine to bits to salvage the useable parts. Hoppy loved that. He had this fantasy about being a famous inventor when he grew up, dreaming up amazing devices that would make him a fortune. Then he'd drive around in a flash car and mirrorshades, impressing the girls and giving the fingers to all the gobshites who'd tormented him. But deep down, Hoppy suspected that nothing as good as that ever happened to kids like him. He'd just end up on the dole, like his Da, and just about everyone else around here. On the scrapheap.

'Ah,' he muttered as he uncovered something. 'That looks like it could be useful.'

He dragged out a metal bar from under the junk. It was a light axle from a small trailer, about four feet long, and with a small wheel rim still attached to one end. He dug about till he found the other wheel rim, and banged it onto the axle.

'Just the job,' he told himself, admiring his handiwork.

He was so engrossed by the fascinating rubbish, he didn't notice the shaven skulls of four or five of the skinheads appearing over the top of the wall above Shera's shed. They looked down with grins of vicious glee.

'Will we do it tonight?' one of them whispered to Quinlan, the squash-faced leader.

'Na!' he leered quietly, watching the oblivious Hoppy below. 'We'll wait a while. Lull them into a false sense of security. Then we'll do a right job on him.'

They smirked an evil smirk at each other, and slid away. Below in the yard, Hoppy prodded happily among the rusting junk, and Shera went on munching from the battered bath tub.

3

The Farm

THE TEN DAYS BEFORE their departure was like a high-speed dream to the girls, as Garry and Monica rushed around getting things ready. Garry, in his usual efficient fashion, had a plan all worked out. Everyone else just had to follow his instructions, even though most of the time they didn't really know what was going on.

Monica and Nina, still dazed and bickering, were dispatched back to London to pack, and to find someone to take over their flat while they were away. It's only a trial, Monica kept insisting, we want to have some place to come back to if it doesn't work out. Quite right, Garry agreed smiling, quite right. And handed them another list of things to do.

Sam, Jenny and he set about clearing their cottage and packing the van. There was a lot of argument about what they could take and what had to be got rid of or stored with friends. But Garry was unyieldingly ruthless: essentials only to begin with, we can come back for the rest later.

Monica and Nina drove up from London the day before they were all due to set off, their small car absolutely stuffed. Garry managed to cram everything into the van, then took the Renault 4 away to a friend who was going to mind it. Finally they were all set to go.

On a bright Friday morning, they piled into the two rows of seats in the big front cab of the van. Garry locked up the cottage for the last time, and handed the keys to a waiting official from the demolition company. Jenny and Sam were nearly in tears when they saw an excavator tearing through the old fence at the back of the house, ready to start its work of devastation. But Garry was grimly cheerful as he jumped in behind the wheel and started the van's powerful engine.

'Never look back,' he advised the girls, 'always look forward.'

He jammed the van into gear, and they were off westwards, to Wales and the ferry.

Once on the road, a general mood of adventure took over. Jenny was almost hysterical with excitement, and led the girls singing pop songs in the passenger seats all the way to Holyhead. There, the massive ferry was lying in the docks, and after a short wait in the queue of vehicles, the van bounced up the ramp through the gaping bows. They were aboard.

'Let's go and have something to eat,' Monica suggested once they had climbed up to the passenger decks. But the girls were too hyped up to think of food, and wanted to scurry off to explore the ship. Even Nina seemed to be getting enthusiastic about things.

'All right,' Garry agreed, 'we'll see you on the promenade deck in about an hour.'

The girls raced quickly around the ship, then went to the stern to watch the seamen cast off the ropes. The ferry slowly manoeuvred itself out of the harbour onto the calm open sea, and the Welsh coastline began to shrink steadily away.

'Let's go up the front and look out for Ireland!' Jenny suggested, and sprinted off without waiting for the other two. Sam and Nina followed a little more sedately.

'I'm dead curious to see what it's really like,' Sam said.

'And I'm dead curious to see what Irish boys are like,' Nina replied, eyes ahead.

Sam pounced instantly. 'I thought you said boys were a headache?'

'Yeah. Right. They are.' Nina's cheeks flushed slightly. 'I just wonder if these ones'll be the same headache or different.'

Sam grinned. Nina hurried on to catch up with Jenny.

The voyage lasted only a few hours before Ireland hove into view.

'There it is!' Jenny screeched, jumping up and down at the bow rail. 'Doesn't it look fantastic!'

Nina stared silently, and Sam was unimpressed. 'Looks just like anywhere else to me.'

Garry and Monica had been sitting on a deck bench nearby, reading an Irish newspaper together. They got up to join the girls and watch the land grow steadily larger. The ferry steamed into Dublin Bay, and the city began to take shape.

Garry put an arm round Monica. 'Well, here we are. The Emerald Isle. What do you think?'

'I think we're mad,' she said flatly.

Garry laughed. 'We probably are. But it feels good to me.'

Jenny turned round and grabbed him. 'Dad! Soon as we're settled in, can we go and buy a horse?'

Garry showed her the newspaper. 'Read that first. They still go in for horse rustling over here. A gang kidnapped a famous racehorse recently, and they're looking for a million pounds ransom for it.'

Sam and Nina half-turned, mildly interested. 'A million?' Nina echoed. 'I didn't think any horse was worth that much.'

'This one evidently is,' said Garry.

'Maybe we should just make do with a hamster,' Monica suggested. 'We'll have enough to worry about without watching out for horse thieves.'

The ship approached the ferry port, and they all hurried down to the car deck to get ready for disembarking. An hour later, they were struggling through Dublin traffic jams on their way across the city.

'Looks a bit like London, only tattier,' Nina commented, with a tinge of disappointment. 'And the people don't seem that much different.'

Garry shook his head. 'It's Ireland, not India.' He cursed as another car swerved across the front of the van.

'The driving's probably better in Calcutta,' Monica observed drily.

They stopped for the night at a bed-and-breakfast on the northern fringe of the city, and set off early next morning for County Cavan. Monica had a map spread on her knees, and gave Garry directions. But they mostly turned out to be wrong, or not quite right, and they began to get irritable with each other. Jenny added to the annoyance by yelling every time they passed a horse. 'I want that one! I want that one!'

'Shut up, for heaven's sake!' Sam snapped at her.

Nina whiled the time away playing interminable games on a handheld computer.

It took them almost the whole day to find the place, hunting for hours along twisting byroads beside lakes and low wooded hills and sleepy little villages with strange names. But finally, there it was.

Garry drove the van into the weed-choked yard and cut the engine. They all jumped out and stood surveying their new home. And feeling very unsure about it.

'It didn't look such a mess in the photographs,' Monica muttered as they surveyed the bits of rusting old farm machinery and the low two-storey house. 'Doesn't look as though it's been lived in for years.'

'Let's see the inside before we make any judgements,' Garry advised.

The girls and Monica followed him single file through the low front door. Inside was dark and smelled musty. The wallpaper and paintwork were faded and battered, the door hinges squeaked, and the light switches didn't work.

'Power must be cut off,' said Garry. 'I'll get them to come and turn it on again tomorrow.'

'How will we see in the dark tonight?' Jenny asked.

'Candles,' said Monica.

'Great,' groaned Nina. 'I just love the stench of candle smoke.'

There were two fairly large rooms on the ground floor, and a crude kitchen and a bathroom in an extension at the back.

'That's the first item on the list,' Monica said determinedly. 'We'll die of starvation without a proper kitchen.'

Narrow creaking stairs led to the upper floor, where there were four bedrooms, one large, one medium, and two small.

'Which is mine?' Sam wanted to know immediately. 'I want the one at the front.'

'Hold on,' said Garry. 'You'll all have to share one room for a while till we get the others decorated and get some furniture.'

'Look!' said Jenny. The others came to peer with her through the small window of the middle bedroom. The house and yard were surrounded by a thick belt of overgrown shrubs and low trees. In the far distance, round hills glowed softly in the evening light. A few hundred yards from the house, in the middle of the greenery, nestled the curved corrugated iron roof of a fairly large building.

'What's that?' Nina wondered.

'Probably the barn,' suggested Garry.

'The barn!' Jenny echoed, suddenly excited again. 'That's where we'll keep our horse!'

She sprang round and clattered hurriedly downstairs. 'Hey! Wait for us!' Sam yelled and ran after her. But she stopped at top of the stairs, and turned to Nina. 'You coming?'

Nina shrugged, trying to look cool about it. 'Yeah. Why not.'

She set off at a saunter, then bounded downstairs three at a time in an effort to catch up with Sam.

'Don't be long!' Monica called after them. 'We have to start unpacking!' But they were already out of earshot.

Jenny had disappeared into the greenery when Sam and Nina tumbled out of the front door. They were halfway across the yard when a large dark-blue car with mud-streaked sides stopped on the road outside the yard gates, its engine running. Two men in the front seats looked out at them with blank expressions. The girls stopped short.

'Might be our neighbours,' Sam said out of the corner of her mouth. 'Better act friendly.'

The girls waved and smiled. But the men just kept staring at them as the car moved off again and sped out of sight.

Nina made a rude gesture after them. 'I thought the Irish were supposed to be friendly?'

They hurried on again. On the other side of the yard, they found an old path that cut like a tunnel through the dense growth. They started down it together, but suddenly Jenny came crashing back towards them.

'What's wrong?' Sam demanded, as Jenny shoved past.

'Nothing! You go on!' Jenny called over her shoulder. 'I'm just going to get something from the van.'

Sam and Nina pushed ahead, ducking through low branches and curtains of leaves, till they came to a grassy clearing in front of the barn doors. They ran across and pulled the heavy wooden doors open and looked into the gloomy interior. There were several stalls, one or two feeding troughs, and scattered bales of old straw and hay. A ladder led to an upper platform where more hay bales were stacked.

'Wow!' said Sam. 'Look at that!'

'Perfect,' Nina agreed. 'If we had a stereo system, we could set up a disco in here.'

They wandered in for a closer inspection. On the ground floor they found some old leather harness gear, falling apart with age, and metal tools that might have been used by a blacksmith, but they couldn't be sure. Then they climbed up the ladder to the hay bales.

'This'll be our headquarters,' Sam announced. 'Gimme a hand.'

'Headquarters for what?' Nina wanted to know. 'I'm not really into playing cowboys and Indians any more.'

Sam gave her an exasperated look. 'Slumber parties. Midnight feasts. Anything we don't want Garry and Monica poking their noses into. Use your imagination!'

Nina considered this interesting prospect. Maybe there was another side to Sam she hadn't seen yet. Maybe she wasn't such a boring dummy after all. 'Yeah. Right.' Nina bent down to help.

They pulled some of the bales around to form a rectangular nest, and were sitting inside savouring the feeling of having somewhere secret to hang out away from the adults, when Jenny hurried into the barn below. She was carrying a little rocking horse, one that had stood beside her bed back home in England.

'Sam! Nina! Where are you?' she called out.

A shower of loose hay fell on Jenny's head from above. Sam and Nina looked down laughing as she pulled it from her face.

'Hey! Where'd you get that from?' Sam demanded when she noticed the rocking horse. 'We weren't supposed to bring any junk.'

'I hid it under some stuff in the van while Garry was busy packing,' Jenny explained, highly pleased with herself. 'This can be our horse till we get a real one.'

Jenny carried the rocking horse over to one of the stalls and carefully put it down. She stood back, smiling, then picked up some hay and offered it to the little toy creature's battered muzzle.

'Din-dins, Rainbowbright?' she coaxed in a baby voice.

Up in the hay den, Nina and Sam exchanged an oh-no-I-don't-believe-it look.

'At least,' Nina chuckled, 'we won't have to worry about horse thieves stealing that thing!'

4
Missing

DISASTER BEFELL RORY the day school broke up for the summer holidays. The bell rang, the school doors exploded, and out they charged, yelling and roaring in anticipation of the weeks of freedom ahead. Rory tumbled out in the midst of them, arguing and horsing around half-heartedly with some classmates. Arrangements were being made for soccer matches – or brawls as they more often turned out – fishing trips to the canal, or bike jaunts across the city to Dollymount strand. But Rory shook his head at the invitations to join in. He had to get home, he had other things to do.

'Hey, Rory!' one girl called after him. 'Carla Doolin says will you walk her down to the chipper at eight o'clock tonight?'

The other boys turned to look at him with expectant grins, but Rory ignored the question, and hurried off through the gates. Carla Doolin was the best-looking girl in his class. She'd never be interested in him. Somebody trying to set him up for a laugh, obviously. But strangely, his ears were suddenly burning.

He mingled with the dispersing crowd of excited youngsters till he reached the corner of the block, then crossed the road to head down a side street. Just then he thought he heard a familiar voice in the distance behind him. Hoppy. He turned and went back to look. But there was no sign of him. He turned again to continue on his way, when Hoppy's distinctive high-pitched tones came to him again, angry, and a bit muffled.

Rory walked out to the middle of the road and looked both ways. On the far side of the front of the school, three boys were gathered around some dustbins that had been put out for collection. They were gleefully struggling with something they were trying to force into one of the bins. Someone. Hoppy.

Rory immediately sprinted off towards them, sizing up the situation as he ran. The three were troublemakers from Hoppy's class who were always picking on him because his small size and bad leg made him easy prey. Few things made Rory as angry as seeing bullies picking on somebody weaker. He'd had too much of that himself from Quinlan's louts, and from Anto. Fired up with fury, he knew he'd be able to handle any one of Hoppy's tormentors easily on their own. But three together was a different matter.

Halfway between him and the struggling group at the bins, an old woman came out of her house to put a bucket of ashes by the roadside for the refuse lorry. As she turned to go in again, Rory swept past and snatched up the bucket without stopping. The three were so engrossed in their fun with Hoppy, they didn't hear Rory come up behind them.

'Hi, guys!' Rory said cheerfully.

The three looked up together, and were instantly hit full in the face by a cloud of choking ash. Blinded and spluttering, they dropped Hoppy and staggered away. Rory hauled him to his feet. Hoppy's normally white face was crimson with rage, and when he saw his tormentors helpless, he took full advantage.

'Ye scum!' he snarled as he tore into the blinded trio with carefully aimed punches. Rory grinned as he watched them crumple under Hoppy's rabid onslaught. They fell over the bins, scattering the stinking contents all over the street, and toppled into it, writhing.

Suddenly a door opened and an outraged householder emerged, brandishing a walking stick. 'Get outta that, ye little hooligans!' Rory grabbed Hoppy and hauled him away as the man bore down on the still-sightless tearaways and began whacking their legs with the stick.

'Thanks, Rory!' Hoppy said breathlessly once they had got to a safe distance. 'I enjoyed that! Did you see the way I landed the big one right in the gob? I'll do your homework for a month once school starts up again.'

'Forget it,' Rory assured him, still grinning. 'That's me paid you back for clocking Quinlan the other week.'

They turned down the side street, and slowed to let Hoppy get his wind back.

'Anyway,' Hoppy went on, 'you won't have to be acting as my minder for much longer.'

'How come?'

A secretive look of self-satisfaction came over Hoppy's face. 'Keep this to yourself. I'm taking up bodybuilding.'

'Bodybuilding?' Rory echoed, disbelieving. 'You?'

'Yeah, me!' Hoppy shot him a defensive glare. 'Why not? I'll build me up a physique like Arnold Schwarzenegger, then them creeps'll be too scared to even look at me!'

Rory had an instant mental image of his undersized mate bulging with enormous knotted muscles, like Popeye after a dose of spinach. He had to turn his face away while he fought down a splutter.

But Hoppy wasn't looking. He was rolling up his shirtsleeves to flex his spindly white arms. 'I've been training at home with some weights I made up from scrap stuff out of the yard. My biceps have nearly doubled already. Look!'

Rory looked. Hoppy's tiny muscles stiffened for a moment, then sagged with the effort, exhausted. Rory moved on, battling the vibrations in his belly.

'You're right,' he lied. 'They're really something.'

Hoppy galloped after him, rolling his sleeves down again.

'You got anything planned for the holidays?' Hoppy inquired eagerly.

Rory shrugged. 'Nothing much. Hang about. The usual. Why?'

'Well. I was just thinking. You and me could join a gym. Work out together in the mornings. Pump iron and build up some beef.' His pale face was alight with enthusiasm.

Rory shook his head. 'Can't spare the time, Hoppy. Shera needs to be fed and watered every day.'

'Ah come on!' Hoppy protested. 'You can do that in the afternoons. Or get somebody else to do it. Your Da. Anto, even.'

'Anto? Don't be crazy.'

Somebody behind them called Rory's name. They turned to see a girl of about ten speeding towards them on a bike. Rory recognised her; she lived a few doors away on his street.

'Rory!' she panted as she skidded to a halt just in front of him. 'That horse of yours is out on the streets on the loose. My Ma says she saw some lads driving her out of the lane this morning!'

Rory froze into stone for a moment. Then, without a word, he tore off in the direction of the yard.

'Hey! Wait for me!' Hoppy yelled, and hobbled quickly after him. But Rory yelled back over his shoulder: 'Can't! See you back at the yard!'

Rory raced all the way to the yard, hoping against hope that maybe Shera had somehow got out by herself, and had found her way back already. He prayed she'd be safely back in her shed when he got there.

But she wasn't.

He stood staring at the empty shelter for a moment, fear gripping his insides. Then he turned and raced out of the yard and up the lane again. On the street, he thundered off to the left, just as Hoppy, pink-faced and puffing, rounded the far corner to the right.

'Wait, will you!' Hoppy called out breathlessly. But Rory was gone again. Hoppy bunched his mouth in annoyance, and speeded up his agile hobble.

The skinheads were gathered in their usual spot on the wasteground, tossing coins and drinking cider, snarling and shoving at each other like a pack of baboons. Rory slowed down when he saw them, and kept a careful distance as he ran along, looking up and down for Shera. Then one of the skinheads spotted him and alerted the others.

'What's up then, son?' Quinlan the squash-faced leader called out to Rory. 'Lost something, have we?'

The others chortled and grinned baboon-like grins at each other.

'Only gone and lost that oul' nag he calls a horse again, hasn't he?' jeered one of the others. The grins got wider.

That gave Rory the proof that it was they who'd let her out.

'Where is she?' he yelled at them.

'Sure we don't know nothing, do we lads?' said Quinlan, looking around his gang with mock innocence. 'We're just honest citizens minding our own business.'

'Maybe it got kidnapped like Sir Gert. How much ransom you got, kid – fifty pence?'

The gang guffawed. Rory stood helplessly glaring across the distance at them, then realised he was wasting his time. They were just winding him up. He moved off again to continue the search.

'If you've done anything to her,' he called back, 'my Da'll kill the lot of ye!'

'Yer Da's an oul' woman!' Quinlan sneered.

'Hey! Let's go down to the chipper and see if they've any horse burgers!' the smallest skinhead suggested. The others laughed coarsely, and then turned back to their game of coins.

Rory ran off into the maze of streets nearby. Just as he disappeared, Hoppy arrived at the other side of the wasteground. Unnoticed by the skinheads, Hoppy gave them the fingers and scuttled past in pursuit of his friend.

Rory looked everywhere. He asked everyone he met. But there was no sign of Shera anywhere.

In despair, the last place he tried was Eugene's, a little corner grocery shop that was open from earliest morning till latest night. Eugene was a bald grumpy old man with a wide belly and bad breath, who knew everybody in the district and everything that happened to them. Maybe he would have some information.

Rory pushed open the glass door and a bell tinkled. A large hand-painted sign on the wall opposite the door warned 'SHOPLIFTERS WILL BE HAMMERED'. Eugene, in a grey shopcoat, was totting up pencilled figures in a dog-eared notebook at the counter. He gave Rory a look that was warning and questioning at the same time. He waited silently for Rory to speak first.

Rory thought it wiser to buy something before asking. He picked a packet of chewing gum from the sweets display and held out his money.

'Did you see a horse round here this morning?' he asked as Eugene rang up the sale on the gleaming new electronic cash register.

'I see tinkers' horses round here many's a morning,' Eugene growled. 'Damned disgrace letting them roam the streets like that.'

'But did you see mine?' Rory pursued. 'Small little mare, white with big brown patches.'

Eugene paused blankly before replying. 'Yeah, there was one like that this morning all right. Two of them skinhead fellahs came in and asked to make a phone call about it. Surprising show of public concern from types like that, I thought.'

'Phone call?' Rory echoed.

'To the animal cruelty place,' Eugene informed him, as though it was obvious. 'They were here within half-an-hour to take the beast away. Shame the rest of the country isn't as efficient.'

He held out Rory's change, but Rory whirled around and flew out the door. Eugene looked after him, then dropped the coins one by one into a charity collection box on the counter.

'Must be all them E numbers in the sweets that's making them crazy,' he muttered, and went back to his figures, shaking his head.

Outside, Rory almost knocked Hoppy over as he exploded from the shop. He grabbed the gasping Hoppy to stop him from falling.

'The animal cruelty's got her!' Rory hissed. 'We've got to get Da!'

And he was off again at top speed.

Hoppy slumped against a nearby car, worn out and disgusted from the long chase. Then a boy on a mountain bike hove into view. Hoppy hopped out in front of him.

'Give us a lift, Farrelly, will you?'

'Sure! Hop on!' the boy agreed, proud of his machine.

Hoppy straddled the rear carrier, and the cyclist wobbled off.

Scrapper's lorry was outside the house when Rory toiled up to the front gate. It was an odd time for it to be there, Rory thought, but a stroke of luck anyway. He bounded up the front steps, through the door and along the hall, heart pounding.

'Da! She's gone again!' he blurted out as he burst into the kitchen. 'The skinheads let her out. The animal cruelty's got her!'

He stopped short. Scrapper was sitting at the table, his left hand heavily bandaged and his arm in a sling. His face was white. Ma was stirring sugar into a cup of tea for him, her expression full of unaccustomed concern.

'Cut out that shouting, Rory!' she snapped at him. 'Yer Da's just had a bad accident.'

Rory stepped closer to look. 'What happened?'

'I was picking up a wrecked car this morning,' Scrapper told him, almost embarrassed. 'It slipped off the hoist and chopped the top off my finger. My own fault. Carelessness.'

Rory stared at the bandaged hand, horrified but fascinated.

'Don't worry,' Scrapper assured him over the rim of the raised tea cup, 'it's not the one I pick my nose with!'

Ma glared at him from the sink. 'It's no laughing matter. It could've been yer whole hand – then where would we be?'

Scrapper gulped from the cup and put it down. 'Now then,' he addressed Rory. 'What's your problem?'

'Shera's gone!' Rory said again. 'Eugene The Shop says the animal cruelty people took her away.'

'Can't say I'm sorry to hear that,' Ma muttered at the sink without looking around. 'Damn horse!'

'How'd she get out?' Scrapper frowned.

'Quinlan's mob,' said Rory. 'It was they rang the cruelty.'

Scrapper stood up, a bit clumsily. Ma turned. 'Where d'you think you're going?'

'To phone the cruelty about the horse,' Scrapper answered as he pulled his jacket from the back of the chair onto his shoulders. He guided Rory out into the hall with his good arm.

'I just hope it's gone for good!' Ma muttered to herself as the front door closed behind them.

Scrapper rang the ISPCA number from a phone booth down the street. Rory waited outside, dancing with nerves in anticipation of the good news. But Scrapper's face was clouded when he hung up the phone and came out.

'She's not there,' he announced.

Rory couldn't believe it. 'What? But Eugene told me –'

'Well, they definitely haven't got her up at the animal pound.'

Rory stared up at him, stunned. 'Who has, then?'

'Let's go check it out.'

They walked over to Eugene's and got him to tell the story again. This time it was a bit different. He hadn't actually seen Shera at all. The skinheads had told him there was an old piebald mare loose in the streets. Nor had he seen her being rounded up by the animal cruelty people. The skinheads had come in and told him about that too.

'Think we'd better go and talk to that Quinlan character,' Scrapper said darkly.

But there was no sign of Quinlan and his gang at the wasteground or anywhere else they searched. Eventually, Scrapper stopped and let out a deep breath. 'I'll have to head home now, son. Starting to feel a bit rough. Must be delayed shock.'

They turned and walked slowly back. Rory was in the depths of despair.

'She'll turn up, don't worry,' Scrapper tried to assure him. 'They probably just chased her off somewhere, and spun a yarn to Eugene so we'd go off on a wild goose chase. Somebody'll find her and bring her back.'

But Rory stayed silent and gloomy.

When they came to the entrance of the yard lane, Scrapper led him in. 'Come here. I've got something that might cheer you up till she comes back.'

In the yard, Scrapper pulled a mucky tarpaulin from something hidden behind a heap of junk. It was a racing bike, a bit scraped and chipped, but still in rideable shape. Scrapper wheeled it out and stood it in front of Rory.

'I was keeping this for yer birthday, but I'd say now's the better time for you to have it.'

Rory grasped the bicycle by the saddle and bars. 'Thanks, Da,' he croaked. Two tears trickled down the sides of his nose.

Scrapper reached over the bike with his good arm and gave Rory an awkward reassuring hug. 'We'll find her, lad, we'll find her. But we'll have to leave it today. I'd better get home before I keel over. Lock the gates, will you?'

Scrapper turned and hurried away, looking decidedly ill. Rory wiped his wet cheeks, looked at the bike, then pushed it out into the lane and locked the gates. He mounted and pedalled to the top of the lane, just as Hoppy appeared, pink-faced and annoyed.

'I've been hunting the world for you!' Hoppy protested. 'Did you find her?'

Rory skidded the bike to a halt. 'The cruelty people haven't got her at all! I don't know what's going on!' His face registered helplessness and rage as he looked pointlessly this way and that along the street.

'Maybe if you'd stop for a minute and think, instead of charging around like a headless chicken, you might figure something out!' Hoppy was exhausted and irritable.

Rory shook his head and stepped on the pedals again. 'Got to keep searching before the trail goes cold. See you later!'

'Hey! Wait!' But Rory was gone again. Hoppy swore. He kicked at a nearby can in anger, lost his balance, and fell onto his bum. 'That's it!' he spat, sitting there. 'That's definitely it!'

Rory scoured the whole district and well beyond on the racer, but there was not a trace of Shera anywhere, and nobody he stopped to ask had seen anything of her. When daylight eventually began to fade and the street lights came on, he turned back for home, grimfaced and desolate.

On the way, he passed the wasteground. The skinheads were congregated round a little wreck of a motor bike. Quinlan was sitting on it, revving the smokey engine loudly while some of the others tinkered with the electrics.

'Hey!' called the smallest one when he looked up and saw Rory glaring hatefully at them as he coasted past on the road. 'Had any good horseburgers lately, hah?'

The others looked up and laughed at the joke again.

'Ah give over!' Quinlan jeered. 'The poor little sod's broken-hearted. I mean, how'd you feel if yer pet horse had just been put through the butcher's mincer?'

The other skinheads chortled mightily at this. Suddenly, the little bike jumped and roared slowly away, belching smoke.

'Weyhey!' whooped Quinlan. The others galloped after him.

Rory stopped to watch. They had left their ghettoblaster standing silent on the old oil drum. Rory waited till the whole gang had jogged off down a side street in pursuit of Quinlan and the spluttering motorbike, then he bumped the racer quickly across the wasteground to the oil drum. Checking that nobody was watching, he grabbed the ghettoblaster, turned the bike, and hared away as fast as he could.

Anto was coming down the stairs when Rory came in the front door. Anto's eyes lit up at the sight of the ghettoblaster.

'Hey, that's a serious piece of kit, that is! Where d'you get it?'

Before Rory could answer, Anto grabbed the machine and turned it on. Savage heavy metal sounds filled the hall. Anto started bopping enthusiastically, dodging all Rory's attempts to snatch back the ghettoblaster.

'Cut out that racket there!' Ma complained from the kitchen.

Anto hurriedly switched off. Rory made another lunge for the machine, but Anto shoved him back against the wall.

'Where'd you get it?' Anto asked again, in a low voice.

'I bought it off a friend,' Rory lied. 'Now give it back!'

Anto shoved away another lunge by Rory.

'You robbed it, more like. How much d'you pay for it, then?'

Rory hesitated. 'Ten quid.'

Anto dug into his jeans pocket. 'I'll give you five. Here.'

He jammed a crumpled note into Rory's shirt pocket, then bounded upstairs with his prize before Rory could object.

'Buy yerself a new horse with it!' Anto called down in a low voice before he disappeared into their shared bedroom.

Rory started to mouth an angry retort, but stopped. He didn't really care about the ghettoblaster. The business of Shera had taken all the fight out of him. He pulled the crumpled fiver out of his shirt, straightened it out, and put it back again.

'I'll buy her some feed with that,' he told himself. 'She'll turn up tomorrow. Bet she does.'

And he went into the kitchen to face another scolding for being late.

5
A Strange Thing

GARRY SET TO WORK immediately, bustling around from morning till night tearing things apart and patching things up. Monica and the girls were expected to be on hand all the time to act as his assistants, but pretty soon they got fed up with this.

'We need an agreed plan of action,' Monica insisted, 'so we all know what's going on and what we're supposed to be doing.'

So they gathered round the kitchen table one morning for a council meeting. Jenny insisted on being chairman, so they let her, just to shut her up.

'Silence in court!' she yelled, banging on the table with a spoon.

'Right,' Garry began. He was keen to get this over as fast as possible so he could get back to work. 'For the next couple of months, we'll concentrate on getting the house comfortable for the winter.'

Everybody agreed this was sensible. But Monica added pointedly: 'Assuming we're still here when winter comes.'

Garry shot her a look of forced patience and carried on: 'Once that's fairly okay, we'll turn our attention to the land, so we can begin planting next spring. We'll have to look as though we're serious about it if we're going to get any grants.'

Everybody agreed again. In fact, they all agreed with everything Garry suggested.

'I love drawing up plans!' Jenny said enthusiastically.

'I'd like to know when we get to visit Dublin,' said Nina.

'And I need a telly,' Sam chimed in. 'I can't live forever without "Top of the Pops" and MTV.'

'All in good time,' Garry assured them. 'We only just got here. Now, can we sort out who's going to do what?'

The girls agreed to help Monica with the redecoration while Garry got on with the big construction jobs. This arrangement worked great for a whole day. Then the girls got bored. The novelty of the situation was beginning to wear off already. Sam grew grumpier and Nina irritably tuned around her portable radio looking for a decent music station.

'When are we going to get our horse?' Jenny wanted to know.

'We'll have to see how far our money goes,' Garry told her, while he fixed up the leaky plumbing in the bathroom. 'I'm afraid a horse is well down the list of priorities.'

Jenny frowned silently and turned away.

The girls made a new deal with Monica: help her in the mornings, have the afternoons free. The next day, straight after the midday meal cooked on the camping stove Monica had been clever enough to bring, the girls disappeared into the shrubbery jungle.

'We'll have to think about school for them if we do decide to stay on after the summer,' Monica told Garry as she poured their coffee. 'They'll go mad hanging about here. And they'll drive us mad with them.'

Garry nodded. 'It's a totally different way of life for all of us, but they'll get used to it soon enough. Once they settle down, they'll start finding things to do. You'll be surprised.'

The girls went to the barn, hung out in the hay den for a bit, then decided to go and see what lay beyond the dense belt of greenery around the farm.

There was no real path from the barn to the outer edge of the shrubs. They had to fight their way through the vegetation with sticks, like explorers hacking through the jungle. Then suddenly they were looking through the last of the branches at a flat valley of boggy land with a little stream winding down the middle.

'Come on!' Jenny urged. She was about to crash out of the greenery when Nina grabbed her and Sam by the wrist and held them back.

'Look! Over there!'

On the side of the low hills on the other side of the bog valley, a jeep was leading a heavy container lorry along a dirt track. Behind them followed a third vehicle – the mud-spattered blue car that had stopped outside the farm gates the day they arrived.

The girls watched as the distant lorry reversed into a spot almost totally surrounded by hawthorn bushes. Several men then got out of the cars and helped to unhitch the container. This done, the lorry's front end drove off. Most of the other men got into the jeep and followed, leaving two men and the blue car behind with the container. The men opened the back of the container for a moment, and looked in. Then they closed it again and stood around smoking and talking.

'What are they up to?' Jenny wondered.

'It's a strange place to park a thing like that,' Sam agreed.

'It almost looks like they're trying to hide it,' said Nina.

'Will we go any further?' asked Jenny. The tone of her voice said she didn't really want to now. The others shook their heads too. Something felt a bit odd about what they had just seen. Their instinct was to stay away from it.

They turned back to the barn, widening their newly-cut path as they went.

'Do you think Garry will buy us a horse ever?' Jenny wondered.

'You and your horse!' Nina said impatiently. 'Do you ever think of anything else?'

'No, I don't!' Jenny informed her defiantly.

'If we had bikes,' Sam suggested, 'we could go exploring the area. I saw a couple of villages nearby on the map Garry has. There might be something happening there.'

'Oh yeah!' Nina sneered. 'Cow-milking contests. Traditional bog dancing. I can't wait.'

Sam felt put down. 'Well, there must be something to do out here.'

'Sure there is,' Nina said. 'Watch the grass grow. Collect dung flies. Breed snails. The possibilities are endless.'

'Maybe we'll stumble across a gang of terrorists up to something nasty!' Jenny suggested brightly.

'Don't say that!' Sam snapped.

'Pah!' said Nina. 'Bet you all those stories are just dreamed up by the newspapers to keep everybody entertained. Things like that never happen in real life.'

'They do so!' Jenny objected.

'Well if they do,' Nina went on, 'they never happen to people like us.'

They trudged back to the barn, dispirited and silent.

6

Shera Turns Up

RORY AND SCRAPPER continued the hunt for Shera. But the days went by with no news, no sightings, nothing.

Scrapper's injured hand meant he couldn't go working, and at first he was glad of an excuse to get out of the house and away from Ma's nagging tongue. But eventually, his interest in the search began to flag. And sensing this, Rory's last shreds of hope finally crumbled.

'It's useless, Da,' he admitted dejectedly when they came home one lunchtime from another fruitless visit to an itinerants' caravan site on the outskirts of the city. 'She's gone for good. We'll never find her now.'

This time, Scrapper had nothing encouraging to say. He put his bandaged hand on Rory's shoulder and snorted quietly with resigned frustration. 'Maybe you should just try to forget about her,' he suggested uncomfortably.

The kitchen table was set, and the air was thick with the smell of frying food. Ma, busy at the cooker, only gave them a sharp glance by way of a greeting. Scrapper and Rory sat down at the table in glum silence.

Ma came over and shovelled the contents of the frying pan onto their plates.

'There was a phone call for you while you were out,' she said curtly.

'For me?' Scrapper responded. 'Where? Who from?'

'At Betty O'Brien's down the street. She's none too pleased at you for giving out her phone number.'

'Who was it?'

'They left a number for you to phone.' Ma dug in her apron pocket and slapped a crumpled note on the table, then turned away. Frowning, Scrapper peered at the scrawled figures while Rory picked miserably at his food.

'I don't know anybody with that number,' Scrapper told himself. Then his face changed. 'Hang on a minute!'

Abruptly, he jumped up, knocking over his chair. He grabbed Rory and pulled him towards the door.

Ma spun round, hand over her heart. 'Janey Mac! What's all the panic!'

'What is it, Da?' Rory demanded.

'It's the animal cruelty number!' Scrapper told him, face alight. 'Bet you they've found Shera! Come on!'

They ran to the street phone booth and crammed inside. Scrapper rang the number and explained who he was. Rory waited, stomach in knots, while Scrapper listened and nodded. Then Scrapper grinned and gave Rory the thumbs-up.

'Yeah, yeah, that's her all right,' Scrapper said into the phone. 'That's the young lad's horse!'

A wave of goosepimpling emotion washed up from Rory's legs to the top of his head. A huge grin broke all over his face, and he jumped and let out a whoop of joy.

Scrapper quickly waved a hand at him to tell him to be quiet.

'And she's all right?' Scrapper asked the voice at the other end of the line.

Scrapper listened and uh-huhed, his face gradually going serious. Rory stood beside him trembling, scarcely able to contain the explosion of energy the good news had set off in him.

A small figure hobbled up outside the booth, and Hoppy's face pressed itself against the glass. Rory instantly burst out and grabbed his little friend, whirling him around in a mad dance of delight.

'They've got Shera! The animal cruelty's got her! She's okay!'

Hoppy's face lit up. 'Brill! Mega! But how'd they find her? Where's she been all this time?'

'Dunno! Da's checking it out! Main thing is she's found!'

Rory whirled Hoppy around till Scrapper came out of the phone booth, then nearly dropped him on the ground.

'Can we go and get her now, Da?' Rory wanted to know.

There was an odd look on Scrapper's face.

'Hang on, son. There's a bit of a problem.'

'Problem? What problem? She's all right, isn't she?'

Scrapper sucked his lips, and took a breath.

'Turns out they had her all the time,' he explained. 'There was some kind of office cock-up last time I rang. The guy I spoke to didn't know she was there, and didn't mention us to anybody else. She's been there more than two weeks now, and they say we have to pay for her keep before we can have her back.'

Rory gawped. 'Keep? How much is that?'

'Six hundred pounds,' Scrapper said flatly.

'Six hundred?' the boys spluttered together.

'That's a bleedin' ransom!' snorted Hoppy.

Rory was stunned. 'Where'll we get that much?'

Scrapper shook his head. 'There's no way we're paying that,' he said emphatically. 'It's more than she's worth.'

'But Da ... !'

Scrapper held up his injured hand. 'We haven't got it anyway, son. I'm out of work. Remember?'

Rory sagged like a deflating balloon. Scrapper turned him around and guided him back along the street. 'We'll eat first, then go up there and talk sense into them. Don't worry, son — she'll be back in the shed tonight.'

Rory stumbled along between Scrapper and Hoppy, looking dazed. Then his step became harder and his lips tightened.

'Nothing's gonna keep me and Shera apart,' he hissed to himself. 'Nothing!'

The pound where stray horses were kept was deep down in the south of the city, where it rises up towards the humpbacked Dublin Mountains. The place had originally been a group of old farm buildings. Now it was swallowed up by housing estates, street after street of boxy little houses with neat front gardens.

Rory, Hoppy and Scrapper drove there in the lorry. Rory was so wound up he didn't speak the whole way, but Hoppy, as usual, filled up the space with his non-stop gabble.

'Tell you how we can raise the money to get Shera back,' he grinned, abruptly changing the subject from whatever it was he had been gabbling about before. 'We can rob a racehorse, like them other fellahs did. Demand a big ransom. And we'll keep the change for ourselves. D'you think they got their million for Sir Gert yet, Scrapper?'

Scrapper snorted, eyes on the traffic. 'No way. Them rich fellahs never do it like that. They'll just claim the insurance and go buy another one. Here we are.'

He swung the lorry off the road and in through the gates of the pound. Before it had properly halted, Rory threw the cab door open and jumped down to race off in search of Shera.

'Wait for me!' Hoppy yelled, and almost fell out in his hurry to follow.

Rory had already found her when they caught up with him in the stables. He had his arms thrown around her neck in a swinging hug, joy written all over his grinning face. Shera seemed just as delighted in her cool horsey way, and kept snorting and twisting her head round, as if she wanted to kiss him with her rough black lips.

'We'll take you home now, Shera!' Rory assured her fervently. 'Don't worry. We're going home. Together!'

Scrapper and Hoppy stood watching outside the horse stall, exchanging would-you-ever-look-at-your-man glances. But secretly, they were delighted too.

Then one of the pound officials appeared. A grey-faced, grey-haired man who looked as though he was expecting a problem.

'Something we can do for you?' He addressed Scrapper warily.

'Howya. Yeah. I'm the fellah that rang about this horse. The one you didn't know was here. Remember?'

'Ah. Right.' The man looked quickly up and down Scrapper's roughly-dressed bulk, and took a step back.

'Now about this six hundred quid business,' Scrapper began. He was about to close the gap between himself and the offical again, when Rory led Shera from the stable and passed between them. Rory walked her up to the top of the yard and waited, talking soothingly to her, while Scrapper and the official argued. Hoppy watched and listened, head flicking from side to side like a tennis spectator.

'You can't take the animal back till you've paid,' the official informed Scrapper, trying to sound impressive.

Scrapper was unimpressed. 'The horse is ours. Nobody asked you to bring it up here. If you'd left her where she was we'd have found her straight away.'

The official kept his eye on Scrapper's good arm, and the big meaty fist at the end of it.

'The fact is the horse was wandering the streets, a danger to herself and to the public. We answered a call and took her in. That's our job.'

Scrapper's chest was getting bigger. Hoppy's mischievous grin widened expectantly.

'That call was from the little gurriers that let her out in the first place,' Scrapper growled at him. 'It was a set-up.'

The official turned away, deciding it was time to retreat.

'The rules are the rules. The animal's been in our care for nearly three weeks, and if you want it back, you have to pay the six hundred pounds it's cost us to look after it.'

He set off towards the office. Scrapper followed, and so did Hoppy. 'It doesn't cost that much to keep an old nag like her.'

The official began to hurry. 'Well, you'd better take that up with head office. I'm only doing what they tell me to do.'

Scrapper's chest was almost at bursting point. He loped alongside the official and held up his injured hand.

'But we haven't got that kind of money. I'm out of work.'

'I'm sorry, but I can't do anything about that,' the official told him snottily.

'And what happens to her if we don't pay up?' Scrapper demanded as they marched on together.

'She'll be auctioned off to the highest bidder. There's a sale on Wednesday at two p.m.'

Scrapper grabbed the man's arm and pulled him to a halt. 'You can't do that! The young lad'll crack up altogether.'

The official froze in Scrapper's iron grip. 'If you don't let go of me, I'll get somebody to call the Guards,' he warned. There was a tremble in his voice. Scrapper let go, and the man walked quickly up to Rory and Shera.

'Is it okay, Da?' Rory asked Scrapper anxiously. 'Can we take her home now?'

Scrapper stood there, too angry to speak. But Hoppy hobbled up and blurted out the news to Rory, as the official took the halter rope and turned Shera back towards the stables.

'She's to be sold – at an auction.'

Rory's mouth fell open as Shera and the official walked away.

'But they can't do that. She's mine!'

Scrapper glared after the official and the horse for a moment, then turned away, his lips thin with rage.

'Come on. I'll borrow a couple of hundred off some guys I know, and we'll bid for her ourselves. Nobody else'll want an old nag like her. We'll get her back for half what these bandits want.'

Scrapper stomped off towards the lorry. Rory stood watching Shera disappear back inside the stable. Then Hoppy shook his arm.

'Scrapper's right. You'll have her back on Wednesday.'

Rory turned and followed him back to the lorry.

Anto was lying on his bed reading a magazine and listening to the ghettoblaster, when the door of the untidy bedroom burst open and Rory charged in.

'Hey! Less noise!' Anto glared at him.

But Rory was already in the wardrobe, throwing things out onto his bed – hurley stick, helmet, BMX gloves, a skateboard with the front wheels missing. Anto watched, frowning.

'What's the panic?'

'I'm collecting,' Rory told him tersely, without looking round.

'Collecting what?'

'Things to sell. They're gonna auction off Shera. And we're gonna buy her back.'

Once he had selected everything saleable, he scooped up the pile from the bed and turned to go. He was hardly able to see over the top of the armful of stuff, but his eye fell on the ghettoblaster. Anto slapped a protective hand over it.

'Don't even think about it,' he warned. 'I paid you for it fair and square. It's mine.'

Rory darted him a quick hostile look and left. Anto kicked the door shut without getting up, and turned back to his magazine.

'Bleedin' horse,' he muttered, in exactly the same tone as Ma.

Rory hawked his belongings around the neighbourhood, counted the money, and hid it in Shera's shed, where Anto couldn't get at it. Then he started counting the hours till the auction. He was dying to ask Scrapper how much he had managed to raise, but didn't dare because of the brooding look on his father's face. Scrapper despised all kinds of officialdom, and the encounter at the animal pound had left him nursing a simmering grudge.

Auction day finally arrived. Rory was pink-eyed from hardly sleeping, but he got up early and went down to the yard to get Shera's shed ready for her return. He swept and shovelled the place spotlessly clean, then put in the new straw and hay Scrapper had bought the day before. He even got an old pot of paint and painted 'Welcome Home Shera!' above the shed door. Everything was as perfect as he could make it by lunchtime, so he stacked the tools away, locked up, and hurried home.

On the way, Hoppy came hobbling out of a side street.

'The big day at last, eh?' he grinned with his usual optimism as he hopped along beside Rory. 'Suppose we'll be having a party tonight, to celebrate.'

'You coming up with us?' Rory asked him.

'Can't. Have to go to the hospital this afternoon. Some specialist thinks he might be able to fix the leg for me.'

'Yeah? Great!' Rory was disappointed Hoppy couldn't come, but felt he shouldn't show it under the circumstances.

'I'll go straight to the yard as soon as I get back,' Hoppy promised. 'Good luck.'

Hoppy slowed and let Rory hurry on.

Scrapper was wolfing his food when Rory got home. He seemed more cheerful, which raised Rory's spirits too. Ma silently dumped a plate of food in front of Rory, and he and Anto exchanged cold glances as they started to eat.

Rory chewed silently for a few minutes, but then he couldn't contain his tension any longer. 'Did you get the money, Da?'

Scrapper, mouth full, winked at him across the table and patted his shirt pocket. 'Eat up. We'd better get over there early.'

Rory grinned and gobbled hurriedly as Scrapper stood up.

'It's a pure disgrace spending good money for an old flea bag of a horse!' Ma complained. 'There's plenty of things around the house that need the spending more.'

Scrapper ignored her as he waited at the kitchen door for Rory, who crammed in one last forkful before bolting after him.

'You can see Rory's well on the way to being just like his da,' Ma scowled once the door had closed on the two of them. 'Pure selfish.'

'You're dead right there, Ma,' Anto agreed piously, as he reached across to hijack Rory's half-full plate.

When they got to the animal pound about quarter of an hour before the auction was due to start, there was no one else there at all. Rory's heart leapt.

'Look's like we'll get her back for a fiver,' Scrapper grinned.

But about five to two, a small red BMW with dark windows pulled up, and a well-dressed woman and a girl of about ten got out. They ignored Rory and Scrapper and went straight to the stables. Handwritten notices had been pinned outside the stalls of the animals that were for auction – Shera, an exhausted-looking old gelding, and two small ponies. The woman and the girl read each sheet of information carefully, and peered into the stalls, being ultra-careful not to get anything nasty on their nice shoes. Rory hated them instantly, but Scrapper only watched them with disdain.

'Don't worry,' he assured Rory. 'Shera's too scruffy for madams like that.'

Sure enough, they pulled small faces of displeasure at Shera's stall, and turned away. Rory was relieved, but still hated them even more for their contempt of Shera.

At precisely two, the official appeared from the office. He gave Scrapper a nervous nod of greeting, then looked around in resigned disappointment at the only other bidders, the woman and the girl.

'Suppose we'll just have to get on with it,' he muttered, and trudged off to bring out the animals and tether them in the open yard.

Rory had to struggle with his impatience while the woman and the girl dithered over which pony to buy. They settled on a little brown mare which they got at an absolute bargain price. They paid by cheque, made arrangements about collecting the animal, and then swept off in their swish car.

The official eyed Rory and Scrapper grudgingly. 'Well, we all know why you're here, so I suppose we'd better do her next.'

'We'll open the bidding at a tenner,' Scrapper smirked at him, and winked at Rory.

The official glared back, clutching his clipboard. 'You've seen the reserve price on the notice. That's the minimum.'

Before Scrapper could reply, two men hurried into the yard. They were youngish and dark-haired and dressed in working clothes. They nodded to the official and went straight to inspect the tethered animals. The official gave Scrapper a smug smile and waited. The two men handled the animals confidently, and obviously knew what they were about. Rory's stomach tightened into a knot.

'Travellers?' he whispered anxiously at Scrapper.

Scrapper watched them with narrowed eyes, and shook his head. 'Scrap dealers,' he whispered back. 'Think I've seen them up at the foundry.'

One of the men came over to the official. 'What's the reserve on the brown mare?' he asked.

'She's sold, I'm afraid,' the official told him.

The man went back to his companion and they conferred in low voices, looking critically at the patient animals. Then they came back together. They nodded to indicate they were ready.

'We were just about to do the piebald,' the official told them.

'Reserve?' asked one of them.

The official handed them an information sheet and they pored over it, frowning. 'We'll open at that,' the first one told him.

The official smiled officially. 'Three hundred. Any advance on three hundred?'

Scrapper glared. 'Three twenty.'

'Three fifty,' the man countered, keeping his eyes on the official.

Scrapper felt the wad of money in his shirt pocket. He looked worried. Rory's mouth had suddenly gone dry.

'Three ... eighty.'

The two men exchanged a glance. 'Four hundred,' said the first.

Scrapper looked down at Rory's pleading face. He shook his head.

Rory abruptly pulled an untidy bunch of notes from his denim jacket and shoved it into Scrapper's hand. Scrapper quickly counted them.

'Four hundred and twelve,' he said, scarcely opening his teeth.

'Four fifty,' announced the first man, with a little smile.

Scrapper's shoulders fell. The official looked at him, eyebrows raised. Scrapper let out a small snort of frustration and shook his head.

'Four hundred and fifty it is then,' said the official, and wrote something on the clipboard.

'Da!' Rory cried, dumbfounded. But Scrapper only shook his head.

'We haven't got it, son. We just haven't got it.'

Rory stood transfixed while the first man paid the money and gave his details to the official, and the other untethered Shera and began to lead her across the yard. Her watery brown eyes looked at Rory as if to ask what was going on.

Scrapper suddenly bounded over and took the second man by the arm.

'Hey listen, that's the kid's horse you've got. Why don't you take one of the other ones?'

The man looked at Scrapper coldly, shrugged off his hand, and walked on with Shera. 'She's ours now. Bought and paid for.'

Scrapper walked with him, waving the bundle of notes at him across Shera's back.

'Okay. I'll do a deal with ye. I'll give ye this four hundred now, and another hundred in two weeks.'

The man ignored him. Rory, in a frozen panic, followed them.

'Okay then. Two hundred. Be reasonable. It's the kid's nag.'

The other man, his business completed, caught up with them.

'Sorry, friend. We wanted this one and we got her. Sure, you can get the kid that other little pony back there. That'd be a better nag for him altogether.'

With that, they led Shera out of the yard towards a van and horsebox parked on the road outside. Scrapper stopped, looking defeated.

'Ah come on, lads! Have ye no heart at all?'

The men silently pushed Shera into the horsebox, shut the tailgate, and got into the van. Rory watched, his heart racing, as the van started up and pulled away.

Scrapper swore. 'That's her gone. They probably want her for pulling a cart for somebody.' He looked at Rory, guilt and anger behind his spectacles. 'I'm sorry, son. There's nothing to be done about it now. Let's go home.'

He trudged off to the lorry. Rory, disbelieving, watched the horsebox dwindle into the distance, then disappear around a corner. A trembling noise came from his throat, and he spun around as if looking for help. Back down the yard, the official was leading the other animals back into the stables. His clipboard lay on top of several bales of straw. Rory raced across, ripped the top sheet from it, and stuffed it into his pocket as he ran back to the yard entrance. Tears welled in his eyes as he looked down the empty road.

'I'll get you back, Shera,' he whispered. 'Somehow. I promise.'

Scrapper's lorry drew alongside him and he clambered in.

7

Captives

THE FARM BEGAN to change as Garry's carefully thought-out plans were put into effect.

Cracked and broken windows were repaired, ill-fitting doors made windproof, and missing slates replaced. Then they cleared the rubbish out of the front yard to make way for deliveries of concrete blocks, sand, cement and timber.

'First priority is the kitchen,' Monica insisted. 'We can survive like gypsies in the rest of the place, but only if we can eat properly, and in comfort.'

The girls stuck grudgingly to the deal they had made, and slaved away every morning helping the adults make a start on the renovation.

'After the kitchen,' Garry promised sweatily as he tore down ancient ramshackle cupboards, 'we'll do the bedrooms. A decent place to cook and eat, and a comfortable place to sleep, and we're halfway there.'

Working on the house was a real chore for the girls. But the afternoons, as agreed, were strictly theirs, and straight after lunch, rain or shine, they headed off through the bushes to the old barn.

The hayloft was converted into a secret den where they couldn't be seen from below. Hidden up there, Sam spent most of her time absorbed in teenage romantic novels, while Nina listlessly prodded away at her Gameboy computer. Below, Jenny laboriously hauled the rusty junk out of the two horse stalls below, and generally tidied the place up.

'Everything has to be perfect for when the horse arrives,' she told herself, ignoring the sceptical sniggers from above.

In between hanging out in the den, they hunted aimlessly through the surrounding scrubby jungle, widening the long-disused paths, and cutting new ones where there were none.

'I wonder who our nearest neighbours are?' Nina thought out loud as they looked out from the leafy tangle at the empty countryside beyond.

'We don't seem to have any,' Sam commented. 'I haven't seen any other houses yet.'

'I hope we're not the only kids around here,' Nina grumbled. 'That would be the absolute pits.' She turned and launched herself back into the greenery, slashing aggressively with her long thin stick.

When they re-emerged, they found themselves looking out across the flat valley to where the big lorry container stood alone on the low hillside opposite.

'It's still there,' Sam observed curiously. 'Wonder what it is?'

'It's just an old bit of a lorry,' Nina said dismissively. 'Come on, let's go back.'

She turned to go, but Jenny stopped her. 'Why don't we go and have a look?'

The others hesitated, unsure. 'There's nobody around,' Jenny assured them.

Silently and warily, they emerged from the cover of the bushy trees and set off across the flat valley.

The ground was boggy and had a little stream running through the middle of it, and it took them about ten minutes to reach the other side. Once they reached the hedgerows at the bottom of the low hill, they stopped to look around and listen. A low breeze rattled quietly among the long grass, and birds chirped faintly on the slope above. Sam shivered.

'Let's go back,' she urged. 'There's something about this place that makes me feel creepy.'

'Oh don't be such a scaredy,' scoffed Nina. 'We're only having a quick look around.'

She led them forward through a gap in the hedge and up the side of an unkempt field. The container lay on the other side of a straggly cluster of hawthorn and elder bushes. They bent low to creep through them towards it, but halted at the other side, unsure.

'Oh come on!' said Jenny impatiently and scuttled out of the covering bushes towards the container. She was looking at the ground beside the container when they caught up with her.

'What is it?' asked Nina, almost whispering and looking around nervously.

'Dunno,' said Jenny. 'They look like hoofmarks.'

A sudden noise made them freeze on the spot.

'What was that!' Nina hissed. They all edged closer together.

'It came from the container,' whispered Sam. 'There must be something inside it.'

They stood looking at each other for a moment, wondering what to do. Then Jenny skipped forward and put her ear to the wall of the container.

'I can hear something!' she hissed. 'It's ... it sounds like breathing. Like a big animal breathing.'

The other two were about to join her when the sound of an approaching car engine gave them another shock.

'Somebody's coming! Quick!' squeaked Nina, and threw herself back into the bushes. Sam and Jenny plunged in after her, ignoring the sharp thorns, and all three dived flat on their faces on the damp soil.

Moments later, a big dark-blue estate car with mud streaks all over its sides, appeared on the track that came round the crest of the hill. It pulled up beside the container, and two men got out. One of them was big and balding, with a face full of cracks and lines. The other was younger and smaller, with dark unfriendly eyes.

Cradled in his arms was a large, heavy shotgun.

The balding man went immediately to the container and checked round it. The one with the unfriendly eyes first yawned and stretched, then scanned up and down the valley as if to check whether they were being observed. His eyes narrowed. He moved a few paces towards the bushes where the girls lay hidden, motionless and unbreathing, watching his legs through the thorns and leaves.

'Hey, Hanley!' the man with the cracked face called out.

Hanley, the one with the shotgun, turned and walked towards his companion. Under the bushes, the petrified girls quietly let out their pent-up breath.

At the car, the crack-faced man took out a small black bag and opened it. From inside it, he pulled a large injection syringe, the kind that vets use, and proceeded to fill it from a sealed brown bottle. Behind them, a thump came from the container.

'Getting restless again,' Hanley, the unfriendly-eyed one, said drily.

The crack-faced man tested the syringe. 'He'll be grand once he gets his medicine,' he chuckled nastily.

Under the bushes, the girls listened, too scared to be able to grasp what was being said. They watched as the two men went to the back of the container, opened it, and clambered cautiously inside. As soon as the men were out of sight, the girls slithered backwards as fast as they could till they were out of the bushes. Then they turned and hurtled downhill in a crouching run, keeping out of sight behind the hedgerows, till they reached the valley.

'If we go across, they might come out and see us!' Nina hissed.

They all huddled in a wet ditch, hearts thumping.

'Did you see the gun!' Jenny gasped.

Nobody answered. Sam looked around nervously.

'We'll go further up the valley till we're out of their sight. Then we'll cross over.'

The others accepted her order silently. They set off in a low scuttle behind her, stumbling and tripping over in their fear.

Garry was sawing up lengths of smooth new timber in the yard, when the three girls exploded from the surrounding greenery and charged towards him.

'Garry! Garry!' they babbled in unison, out of breath.

Garry straightened up, frowning, and switched off the power saw.

'There's something in the big container!' Sam blurted out as they skidded to a halt in front of him.

'We saw these two horrible men!' Nina gasped. Her dark eyes were enormous.

'And they've got a huge shotgun!' Jenny cut in, and clutched him for protection.

'Hang on a minute now. One at a time. What container? What men?' he said.

The girls exchanged a quick glance and silently agreed to let Sam do the explaining.

'There's a big container thing, you know, off the back of a lorry, over on the hill beyond the wood. We noticed it before, and today we went to have a closer look,' she related breathlessly. 'We saw hoofprints around it, and we heard something inside. Then these two weird men came in a car, and we hid. One of them had a shotgun, and the other had a big injection thing. They opened the container and went inside.'

The girls waited for his reaction, still panting from the effort of their flight. Garry looked around for a moment.

'So?'

The girls were nonplussed.

'They must be up to something!' Nina insisted.

Garry gave them a patiently reproving look. 'How do you work that out?'

'They've got an animal locked up in that thing, we're sure of it!' Sam insisted.

'So what?' Gary asked.

This pulled the girls up short. 'It's cruel!' Jenny spat angrily.

'Well, maybe they have,' agreed Garry. 'But you don't know why. It might be a sick beast that they have to keep in quarantine.'

This idea hadn't occurred to the girls.

'But the gun!' Nina objected. 'They had a shotgun!'

Garry smiled. 'But every farmer has to have a shotgun. To shoot predators like foxes and rats.'

That too hadn't occurred to the girls. They looked deflated.

'But ...' Sam persisted, unwilling to give up their version of what they had just seen.

'Listen,' Garry told them seriously. 'You've obviously got yourselves all worked up about something that's doubtless quite innocent and normal around here. And anyway, it's none of our business what goes on on somebody else's land. You'd no right to go poking your noses over there in the first place. That's trespassing. Remember, we're new around here and we're foreigners. The locals won't like it at all if they catch you spying on them on their own territory. Understand?'

The girls didn't know what to say, and just stood there looking guilty and perplexed. Then an upstairs window in the house opened and Monica, in paint-smeared overalls, leaned out.

'Hey, girls!' she called down to them. 'Come up here and give me a hand. I want to finish painting the bedrooms. You can all tell me what colours you want.'

The girls hesitated before trudging obediently to the house.

On the way, they passed a big rusty piece of machinery that hadn't been in the yard before.

'What's this?' Jenny called to Garry, in a sudden change of mood.

'It's an old horse-drawn seed planter I found. I'm going to clean it up and try to get it going again,' he called back.

'With a horse?' She was bright with anticipation again.

'Maybe. At least it would be a practical reason for having one.'

Garry switched on the saw again and bent down to the timber. Jenny ran after the others to tell them what he had said.

Rory sat quiet and expressionless at the kitchen table while Ma poured tea for him and Scrapper. He could see she was secretly pleased to think that Shera was gone for good, but was saying nothing because of the sour, disgusted look on Scrapper's lumpy face. One word, Rory knew, and Da would explode.

The silence was heavy as the three sat at the table sipping from their cups. Rory's eyes blinked from time to time as his mind worked secretly at something. Then, after a long five minutes or so, he spoke. His voice had an unexpected strength.

'Da, can I have my money back, please?'

Scrapper was nudged out of his dark thoughts. He hauled out the wad of notes and peeled off Rory's little bundle. Then he peeled another note off the main wad.

'There's an extra twenty,' he said awkwardly as he passed the money across to Rory. 'Go and buy yourself something.'

Ma sucked her breath in sharply as a prelude to protest, but Scrapper flashed her a just-you-dare look, so she stuck her cup back to her lips. Rory took the money calmly.

'Thanks, Da.'

He stood up to go. Scrapper put his big battered hand on Rory's shoulder.

'I'm really sorry, son. Really.'

'I know, Da. You did your best. It's okay.'

Rory left the room. Scrapper looked out of the window and let out a noisy breath through his nose.

Rory went upstairs to the bedroom. Anto was out. Good, he thought.

Quickly, he took two plastic carrier bags from the wardrobe and began filling them with clothes from the chest of drawers. Most of the things he took were his own, but some were Anto's, his favourites.

From under his bed, Rory pulled out a tightly-rolled sleeping bag which filled one carrier. Then he collected up odds and ends like his multipurpose knife, a baseball cap, a pair of old gloves, and a fold-up nylon parka. These stowed in the bags, he looked around. His eye fell on the ghettoblaster on the chest beside Anto's bed. He considered it for a moment, then shook his head.

In front of the ghettoblaster lay a plate with a half-eaten burger which Anto had left there the night before. Beside it was a bottle of ketchup from the kitchen. A small smile twitched Rory's mouth. He pulled the cap off the ketchup, went back to the wardrobe, and carefully squirted most of the red pungent sauce into something lying on the bottom shelf.

That done, he put on his denim jacket, checked that no one was about, then sneaked downstairs and silently out through the front door.

Hoppy looked even more cheerful than usual as he galloped lopsidedly down the lane to Scrapper's yard, a battered football under one arm. But he stopped short when he saw Rory locking the yard gates, and the bicycle leaning against the nearby wall.

Rory turned. 'Hiya.'

Hoppy advanced, but slower. He could sense something was wrong. 'Is she back? Is she okay?'

'She's sold,' Rory told him flatly.

'Sold? To you, you mean?'

Rory shook his head, avoiding Hoppy's eyes. 'Somebody else got her.'

Rory went to the bike. Hoppy watched him, his pale face turning paler. 'But ...'

Rory started wheeling the bike up the lane. 'How'd you get on at the hospital?'

'Great,' Hoppy told him, stunned and confused. 'Doctor says he'll fix me up with a plastic knee joint, so's I'm normal. I've to go in for an operation.'

'Brill,' said Rory flatly. He wished he could feel more happy for his friend, but right now he was too screwed up inside.

Hoppy followed him up the lane, looking at the bags strapped to the back of the bike. 'You going camping?'

Rory stopped pushing the bike and prepared to mount up.

'Listen, Hoppy. If anybody asks, you never saw me. Right?'

Hoppy nodded, open mouthed. 'Right.'

He stood watching as Rory straddled the bike and got ready to push off. Then Rory gave him a strange look and held out his hand.

'Thanks, Hoppy. You've been a great mate. Good luck.'

'Been?' Hoppy echoed, bewildered, as he shook the outstretched hand. Rory leaned on the pedals and the bike rolled forward.

'Hey, Rory. Wait a minute. Come here.' But Rory was already out onto the street and away.

Rory cycled hard for more than half an hour, weaving his way through the traffic, stopping occasionally to check his bearings with a passerby.

Eventually, a bit out of breath, he halted at the top of a sloping street of old low houses in the north-west corner of town. They looked as though they might once have been a workers' village that had been swallowed by the swelling city. On the other side of the road, further up, were yard gates much like those at Scrapper's place. Rory pulled a piece of paper from his pocket and checked it. It was the sheet he had stolen at the auction.

'This is it all right,' he told himself.

Further along from the yard gates was a lane entrance. He pushed the bike closer, then crossed the road and checked around before nipping quickly into the lane.

Down at the bottom of the lane stood the van that had towed Shera and the horsebox away from the auction.

Rory gently laid his bike against the wooden walls of the yard, then reached up and hauled his head to the top of the timber. On the other side, was the familiar sight of a scrap yard. And there, to one side of it, stood Shera, tethered forlornly to the rusting wreck of a car.

Rory's heart raced. 'Shera!' he called softly.

She turned her head in his direction, and let out a snort when she saw him.

'It's me!' he told her. 'Don't worry. I'll have you out of there soon!'

Shera pulled impatiently at the tether rope.

'Just hang on. I'll be back later. Okay?'

Rory slid to the ground again and rubbed his fingers, stinging from gripping the rough top of the wall. Then he took his bike and went back up the lane, checking again before he emerged. He hurried along the street before crossing over and stopping at a low wall in front of a long, overgrown garden. From here he could still see the lane entrance and the houses beside the yard.

'This'll do grand,' he told himself.

He untied the carrier bags from the back of the bike and dropped them over the wall. He looked at the bike, brows furrowed. Can't leave it lying around, he warned himself, it's evidence. He sat down on the wall to think. Then a boy of about ten, on his way home from school, came up the hill towards him on the other side of the road.

'Hey, kid!' Rory called out as the boy passed by. The boy looked at him suspiciously. 'Want a bike?' Rory smiled.

The boy stopped, wondering if he was being wound up. Rory held the bike forward.

'Serious. If you want it, take it. I don't need it.'

The boy crossed over warily, and looked from the bike to Rory with narrowed eyes.

'What's the catch?' he demanded.

'Nothing,' Rory assured him. 'Just take it.'

He thrust the bike at the boy, who grasped it by the saddle and handlebars. 'Go on,' Rory encouraged him. 'It's yours.'

The boy hesitated, still disbelieving. Then he began wheeling the bike slowly away, keeping his eyes on Rory in case he was going to jump on him and beat him up. But Rory just sat there smiling. So the boy began wheeling the bike faster, and eventually, at a safe distance, hopped onto the saddle and began to pedal off.

Rory waved after him. 'Good luck!'

But the boy was already sprinting over the crest of the hill, his face ablaze with delight and astonishment.

That done, Rory jumped over the low wall and huddled down on one of the carrier bags. He took out a bar of chocolate and munched it, checking his watch.

'Three or four hours,' he told himself. 'Not long.'

'Rory, you little –!'

Anto's enraged yell came down through the kitchen ceiling and made Scrapper look up from his newspaper. Ma interrupted her low mutterings at the sink, where she was washing dishes.

'In the name of heaven, what's up now?'

They didn't have to wait long to find out. Moments later, Anto appeared at the kitchen door, his best Doc Marten boots in one hand, ketchup bottle in the other, his face pink with fury.

'Look what he did! Lookit!'

They looked. Anto's white socks oozed dark red squelchy stuff. Behind him lay a trail of what looked like bloody footprints.

'Oh my God!' Ma moaned slowly. Scrapper fought back a grin.

'Where is he? I'll kill him so I will!' Anto spat through his teeth.

Ma sprang into action with a dish cloth, wiping the mess from the floor. 'No, you won't! That'll be my privilege! Take them socks off!'

Anto obeyed, balancing unsteadily on one leg at a time. Scrapper watched, wrinkling his nose at the pungent odour of the sauce.

'Well, at least it smells a bit more appetising than your usual whiff,' he commented, and went back to his paper, looking considerably cheered up.

Banging and voices startled Rory from a doze. It was dusk. For a moment he didn't know where he was. But then he remembered, and jumped up to peer over the wall.

Along the street, the van from the lane stood outside the open gates of the yard. The two men who had bought Shera were finishing loading something into it. This done, they locked the yard gates, climbed into the van, and drove off.

Rory waited till the sound of the van had died away. Then he grabbed up his carrier bags and bounded over the wall.

He crossed the street quickly and hurried into the lane. There, he threw the bags over the wooden yard fence before jumping up and hauling himself over the top. Shera heard the scrabbling noises and looked around with a shake of her head and a snort. Rory dropped to the ground on the other side, crouched for a moment to make sure there was nobody there, then grabbed up the bags and scuttled over to her.

'Shera!' He clutched her head and kissed it, drinking in her familiar horse smell. She in turn snorted with pleasure.

'Come on, we can't hang around!' he told her as he quickly tied the bags together with a piece of string and threw them across her back, cowboy style. 'They might be back soon.'

He untethered her and led her across to the gates. They were old and half-rotten, so it was no problem for him to prise off the lock bolts with a handy piece of scrap metal. He pushed the gates open a few inches and peered out. Nobody around. Good. Quickly, he opened the gates to let Shera out, then pushed them closed behind him. He hauled himself onto her bare back, holding the halter rope as reins, and kicked her gently into a trot. Shera needed no urging. She seemed to understand what was going on and cantered forward eagerly. They clopped over the top of the hill, and disappeared down the other side, towards the fading light of the sunken sun.

8
Gone

SCRAPPER GOT UP LATE the next day and stumbled downstairs, tousle-headed and yawning.

'Morning,' he greeted Ma flatly in the kitchen where she was at her usual business. She seemed to spend most of her life within ten feet of the kitchen sink, except for the daily lightning raid on the local shop.

'How's the hand?' she inquired gruffly without interrupting her ceaseless domestic activity.

Scrapper held it up to look. The grubby bandage had been replaced, and the damaged forefinger was covered by a plastic tube tied to his wrist. 'Better. I'll go up the hospital this afternoon and have it checked.'

Ma dumped the teapot and a packet of cornflakes in front of him at the table. 'You'll have to be thinking about getting back on the road sometime. I'm running very short.'

With a slow sigh, Scrapper pulled the bundle of notes from his shirt pocket and peeled off a few.

'You might as well have some of this so. It's not going to be used for what it was intended.'

Ma took the notes wordlessly and went back to the sink. Anto came in, combing his gelled hair.

'Hello, love,' Ma greeted him, with a sudden switch of expression that was almost play-acting. Scrapper grabbed up the morning paper and opened it noisily.

'Hi,' Anto muttered, and sat down to pour himself a bowl of corn-flakes. Scrapper lowered the morning paper to look over it at Anto.

'Morning, love,' Scrapper smirked in a soft mocking voice. Anto flashed a timid glare at his father, then devoured the cornflakes aggres-sively.

'Where's Rory?' Anto demanded after a while. 'I still got a score to settle with the little vandal.'

'Still in bed, isn't he?' said Ma.

'No, he isn't.'

Ma looked around, frowning. 'Did you see him this morning?' she demanded of Scrapper.

'I just got up didn't I?' Scrapper responded, shaking the newspaper irritably. 'He's probably out playing football.'

Ma wiped her hands on her apron and went to look upstairs. Anto ate more slowly, flicking his eyes at Scrapper.

'Da,' he began sweetly and cautiously. 'Any chance you could lend us a tenner? Till Friday?'

Scrapper laid down the paper and smiled an artificial smile at him. 'Sure, love. Anything for you. Love.'

He threw the note across the table, and Anto took it with a look of humiliated annoyance.

Ma returned quickly, her face changed. 'Rory's bed's not been slept in. And some of his things are gone.'

Scrapper laid the paper down again. 'Was he there last night?' he demanded of Anto.

Anto looked furtive. 'I thought he was. I ... got home a bit late. Didn't put the light on. Didn't notice really.'

Scrapper and Ma looked at each other. 'Maybe he spent the night with that little pal of his. You know. The one with the bad leg,' Scrapper wondered hopefully.

'He's never done that before. He would have said.' Ma was annoyed, but genuinely worried now.

'Oh my God,' Scrapper said to himself in a low voice. 'He was a bit queer after the auction, now that I think of it. Broody. I hope he hasn't gone and done something stupid.'

Scrapper stood up quickly and got himself ready to go. 'I'll go ask whats-his-name, Hoppy, if he's seen him. Anto. You get out and have a scout around.'

'Ah, Da. I'm wrecked. And I haven't finished my breakfast yet.'

'Do as your Da says!' Ma told him with unaccustomed severity. Taken aback, Anto put down his spoon and stood up to obey.

Hoppy was kicking a football around on the road outside his house when Scrapper came hurrying along. His mouth fell open when he heard what Scrapper had to say.

'Last time I saw him was yesterday afternoon at the yard,' said Hoppy. 'He was going somewhere on the bike. He had a couple of bags tied on the bag of it. And he was talking funny. Nearly like he was saying goodbye or something.'

Scrapper looked helplessly around. 'He's run off. That's it. And there was me feeling sorry for myself. Where d'you think he might have gone?'

Hoppy frowned, thinking. 'Betcha he went looking for Shera. Who's got her? Where'd they live?'

Scrapper became suddenly determined. 'Dunno. But I'll find out.'

He turned and strode away. Hoppy kicked his ball into the front garden of his house, almost toppling himself over. Then he loped after Scrapper. 'Hang on! I'm coming too.'

Anto meanwhile was grudgingly trudging the streets as instructed, stopping local kids and asking if any had seen Rory. He had brought the ghettoblaster with him for entertainment on the way. But with every no and shake of the head that greeted his inquiries, his interest in the job dwindled, and his attention to the music grew.

After a while, he found himself at the wasteground. The skinheads were there as usual, still fiddling with the motorbike and arguing among themselves. As Anto passed by, one of them cocked his head at the sound of the music and nudged the others. They stopped squabbling and looked around. Quinlan's mean eyes fell on the ghettoblaster. He nodded, and they all moved off in the direction of the unwitting Anto.

'Hey! Where'd you get that?'

Anto was startled to find himself suddenly surrounded by the skinhead gang. The ghettoblaster was wrenched from his grasp.

'Give that back!' he snapped 'It's mine!'

Quinlan pulled the ghettoblaster out of reach of Anto's hands.

'That a fact?' Quinlan mocked. 'So where'd you get it?'

'I bought it,' Anto answered, getting nervous. 'What's it to you anyway?'

Quinlan looked around at the others with a sneering grin. 'Listen to him. He bought it.' He moved closer to Anto. 'You'll have to think of something better than that, craphead.'

Anto suddenly found himself being lifted bodily into the air and carried quickly across the wasteground. 'Hey! Let go, will you!' he struggled. 'Put me down!'

And they did. Right in the middle of a stagnant pool of sludge.

Scrapper rang the animal pound and eventually got the address of Shera's buyers by pretending he wanted to try to buy her back.

He and Hoppy roared across town in the lorry, Scrapper's injured finger sticking straight out as he hauled the heavy steering wheel from side to side. But when they got to the other yard, they found the police were there before them.

'Uh-oh,' Scrapper muttered as he slowed the lorry to cruise past the police car. The two men from the auction were standing at the open yard gates, showing the forced lock to two policemen.

Scrapper stopped the lorry near the top of the sloping street. 'Nip out and take a wander past them,' he instructed Hoppy. 'See can you hear what they're saying.'

Hoppy slid out of the cab and sauntered back down the street on the other side, while Scrapper watched in his rear-view mirror. The group of men at the yard paid no attention to Hoppy as he hung around at their backs for a moment, listening and looking into the yard. After a few minutes, he sauntered back again, and Scrapper hauled him into the cab.

'Somebody stole a horse off them,' Hoppy reported excitedly. 'Must have been Shera. They're raging mad.'

Scrapper and Hoppy stared at each other as it dawned on them what had happened.

'Rory!' breathed Scrapper. 'The little ...'

His frown of tension gave way to a little grin of admiration. Hoppy was thrilled too. Scrapper restarted the engine.

'We'd better find them before the cops do. Boy on a horse shouldn't be too hard to spot. Now which way would they have gone?'

'He's got to feed her,' said Hoppy as the lorry moved off. 'That means hay. Or grass.'

The lorry crested the slope. Before them lay the last straggling outskirts of the city, and beyond that, to the west and north, distant rolling countryside. Scrapper stared for a moment, then pushed hard on the accelerator.

'They went thataway!'

Something moist and warm brought Rory out of his heavy sleep. He opened his sticky eyes to find himself staring close into Shera's muzzle, framed by the branches and leaves above it.

He sat up abruptly, causing Shera to step back in surprise. Rory looked round. He was in his sleeping bag in the corner of a square field, under the canopy of some windbreak trees. After blinking at the scene for a few moments to remind himself where he was and why, he yawned, stretched and wriggled out of the damp bag. Shera closed in again to give him an affectionate nuzzle, which Rory returned with an energetic hug.

'I suppose you've eaten already, eh?' he said to her, nodding at the lush grass around them. 'You must've been ravenous after last night. We must've covered at least forty miles before dawn. You did a great job.'

Shera snorted and waggled her head in agreement. Rory gave her another hug, but his belly gave a loud rumble in protest at being ignored.

'I'm starving meself,' he admitted. 'I could eat a horse.' He laughed. 'Relax! It's only a saying! Let's see what we've got left in here.'

He picked up a carrier bag and rooted around in it till he found a chocolate bar. He pulled the wrapper off and raised the bar to his mouth.

But before it got there, Shera's muzzle descended on it, and chomp the chocolate was gone.

Rory threw a dirty look at her big innocent brown eyes. 'Thanks, Shera. That was the last one.'

He looked at his watch and thought. 'Listen. We passed through a village a mile or two back. I saw a shop. You wait here and I'll go back on foot and get some grub. 'Spect you'll want some cheese and onion crisps?

'Okay. Keep out of sight. I won't be long.'

Shera stayed motionless and watched as Rory trotted along the hedgerow and clambered over the gate.

The little village – really just two rows of houses on either side of the road – was quiet when Rory got there.

He hurried down the long street, trying to look as inconspicuous as possible, till he came to the shop. He looked in. It was deserted. He pushed open the worn door and went in.

A woman with huge spectacles and three layers of woollen cardigans appeared and eyed him suspiciously from behind the cash register. Rory went quickly about his business. He was surprised to find the goodies selection out here in the wilderness much the same as back home in Dublin. He'd always imagined that beyond the city limits, the only food available was brown soda bread and salty bacon.

Arms full, he approached the cash register, wondering if he could afford to add a few Mars bars to his provisions. If only that owl-faced oul' bag would take her eyes off me for a minute, he thought, I could slip a few in me pocket ...

Outside the shop window, a car pulled up. Rory glanced at it, then stared again in horror.

A police car.

The woman totted up Rory's purchases on the register, sniffing. Outside, a policeman got out of the car and walked to the shop door. Rory's stomach shrank into a knot. The door opened. The policeman walked in. And straight towards Rory.

'Three eighty-two altogether,' the woman said to Rory. But Rory didn't hear. He stood frozen to the spot as the policeman walked up to him, stopped, reached out an arm ... and picked up one of the newspapers that lay on the counter top behind Rory.

'Three eighty-two,' the woman repeated testily, holding out a plastic bag with all Rory's stuff in it.

In a controlled panic, Rory counted out the coins, took the bag and hurried from the shop.

'He a local?' the policeman asked the owl-eyed woman.

'Not at all,' she told him. 'Some little gurrier from Dublin. Got to watch them like a hawk. They'd rob a horse from under your backside, as they used to say.'

The policeman's eyes narrowed as he watched Rory disappear.

Scrapper and Hoppy meantime had made good progress in the same direction, and the lorry was thundering along a winding road not too far away.

'If he stuck to this road we'll catch up on him no problem,' Scrapper thought out loud. 'But if he went up one of them side roads ...'

'He has to eat,' Hoppy reminded him 'That means he has to find a shop.'

The village Rory had just left hove into view. Scrapper slowed the lorry.

'Good thinking, Hoppy oul' son, good thinking.'

Scrapper cruised the lorry down the long street till it reached the shop. There he stopped, jumped out, and went in to talk to the owl-faced woman. Hoppy watched from the cab. Scrapper hurried out again and clambered back in, jubilant.

'He was here. And only about five minutes ago. We got him!'

He roared the lorry off down the street.

Shera was still obediently in the same spot when Rory got back to her.

'We have to get out of here quick,' he told her, out of breath, as he speedily packed and loaded up. 'Cops. They'll be watching for us on the roads. That means we go across country from now on.'

Minutes later, he and Shera were headed out of the field and on into the vast patchwork of farms and woods that spread out north-westward.

Scrapper slowed the lorry down after they had covered several speedy miles.

'They couldn't have gone this far in ten minutes,' he muttered darkly. 'They must be back there somewhere.'

'In a field most likely,' Hoppy agreed.

Scrapper began turning the lorry around to go back. It wasn't easy, because of the thick high hedgerows on either side of the road.

'Damn hedges,' he cursed. 'Better if they'd cut them down!'

He was right. For if he and Hoppy had been able to see what lay on the other side of the thick tangle of twigs and leaves, their search would have been over. A few hundred yards away from them, Rory and Shera were plodding up a gentle slope, heading towards the unknown and unexpected.

Jenny was singing happily to herself as she covered the walls of her future bedroom with paint.

She was dressed in one of Garry's old shirts, which hung on her like a big nightdress. With a dripping brush, she sloshed on paint from a variety of pots, filling out an enormous, childish mural of sun, clouds, flowers, birds and trees.

Behind her, the door opened noiselessly, and Sam and Nina peered in. They gaped at the wall, open-mouthed.

'Jenny!' Sam gasped. 'What the heck are you up to!'

Jenny turned, grinning with pride. 'Painting my room,' she told them, all innocence.

'But you're supposed to paint it all one colour, dummy!' Sam protested, as she and Nina came all the way in for a better look. 'You'll get hell for this!'

Nina was smiling with admiration. 'Well, actually, I think it's kinda cool,' she murmured in a mock American accent.

'Monica!' Sam called out. 'You'd better come and see this!'

Monica, paint roller in hand, arrived. She too stared open-mouthed at Jenny's masterpiece.

'Well. It's not quite what I had in mind ... but it's lovely. Really. I think.'

Sam frowned in annoyance. 'Well, in that case, I'm going to do the same in my room.' And off she went.

'Me too,' Nina agreed enthusiastically. 'Something really freaky!' And off she went too.

Monica drew in an apprehensive breath, then let it out again. She folded her arms and watched Jenny go on painting. 'Well, I suppose at least it keeps you all from annoying the neighbours.'

Jenny painted on and Monica watched. Neither of them noticed, through the window, the car that had pulled up on the road outside the yard entrance. It was the car the girls had seen at the container. It stood there for a moment, then moved off again, slowly and quietly.

Scrapper's lorry coasted noisily along the tight country road, its progress slowed by the constant twists and turns. His lips grew tighter and smaller with every mile that passed.

'He's given us the slip,' he cursed eventually.

'Bet he went across the land,' Hoppy said cheerfully.

'Must have done. We've covered the few roads there are round here. Little brat.'

They rounded another bend to find a car coming towards them.

'We'll ask these heads if they've seen anything,' said Scrapper. He slowed the lorry down, and as the car tried to squeeze past, he wound down his window to shout hello. The driver looked up. It was the crack-faced man who had been at the container. His evil-eyed companion Hanley sat beside him, and from the open boot of the car a bale of hay stuck out.

'We're looking for a young lad on an oul' nag,' Scrapper began. But the men ignored him. The car slid past the lorry, then sped off. Scrapper swore after it.

'Culchies!' Hoppy sneered.

Scrapper roared the lorry forward. 'Ah, come on – let's go find somewhere we can get something to eat. We'll have another scout around later in the afternoon, and if we don't find any sign of him, we'll head for home.'

'But Rory –' Hoppy started to protest.

'Knows how to take of himself,' Scrapper cut in. 'Besides, another night out here in the wilderness and he'll more than likely decide to come home on his own. Specially since it looks like there's a spot of damp weather on the way.'

They both looked up at the thickening grey clouds above the hedge-rows, and exchanged an almost gleeful look. But then Hoppy frowned.

'What if he doesn't? Will you tell the Guards he's around here?'

Scrapper glared at him indignantly.

'Shop me own kid? Na, he's in enough trouble as it is. We'll just come back in the morning and try to pick up the trail again. He has to show his nose sometime. Let's go – I'm starving!'

The lorry turned left at a crossroads and thundered away.

Garry guzzled hungrily in the middle of the chaotic half-rebuilt kitchen. His clothes and face were work-stained, but his eyes were clear and bright as he lectured Monica and the girls on the next stage of his master plan.

'A henhouse,' he announced. 'Two henhouses. We need eggs. To eat and to sell. And chickens. Lots of juicy, plump chickens.'

'What we need is a horse,' Jenny told him with pursed lips.

'Oh, Jenny – not that again!' Monica protested as she stood up to start clearing the table. 'We've more pressing matters to attend to. Even more pressing than a henhouse.'

'Such as what?' Garry demanded to know.

'Such as a decent bathroom. I tried to have a bath this morning in that old tub back there, and d'you know what came out of the taps?'

Garry and the girls waited, jaws motionless.

'Goo,' Monica told them, almost with pleasure. 'Dribbly brown goo, just like –'

'Plumbing needs to be renewed,' Garry interrupted before the fascinated girls found out just what it was like. 'I'll get onto that next week.'

'But Garry, you promised we could have a horse,' Jenny persisted.

Garry wiped his mouth and sat back. 'Okay, okay. I'll do a deal with you. Help Monica finish the bedrooms by the weekend, and I'll find out if maybe one of the locals has a mount or two we could rent from them. Agreed?'

'Yeah!' Jenny squealed in delight.

Sam and Nina looked at each other and shrugged, both trying not to look too interested. 'I suppose it's something to do,' Nina drawled.

'Right. It's a deal,' Garry smiled at them.

'And the deal starts right now,' Monica chimed in from the sink. 'You've got a good five working hours before it gets dark.'

The girls got up and went out, Jenny charging ahead as usual.

'And early to bed from now on,' Garry called after them. 'We'll get a lot more done if we start at the crack of dawn every day.'

He and Monica exchanged a satisfied little smile.

And so the girls scraped walls and sloshed on paint till the daylight faded and they were tired. Then, after cleaning up and eating supper, they retired to the room where they were all camping together during the renovations. Jenny conked out immediately on her mattress, while Nina lay in her sleeping bag, reading by torchlight. Sam went to look out of the window while she combed her hair, yawning.

Suddenly, she froze. 'Hey!' she hissed. 'Look. Lights. Over there.'

Nina jumped up to join her at the window. 'Where?'

'Over there. Where that container thing is.'

Nina strained her eyes. In the gloomy distance, she saw one or two brief flashes, then nothing. 'What is it?'

'Dunno,' whispered Sam. Then: 'Will we sneak out for a look?'

Nina hesitated. She was surprised that Sam had suggested this, and dubious about going back to the container, in the dark. But she wasn't going to let Sam think she was chicken. No way. 'Yeah. Sure,' she answered with a cockiness she didn't feel.

'Right!' said Sam. 'Careful not to wake Jenny.'

But when they turned back to the room Jenny was standing on the mattress, pulling on her jeans.

Fifteen minutes later, all three were lying under the hawthorn bushes peering out at the looming shadow of the container.

'Doesn't seem to be anyone around,' whispered Nina.

The moon was trying to break through dense masses of dark cloud that looked ripe with rain. Suddenly, bright light erupted around them.

'Jenny! Switch that torch off!' Sam hissed in alarm.

It went dark again just as abruptly. 'Sorry,' Jenny mumbled. 'My finger slipped on the button.'

They waited a few moments, holding their breath.

'Come on,' said Sam eventually. 'There isn't anyone here. They'd have seen the light if there was. Let's go and have a closer look at that thing.'

They had just started to wriggle forward when they heard noises. Horse's hooves, slowly thudding. And voices. Men's voices. The girls froze, hearts thumping.

Shadowy shapes approached the container from the darkness beyond, and halted at its side. For a brief instant, the moon blazed through the clouds, and the girls saw them all clearly. The two men they had seen the last time, and a horse. A tall magnificent creature with powerful haunches and a sleek, shiny coat. It stood passive at the end of a rope held by one of the men, its big head hung low.

'Let's get him back in, then,' said the crack-faced man.

Cloud smothered the moon and all was dark again. The girls, barely breathing, listened as the container doors were opened, the horse urged roughly inside, and the doors closed again. Then muffled footsteps on the grass, coming closer. A match flared barely ten feet from where the girls lay as Hanley, the mean-eyed one, lit a cigarette.

'I'm getting nervous about him, Myler,' came Hanley's voice. 'Doesn't look in great shape at all.'

'Neither would you if you had that stuff pumped into you all the time,' said Myler. 'Give us a light.'

A match flared again as another cigarette was lit. The girls pressed their faces hard into the damp earth.

'Any word on the pay-off yet?' Hanley asked. The tips of their cigarettes glowed like angry fireflies in the gloom.

'Na. One of the owners' syndicate won't play ball. Some rotten rich Arab. Doesn't give a damn, probably. He'll go just go and buy himself another one.'

'Isn't sounding too good, is it?' Hanley mused. 'Might end up having to shoot the poor git after all. Doesn't seem right.'

Under the bushes, the girls listened intently. The men's accents were thick and strange to them, and they didn't understand everything that was being said. But they all picked up the word 'shoot'. Pinpricks of terror ran over their cowering backs.

Suddenly Nina let out a tiny stifled squeak. A dead thorn she was lying on had finally punctured the fabric of her jeans, and pricked her tense leg.

The men froze motionless, listening.

'What was that?' Myler hissed.

The two began to move around, kicking at the branches of the hawthorns. One of them switched on a handlamp. Fingers of its beam probed through the leaves and branches towards the spot where the girls lay, fighting back screams of panic.

'Put that out!' Hanley's voice ordered nervously. 'Somebody might see it!'

The probing light died. The girls trembled with silent relief.

'Probably just a rat or something,' suggested Myler.

'Let's go anyway,' Hanley told him. 'I'm gasping for a drink.'

Footsteps. The red dots of the cigarette ends dwindled away into the night. A few moments of silence followed, then a car engine sprang to life, revved, and slowly sank into the distance.

The girls lay for several minutes before they dared to move. Then, once they felt sure it was safe enough, they exploded, hugging each other and letting out their fright in quivering gasps.

Nina was first to begin to recover. 'They *do* have a horse in that thing! Will we go and look?'

'I just want to get out of here!' said Sam, and she started to crawl hurriedly backwards. But Jenny grabbed her.

'Wait! We can't just run away like that. Leave that poor animal in there. It's too cruel!'

'It's none of our business!' Sam snapped back at her. 'It probably really is being kept in there because it's sick. You saw it. It looked awful.'

'All the more reason why we should do something about it!' Nina insisted.

'No!' Sam was adamant. 'You heard what Garry said. We don't want any trouble. Especially from those two horrible men!'

She tore herself from Jenny's grasp and disappeared backwards into the dark. Jenny followed after her reluctantly. Nina lay looking at the dark shadow of the container for a moment, before she too scuttled away.

Rain began to fall, slowly at first, then with gathering force, drumming on the roof of the container. From inside came a dull thud, and a low, plaintive whinny.

Then new sounds drifted faintly through the hissing downpour. Slow horse's hooves again, coming gradually closer. And eventually something took shape from the blackness. A small piebald mare with a hunched figure on its back. Rory and Shera.

Shera halted for a moment at the side of the container and sniffed through her dripping nostrils. But Rory, shoulders hunched against the chill cascade from the invisible clouds, urged her on.

'Move, Shera!' he told her. 'We have to find shelter!'

Shera trudged on reluctantly and they disappeared into the gloom. As the sound of Shera's hooves faded, another weak whinny came from inside the container, only to be washed away by the steady thrash of the rain.

The leafy cover of the little wood protected the girls on their mad rush back to the farmhouse, and they were only slightly damp when they finally reached the safety of the kitchen. There, they leaned against walls and cupboards, panting from their frightening experience. Nina's brow was knotted in a determined frown.

'I think we have to tell Garry and Monica and get them to call the police,' she announced. 'Even if that horse is sick, keeping it like that is criminal. And if they're going to shoot it ...'

Sam gave her a look. 'Remember what Garry said. It's none of our business. He warned us not to go back there.'

'Well, if you're too scared, I'll tell him!' said Jenny.

Sam thought. 'No, I'll do it. I know how to handle him.'

The kitchen door suddenly sprang open. Garry, dressed in pyjamas and holding a candle, glared in at them.

'Have you all gone mad!' he demanded. 'Now come on – upstairs and into bed instantly!'

'Garry –' Sam began.

'No buts!' He was on the point of a rage. 'Bed! Now!'

Nina and Jenny looked at Sam. Sam bit her lip for a brief second, then hurried out past Garry. The others followed quickly.

'Congratulations!' Nina hissed derisively at Sam as they scurried upstairs. 'You handled him real well!'

The big door of the girl's old barn creaked open and Rory shone his small handlamp round the interior.

'Perfect!' he whispered.

He opened the door wider to let Shera in, then closed it gently to shut out the wet night. Together they wandered around, inspecting what the handlamp's small circle of light revealed. They came to the two freshlystrawed horse stalls, and exchanged a baffled look at the sight of the little rocking horse in one of them.

'Weird,' Rory shrugged. 'Better not disturb it.'

He ushered the weary Shera into the other stall and watched while she ate gratefully from a bag of hay hanging on a hook.

'You'd nearly think someone was expecting us,' he muttered wonderingly.

He lifted the bags from Shera's back and ate a packet of crisps before rolling out his sleeping bag on a pile of straw in a corner. Then he threw off his wet things and climbed in gratefully. 'I'd say we'll be safe enough here for the night. I'm wrecked.'

He pulled the sleeping bag up to his neck and rolled over. In ten seconds flat, he was fast asleep.

In the stall, Shera munched quietly on. Suddenly, she stopped and her damp ears pricked up. She turned her head to the barn doors.

Outside, beyond the dark dripping trees and the sodden flat valley, the captive in the container called low.

9

A Second Breakout

ANTO SAT silent at the kitchen table, looking bruised and sullen, while Scrapper simultaneously stuffed tea and toast into himself and did up his shirt buttons.

Ma sat at the table too. Her normal compulsive busy-ness had been abandoned, and the place looked messy and unkempt as a result. She distractedly chewed her lower lip, tense and anxious.

'That's two nights he's gone now,' she fired accusingly at Scrapper. 'God only know's what could've happened to him. He could be frozen. Starved. Kidnapped.'

Scrapper drained the last of his tea in a gulp. 'He's not a racehorse. He's a smart young fellah that knows how to look after himself. Not like Mr Smoothy here. What happened to him anyway?'

'That tearaway Quinlan and his skinheads beat him up and threw him in a pool of muck,' Ma explained angrily.

Scrapper snorted as he pulled on his jacket. 'And he let them?'

'What did you expect me to do!' Anto suddenly burst out, close to tears. 'There was half a dozen of them!'

Scrapper looked a bit guilty. 'Okay, okay. We'll settle that score once we've sorted out this Rory business.'

Ma stood up. 'I've had enough of this! If you won't call the Guards, I will!'

She moved towards the door but Scrapper blocked her path.

'Don't even think about it!' he warned her seriously. 'He stole a horse. Remember?'

'But it's his own horse!' Ma retorted angrily.

'The law won't see it that way. Just leave it to me, will you? For today, anyway.'

Ma pulled her apron up over her face and turned away, stifling tears. 'All this over a horse!'

'Well, maybe if you weren't always so hard on him, he wouldn't need to get involved with a horse!' The words had hardly left Scrapper's mouth before he instantly regretted the outburst.

Ma snapped around, eyes blazing. 'I wasn't being hard on him! I was just keeping him in his place after all the spoiling you give him! You'd let him away with anything!'

'Spoiling?! And what d'you call the treatment you give to his lordship here?' Scrapper retorted, pointing at Anto, who was watching and listening with lips parted.

'You leave Anto out of this! At least he gives me a bit of warmth and appreciation, which is more than I ever get from you! You think more of that damn lorry of yours than you do about me! Same way Rory thinks about nothing but the nag!'

She sat heavily onto a chair and put her head on the table, sobbing. Scrapper gave Anto a confused look and sat down beside Ma. Awkwardly, he put his uninjured hand on the back of her shoulder. His expression was serious and uncomfortable.

'Looks like this family's gone off the road somewhere,' he muttered in a low voice. 'We'll have to see what we can do to set it right, eh?'

Ma raised her head, face wet. 'Find Rory first!'

Scrapper looked helpless for a moment, then put a brawny arm round her shoulder. 'Listen. I've a good idea of the general area he's in,' he told her with as much softness as he could muster. 'A stranger lad on a horse is bound to get noticed. You know what country folk are like. I just want to get to him before the law does. Understand?'

Ma wiped her face with the apron and nodded. Scrapper let out a long breath and stood up. 'I'd better get going so.'

He gave her shoulders a squeeze, then turned and left quickly.

Ma sat head bowed after the front door banged. Anto, amazed at what he had just witnessed, gaped at her for a few moments before getting up to put a consoling hand on her back.

'I'll always be here for you, Ma,' he told her in a sugary voice.

But Ma suddenly jerked around and gave him a resounding wallop on the ear. Anto was stunned.

'Ahwa! What's that for!'

'For all the things I turned a blind eye to this last while! For the lies you've been telling! For the way you took advantage of the situation! For the way you've been tormenting Rory all the time! Did you think I was a complete eejit?' She stood up. 'Well, let me tell you this, boy – if and when we get Rory back in one piece, we'll all be making some changes around here. You mark my words!'

She stormed out of the kitchen, sobbing angrily, and slammed the door. Anto held his throbbing ear and gaped after her. He didn't really grasp what was going on, but one thing he understood for certain: his reign as the Golden Boy was over.

Jenny wandered through the little jungle wood, humming happily to herself as she gathered an armful of the bright wild flowers that grew in profusion in the small clearings.

It was a beautiful morning, bright and warm. The overnight rain had given way to a brilliant blue sky, and the whole world felt refreshed and happy. The sunlight and the rich aroma of nature had put the events of the previous night completely out of her mind.

Eventually she arrived at the old barn. She finished munching an apple she had brought with her, and looked around till she spotted a little hole in the ground that might once have been a field-mouse's hideout. Carefully, she dropped the apple core into the hole and firmed earth over it.

'There!' she told herself. 'Next summer we will have our very own apples growing right here!' Then she swung around gaily and carried the armful of flowers into the barn.

In her stall, Shera turned her head when the barn door opened to let the morning sunlight pour in. The horse watched as Jenny, still humming, crossed to the ladder that led up to the hayloft. The scent of the flowers drifted to Shera's nostrils. She snorted.

The sound brought Jenny to an abrupt halt. She turned, stared into the stall, and her mouth slowly fell open. Shera stared back.

'A horse!' Jenny whispered in disbelief.

She walked slowly and carefully towards the stall, as if afraid to disturb the vision and make it disappear.

'Are you real?' she asked in low amazement when she got close enough to smell the horsey smell.

Shera's head moved up and down.

Gently, Jenny reached out to put a trembling finger on Shera's warm flank.

'You *are* real!' Jenny gasped, dumbfounded. 'But who are you? Where did you come from?'

Shera snuffled and stretched her neck to reach the flowers.

Her yellow teeth chomped off a few heads, and she munched them noisily. Jenny held the rest of the bunch out to her.

'Here! Eat them! Eat them all! But don't go away. I'll be right back.'

Jenny dropped the armful of flowers at Shera's feet, and backed off towards the door. Once there, she crept out, closed the doors gently, then flew off back through the wood towards the farmhouse.

Sam and Nina were still fast asleep in their sleeping bags when Jenny burst madly into the room and threw herself on top of them.

'Sam! Nina! Wake up!' she gabbled excitedly. 'It's here!'

Sam jerked awake, looking very bad-tempered. 'Get off you little savage!' she snarled, and pulled the sleeping bag back over her head.

'But you have to get up!' Jenny insisted, shaking her. 'It's here!'

Nina sat up, groggy. 'What is *it*? What's here?'

Jenny leapt across to her and tried to pull her out of the sleeping bag. 'Our horse! It's in the barn! Come and see!'

'A horse?' Nina repeated. 'Serious?'

'Don't listen to her!' Sam's irritated voice came from inside her sleeping bag. 'She's always inventing stories!'

On her knees, Jenny leapt back to Sam. 'But it's true! It ate my flowers!'

Sam erupted from the bag, eyes blazing. 'Liar! Horses don't eat flowers!'

Jenny looked about to explode with frustration. Then she suddenly yanked off one of her runners and stuck it under Sam's nose.

'Here! Smell that!'

Sam sniffed, then pulled back, her face wrinkled with disgust and astonishment. 'Horse shit!'

She and Nina stared at the grinning Jenny for a moment. Then both jumped to their feet and hurriedly hauled on their clothes.

Garry was pushing a barrowload of concrete blocks across the yard when the three girls burst from the house and raced towards the jungle wood.

'Breakfast?' he invited them as they flew past. But they disappeared without even looking at him. He paused for a moment to watch them go, then shook his head and carried on pushing the heavy barrow.

'Gimme a boy any day!' he muttered to himself.

The girls sprinted all the way to the barn, yanked the door open, and just stood there out of breath, staring. Jenny grinned an I-told-you-so grin at the other two. But they didn't notice.

In her shadowy stall, Shera stared back at them with calm eyes. The flowers were all gone.

'See?' said Jenny, smug and triumphant. They all advanced slowly to the stall, and gingerly touched and stroked Shera, their faces full of wonder.

'You're right,' said Nina. 'It's a real live horse!'

'A fairly ugly one, though,' Sam commented.

'But she's ours!' Jenny enthused. 'All ours!'

'No, she isn't!' Nina said. 'She belongs to somebody. But who?'

Abruptly, a figure arose from a nearby pile of straw. The girls shrieked, startling Shera. It was Rory.

'It's okay, it's okay!' he hissed, stepping towards them. 'Don't scream or you'll give us away!'

The girls backed off as he patted and stroked Shera reassuringly.

'Who are you?' Sam demanded, trying to cover over her nervousness. 'What are you doing here?'

'Me and Shera took shelter in here from the rain last night,' Rory explained, nervous himself. 'Is this your place?'

'Yes it is,' Sam informed him. 'And you've no right to come in here and give us such a fright!'

'Sorry,' Rory mumbled, looked around for his bags. 'We'll get going right away. Just don't tell anyone you saw us. Please.'

His anxious tone gave the girls their confidence back. They moved closer again.

'Is this your horse?' Jenny asked him.

Rory nodded. He was trying to stuff his things back into the bags, and pull on his clothes at the same time.

'Do you live around here?' Nina asked him.

Rory shook his head. 'We're on the road. Travelling.'

The girls didn't seem to understand this.

'We move around from place to place,' he explained, glancing curiously at them as he began to notice their foreignness.

'You mean, you've no home?' Sam wondered.

Rory thought, then shook his head in agreement.

'Well, you can stay here,' Jenny invited him, and moved close to Shera again. 'Both of you. Can't they?'

Nina and Sam exchanged a glance. Rory's nervousness had lessened theirs. They edged back towards him.

'Why are you afraid that we'll give you away?' Nina interrogated. 'Why can't we tell anyone we saw you here?'

Rory started untying Shera, avoiding the girls' eyes.

'Just don't. Right?'

A small smile of understanding grew on Sam's lips. 'Is this horse really yours? You didn't steal it somewhere?'

'Her. And she belongs to *me*!' Rory snapped aggressively. 'I only stole her back again!'

Realising what he had said, he stared at the girls. They stared back, then exchanged a look of unspoken agreement.

'This sounds really interesting,' said Sam. 'Why don't you stay here and tell us all about it?'

'Yeah!' Jenny breathed. 'We'll hide you here!'

Rory stared at them, unsure.

'You foreigners?' he asked suddenly.

'From England,' Nina told him. 'We've just arrived. To stay.'

'We don't know any of the locals yet,' Sam reassured him. 'Nobody ever comes near this place.'

Jenny went to his side and grasped his arm.

'Please stay!' she urged him excitedly. 'We'll look after you. And Shera.'

Rory was still unsure. He looked around the place, then at Shera, who also seemed to be waiting for his decision.

'Well. Okay. But just for the day. Then we have to move on.'

Jenny jumped up and down, then rushed to hug Shera. The other two girls glanced at each other, not sure what to do next.

'Hungry?' Nina asked him.

Rory nodded. 'I've been living on crisps and chocolate.'

'Right,' Sam said decisively. 'Stay out of sight in here. We'll be right back with breakfast.'

She and Nina hurried to the barn doors. Jenny took an apple from her pocket and gave it to Shera before racing after them.

Bemused, Rory and Shera watched the door close.

'Foreigners!' Rory thought out loud. 'Think we can trust them?'

Not too far away, Scrapper's lorry was scouting slowly along a side road. Scrapper held the wheel tight as he looked right and left for gaps in the hedge to peer through. Hoppy sat beside him with a map spread out on his bony knees.

'What's them red crosses for?' Hoppy asked as he peered at it.'

Sightings,' Scrapper explained without looking away from the hedgerows. 'Anywhere we stopped somebody who thought they might've seen him, I make a mark. Join up the crosses and you see the direction he's headed in.'

Hoppy turned the map this way and that. 'It's not a line. It goes all over the place.'

'That's the problem,' Scrapper agreed. 'Hang on – here's another one we can ask.'

Up ahead, a farm labourer was chopping at a hedge with a big slash-hook. Scrapper slowed the lorry and wound down his window.

Garry came around the side of the house, pushing a barrowload of sand this time. Once again, the girls erupted from the house and charged past him, clutching various items of food and drink.

'What about breakfast!' Garry demanded in exasperation.

'We're taking it with us!' Sam called back before she and the others disappeared into the greenery.

Garry glared after them. 'There's mountains of work to be done around here!' he yelled. 'Any chance of some help sometime?'

But the wood had swallowed them. Garry turned and looked up at a window where Monica, in painting clothes again, was watching.

'I think it's time to officially end the settling down period and re-establish a bit of normal discipline again, eh?' she shouted down.

Tight-lipped, Garry nodded. Then his gaze went back to the edge of the little wood. 'They're up to something,' he muttered to himself as he heaved the heavy barrow into motion again. 'I can feel it!'

Rory was grooming Shera with an old brush he'd found lying around, when the girls came tumbling in through the barn door. Jenny immediately rushed forward to offer more apples to Shera. But Sam and Nina slowed down to regain their composure before homing in on Rory. Each held out something to him, awkward.

'Cheese sandwich,' Sam told him.

'Ham sandwich,' Nina countered.

Rory looked at both offerings, eagerly took one in each hand, and wolfed them down with alternate, greedy bites. He sank down onto the straw to let his stomach enjoy the feast in comfort. Sam and Nina quietly dropped to their knees to watch.

'You really were hungry,' Nina commented.

'Starving!' Rory agreed through a stuffed mouth. 'I could have eaten a ...'

He glanced at Shera, but she was busy with the apples, so he went on tearing at the food with his teeth. Sam pushed a bottle of mineral water at him, and he drank from it with loud glugging noises. The girls exchanged an involuntary smile.

When the worst of his hunger pangs had been satisfied, Rory's jaws slowed down. He became aware of Nina and Sam staring at him, and stared back.

'What's your name?' Nina asked him.

'Rory. Yours?' he replied between chews.

'Nina.'

'I'm Sam.'

'And I'm Jenny!' came a call from Shera's stall. What's your horse called again?'

'Shera.'

'Well, Shera has eaten all the apples, and I think she might be thirsty,' Jenny advised him.

'There's a little stream nearby we can take her to,' Sam suggested.

Rory didn't like the idea of going out. 'Is there anyone around who might see us?'

'Not that we know of,' Nina answered first. 'But if you're really afraid, we'll go and get some water in a bucket.'

'That might be better,' Rory agreed. 'I can take her out later in the dark and let her feed off some fresh grass.'

Sam jumped up and grabbed a battered bucket from nearby. Nina stayed where she was, but when Sam realised this, she turned back and glared at Nina to come with her. Sam almost pushed her out through the barn doors.

Rory stood up, still eating, and went to join Jenny beside Shera.

'You must love her a lot to get into such big trouble for her,' Jenny remarked.

Rory gave her a quick look and changed the subject. 'Your Ma and Da around here?'

'Garry and Monica are back at the farmhouse. But Monica isn't my mother,' Jenny answered quickly.

Rory decided not to inquire into this any further. 'What does your father do?'

'He's going to be an organic vegetable grower. What does yours do?'

'Drives a lorry,' Rory answered evasively.

Scrapper was still driving his lorry along a nearby road, getting closer to Rory all the time, although he and Hoppy didn't know it.

'That last fellah must have given us a bum steer,' Hoppy complained as he jiggled the map around. 'This road goes well away from all the other sightings.'

Scrapper frowned as he looked out at the hedgerows. 'It's kind of familiar though. Did we come along here yesterday?'

Hoppy looked around and snorted. 'Sure these roads all look the same to me. Here's somebody. They might've seen Rory.'

Up ahead, a mud-smeared estate car cruised towards them. Scrapper slowed and wound down his window, but the car slid past and sped off, ignoring him. Scrapper cursed.

Hoppy caught the glint of a pair of mean eyes inside it as the car went by. 'I think we met that car yesterday and it did the same thing.'

Scrapper started reversing the lorry into a gate opening to turn it around. 'We'll go back to that village shop he was in yesterday. He might have called there again for more grub.'

Nina and Sam returned carrying the full bucket between them, their legs wet from splashes.

'Great!' Rory thanked them as Shera stuck her muzzle into the cool liquid. 'If we just had some more fresh hay now, she'd be right. This stuff's pretty ancient.'

'There's some beside the container!' Jenny blurted out. Then she thought. 'But we can't go back there! Those men!'

'No way!' Nina agreed with a shiver. Sam frowned and nibbled her lower lip thoughtfully.

Rory watched them, curious at the sudden tension and secretiveness. 'What men? What's this container?'

'There's a big lorry container on the other side of the valley beyond our wood. Some nasty-looking types have got a horse locked up in it,' Nina explained seriously.

Rory reflected for a moment. 'I think we passed it last night in the rain. And there's a horse in it? That's cruelty.'

'Yes!' Jenny agreed. 'We should report them.'

'No, don't,' said Rory quickly. 'Not while me and Shera are here.'

Garry's voice suddenly called from outside.

'Jenny! Nina! Sam!'

The girls froze. Rory looked from one to the other, scared.

'Who's that?!'

'It's Garry looking for us!' Sam hissed. 'Come on – he mustn't come in here!'

The girls rushed out through the barn door and closed it hurriedly behind them.

Garry had just emerged from the greenery and was walking towards the barn. The girls ran to meet him, smiling sweetly.

'Here we are, Dad!' Jenny greeted him.

'Right then,' Garry addressed them sternly. 'I want you all to come back to the house and give Monica a hand, just like you promised. There'll be plenty of time to play later, when the work's done. No argument.'

'Sure thing,' Sam answered with a fixed smile. 'We're just dying to get on with it, aren't we?'

The other two nodded enthusiastically and they all trooped off into the scrub wood. Garry watched them, suspicious, then turned his eyes back to the barn.

'What're they up to in there?' he wondered out loud. He started walking towards the barn door, and was almost there when Sam reappeared behind him.

'Dad! Come on!' she urged anxiously. 'We've lots to do! Monica will be fuming.'

Garry looked at his watch. 'And the morning's half gone,' he agreed. He turned away from the barn and hurried after the girls.

Back at the house, Monica was up a stepladder painting a ceiling with a roller and trying to dodge the drips.

'Here we are, Mum. What do you want us to do?' Nina asked as the girls appeared in the room.

Monica wiped a drop of paint from her cheek, leaving a big smear. 'About time,' she told them with the voice of someone not having fun. 'One of you can help me with this painting, and the other two can go and clear up the kitchen mess.'

'I'll stay and help you,' Nina decided quickly.

'And Jenny and I will do the kitchen,' Sam announced.

'But I hate washing dishes!' Jenny complained. 'I want to paint!'

Sam took Jenny's arm and firmly guided her out of the room. 'Shut up and do what I say!' she hissed at her.

She hauled Jenny downstairs and into the kitchen, and closed the door.

'Now listen you!' Sam told her severely. 'You have to play along with everything we say. Right?'

Jenny nodded meekly.

'Right,' said Sam and marched to the sink. 'So let's get on with it. I'll wash, you dry.'

Jenny followed obediently. Neither of them noticed Garry's puzzled face listening and watching outside the nearby window.

Scrapper and Hoppy sat in the lorry cab outside the village shop, noisily devouring ice cream and crisps at the same time.

'And when did she say this oul' fellah spotted Rory and Shera?' Hoppy asked through white-smeared lips.

'Last night,' Scrapper told him as he threw his head back to empty the crisp packet into his gaping mouth. 'Just before dark.'

'On the road?'

'Na. Heading across country.'

'Where we can't get at him.'

'He needs shelter and food,' Scrapper thought out loud as he crumpled the crisp packet and wiped his fingers on his legs. 'That means he has to ask somebody for it. He's around here somewhere, I can feel it. We'll find him all right. And soon.'

'But if we can't,' Hoppy added, 'at least the cops can't either.'

Scrapper started the engine and the lorry drove off down the village street to renew the hunt. Neither of them noticed a mud-streaked car waiting to emerge from a side road between the houses. But in the car, Myler and Hanley stared intently at the lumbering lorry.

'That's the third time in two days that thing's passed us,' said Myler, his cracked face even more cracked with suspicion.

'So what?' Hanley commented drily.

'It's just getting beyond a coincidence.'

'Ah come on,' Hanley sneered. 'Even undercover cops don't drag kids around with them. You're just getting jumpy.'

'Damn right I am,' Myler agreed. 'This business has dragged on way longer than we were told it would. We should have had the money by now and be gone out of it. The longer we have to hang around, the more chance somebody's gonna start noticing something.'

'True enough,' Hanley agreed. 'And the nag is getting worse by the day, cooped up in that box.'

'I reckon we should go and see the boss and find out when the ransom's coming, if it is. Right?'

'He told us to stay put,' warned Hanley.

'Yeah,' said Myler, 'but the staying put time's just about run out now.'

He slammed the car into gear. It shot forward, turned onto the road, and sped off in the opposite direction to Scrapper's lorry.

That evening, as the light faded, the girls hurried out of the scrub wood towards the barn, their sweatshirts bulging with new supplies for Rory and Shera.

Rory was lying up in the hayloft, chewing straw with a bored expression, when he heard the door open below. He rolled over to look down.

'Hiya!' he greeted the girls, who were looking around for him.

Jenny ran to Shera with more apples, while Sam and Nina scrambled up the hayloft ladder to shake out the contents of their sweatshirts in front of Rory. There was bread, cheese, salami, biscuits, fruit, and a couple of Coke cans.

'Don't your folks notice all this stuff disappearing?' Rory wondered as he tucked in, though not so hungrily this time.

'It's our own food,' Nina told him. 'We're allowed to eat out here in return for helping at the house all day.'

'And we were very good today,' added Sam. 'To put them off the scent.' She and Nina exchanged a grin. Jenny called up from below. 'Can we take Shera out now? Please? I'd love to sit on her back. Can I?'

'Okay,' Rory agreed, and stood up. 'It'll be dark shortly. We'll be safe enough.'

'Until Garry comes looking for us,' Nina added.

'Maybe one of us should go back along the path and stand lookout,' Sam suggested.

'You can if you want,' Nina shrugged.

Sam glared at her. 'Let's just forget it.'

The girls followed him down the ladder, and waited while he untied Shera and led her out through the barn doors. He helped Jenny and Nina onto the horse's back, and Sam walked beside him as he led Shera off into the gloom of the scrub wood, where the birds were chirruping their last few notes of the day.

Some twenty minutes or so later, they emerged at the end of the path that led to the flat valley. The sun was gone, and the last light was fading from a sky scattered with stray wisps of brilliantly coloured cloud. On the hill across the valley, the dim outline of the container was fading into invisibility.

'That's it, isn't it?' Rory asked the girls. They all nodded, tension in their eyes as their stared out across the gloom.

'Keeping a horse locked up in that is savage altogether,' Rory muttered darkly.

Sam turned to the other two and tugged at them to get down from Shera. 'Come on. It's my turn on the way back.'

From behind them, in the distance, came Garry's voice.

'Jenny! Nina! Sam!'

The girls jumped nervously. 'Damn!' Sam hissed. 'Now I'll have to wait till tomorrow!'

Nina slid off quickly and helped Jenny down. 'We'd better hurry before he gets to the barn,' she advised.

Jenny hugged Shera's muzzle. 'See you tomorrow!' she promised before diving off into the greenery in the direction of Garry's voice. Sam patted Shera's side and waved goodnight to Rory before following. Nina lingered, looking awkward.

'Will you stay out long?' she asked Rory.

He shook his head, eyes still on the distant spot where the container stood. 'Long enough for Shera to eat what she needs.'

Nina moved up closer to give Shera a final pat. Her arm pressed against Rory's. She looked steadily into his face with a funny half-smile, as if waiting for something. 'Well. Goodnight then.'

Rory felt distinctly uncomfortable. Suddenly Sam burst out of the greenery again. 'Are you coming, Nina!'

Nina scowled at her. 'Yeah, yeah! Okay!'

The two girls disappeared into the scrubwood shadows.

'Spacers!' Rory muttered to himself. Shera snorted as if in sympathy.

Rory turned back to gaze across the dim valley. His brows lowered, and he chewed his lower lip thoughtfully. Then he climbed onto Shera's back, and urged her gently in the direction of the container.

Scrapper's lorry halted across the entrance to the farmyard, engine running. He and Hoppy turned sideways and strained their eyes in the near-darkness to make out the house.

'Well, that's certainly no yellow cottage with roses growing up it,' said Scrapper irritably. 'We're spending more time looking for this famous oul' fellah than we are looking for Rory!'

Hoppy nudged him. 'Look.'

As they watched, Jenny, Nina and Sam burst from the bushes, ran across the yard, and into the house. Seconds later, Garry followed, like a herdsman bringing home his herd for the night.

'Kids!' said Hoppy. 'They might know something!'

Garry was almost at the front door when Scrapper rolled down his window and and called out to him. 'Hello there!'

Garry turned to look. He frowned, then smiled and waved cheerfully. Probably neighbours, he was thinking to himself, better go and say hello. But just as he took a step towards the lorry, he heard the faint sound of Monica's raised voice railing at the girls in the house. Uh-oh, he told himself, better get in there before there's a murder. So he gave another wave towards Scrapper and Hoppy and hurried inside.

'How d'you like that for ignorance!' snorted Scrapper.

'I'll go in and talk to them,' Hoppy offered, and started to open his door. But Scrapper looked at his watch.

'Ah forget it. I've had enough for the day. It'll take us an hour and a half to get home, and we're both beat and starving.'

'But that'll be three nights Rory's been roughing it,' Hoppy objected.

'Well, I just hope he's hungry and uncomfortable,' Scrapper said sourly. 'He's due some misery for what he's putting us through. Come on, we'll find him tomorrow.'

He accelerated the lorry away, and Hoppy closed the door.

Rory and Shera by this time had reached the other side of the valley, where Shera stopped and dropped her head to the juicy uncropped grass. But Rory urged her on.

'Come on, Shera. I want to take a closer look at that thing.'

Reluctantly, Shera plodded up the slope till they reached the hawthorn bushes. There, Rory dismounted and led her along a narrow path between the thorny branches. The dim outline of the container began to take shape ahead of them in the light of a rising half-moon. As they approached it, Shera began to make snuffling noises and shake her head.

'Look, Shera. Hay,' Rory told her as they emerged from the bushes. Shera moved forward past him, but not to the hay bale lying on the ground. Instead she went right up to the container and rubbed her muzzle against it, snuffling. Rory joined her.

'Is there really something in there?' he asked her quietly. 'Can you smell it?'

From inside the container came sounds of clumsy movement.

'Wow!' hissed Rory. 'There is an' all. Let's have a look.'

Shera clomped after him as Rory went to the back of the container where a rough wooden ramp led up to the doors. She waited as he walked up it and tried the stiff lock mechanism. After a few tugs, the levers moved, and one half of the doors began to swing slowly open.

'What a smell!' Rory groaned as the fetid air from the container wafted out over him. At the bottom of the ramp, Shera snorted.

Cautiously, Rory pushed his head inside. But before he had got very far, a horse's huge head appeared in front of his, teeth bared. Rory jumped back in shock, and fell over. The horse snorted, and Shera snorted back. Then the head sank back into the darkness of the container.

Rory got up again and crept back to open the door wider. Weak moonlight filtered into the interior. Mouth agape, Rory watched as the horse sank down onto its bed of filthy straw. It was obviously in great distress.

'It's a racehorse!' he told Shera without looking back. 'And he's in a bad way by the look of him.'

The racehorse lay watching suspiciously as Rory inched towards it. 'What are you doing locked up in here, fellah?' Rory asked in a soothing voice.

He was just reaching out a hand to stroke its head when the distant sound of a car engine made him turn with a start. He jumped back to the doors. Headlight beams were cutting through the gloom, coming this way. Rory's heart raced.

'Sorry, oul' fellah!' he apologised hurriedly to the racehorse as he closed and locked the container door again.

Rory jumped down the ramp, grabbed Shera's halter rope, and pulled her quickly back through the hawthorn bushes as the car drew nearer. On the other side of the bushes, he tied her rope to a branch. 'Don't move. Stay quiet,' he hissed at her.

He scuttled back through the bushes and wriggled into the same spot where the girls had lain the night before. Hardly breathing, he watched as the car slowly approached the container, stopped, and its headlights switched off. Two shadowy figures emerged from it. Myler and Hanley.

'Will we let him out for a bit?' asked Hanley.

'Ah, we'll just give him another blast of tranquilliser,' Myler replied. They both sounded very disgruntled.

'Any more of that stuff and he'll just give up and die. Racehorses are delicate things, y'know.'

'So what? You heard what the boss said. No ransom by tomorrow, and the horse gets the bullet. Bang. It'd be kinder to him if he did pass away in his sleep.'

Hidden in the bushes, realisation suddenly dawned on Rory.

'It's Sir Gert!' he whispered to himself. Caught up in his own drama with Shera, he had forgotten the famous kidnap.

Behind him, Shera suddenly let out a quiet snort. The men at the container ramp froze.

'What was that?' Myler spat in a low voice.

'Came from over there!' hissed Hanley.

The men walked to the bushes and stood right in front of Rory's hiding place, listening. Rory kept dead still, praying that Shera would do the same.

'Ah, it's probably just a sheep or a badger or something,' Hanley decided after a few silent seconds. 'Let's take a look at our friend and get out of here. If he's happy enough we'll just leave him be for the night. It might be his last.'

They turned and went back to open the container. Once they were inside, Rory slid gingerly backwards under the bushes till he emerged beside Shera.

'Quiet now!' he whispered as he untied her. 'It's that kidnapped racehorse Sir Gert that's in there. Sounds like they're planning to shoot him. We have to do something!'

Shera seemed to understand, and trod delicately as Rory led her away into the darkness of the valley.

At the farmhouse, the girls had silently suffered a thorough telling-off from Monica and Garry, then obediently trooped upstairs to bed.

Jenny chattered on in a non-stop whisper about Shera, and how exciting the whole business was, while they washed, brushed their teeth, and undressed. Sam and Nina, quietly lost in their own thoughts, didn't interrupt her or even tell her to shut up. Finally Jenny got into her sleeping bag, and after a few minutes, the chattering stopped in mid-sentence. Her eyes were closed and her mouth hung open in apparent deep sleep.

Nina got into her sleeping bag and lay back, hands behind her head. But Sam felt too restless to lie down. She paced around the free floor space, brushing her hair and fidgeting with anything that was lying around. She still couldn't believe this was really happening. It was like something out of a book. And Rory. He was really mysterious. And good-looking.

'Hard to believe this is really happening,' Nina suddenly said from behind her. 'It's like something out of a book.'

Sam gave her a quick glare. 'Don't get carried away with any romantic ideas – it's a serious business.'

But Nina stared up at the peeling ceiling, paying no attention to her. 'And Rory's really mysterious. Pretty good-looking too.'

'He's nothing special. Just another dumb boy. And you don't know what he's really done, he might be some kind of delinquent.' Sam wondered why she was talking like this, and why she felt so hostile.

Nina gave her a strange look. 'Yeah,' Nina said. 'Could be. Maybe we should tell him to go before he gets us into trouble too.'

'Maybe we should,' Sam agreed. Their gazes crossed, and Nina rolled over to go to sleep. Sam went on brushing her hair.

Rory had put Shera back in the barn, then raced off through the dark scrubwood along the path the girls had cut, tripping and stumbling. When he poked his head through the greenery around the yard, there were lights on in the ground floor of the farmhouse, and in one upstairs room. He tiptoed quickly across to a pile of concrete blocks and crouched behind it, looking up. After a few moments, Sam's head passed across the upstairs window. Rory scraped up a few pebbles and moved closer.

His first throw missed. But the second rattled against the glass. Then another. Sam appeared and pushed the window open. She peered around nervously till she saw Rory crouching in the shadows below. He signalled to her to come down, and she quickly closed the window again.

In the bedroom, Sam pulled on her sweatshirt and tiptoed carefully past the mattresses where Jenny and Nina lay, eyes closed and breathing deeply. But as soon as Sam had gone out and closed the door, Nina sat up, and hurriedly began to dress. This done, she too crept out and silently closed the door.

Immediately, Jenny opened her eyes, jumped up, and began to pull on her clothes too.

Garry and Monica were arguing in low voices behind the closed door of the kitchen as Sam crept past.

'I'm getting pretty fed up with this constant work, work, work myself!' Monica was saying. 'We came here to get away from the rat race, and here we are slaving day and night in our very own labour camp!

The kids need a break now and then. I need a break. Even you need one, Garry.'

'Okay, okay,' Garry sighed. 'I suppose you're right. Maybe we'll take a couple of days off and go down to Dublin for the weekend. We'll talk to the kids about it in the morning.'

Their voices droned on as Sam ever-so-quietly slipped out through the front door. She scurried across to Rory at the pile of blocks, and crouched beside him, smiling.

'Did you want to see me?'

'Yeah,' he replied seriously. 'There's a kidnapped racehorse in that container. And I heard two guys say they're gonna kill it tomorrow if there's no ransom.'

Sam was shocked. 'Is that the horse that was in the newspapers?'

Rory nodded. 'It's got to be Sir Gert!'

'I'll tell Garry and Monica and get them to phone the police!' Sam half-turned to race back to the house but Rory grabbed her by the arm. 'No! If you call the Guards, I'll get done too! Me and Shera are on the run too – remember?'

'But we have to do something!' Sam pleaded.

'I know. Come on!' He turned and scuttled off into the scrub wood. Sam hesitated, then hurried after him.

Not long after, they were back among the hawthorn bushes near the container, looking out at it.

'Looks like they're gone,' Rory whispered to Sam, who huddled close to him, almost touching.

'Who are they anyway?' she asked.

'Could be the IRA,' he answered grimly.

'Terrorists? Oh not that, please!' Sam breathed.

Suddenly Rory grabbed her arm. 'Ssssh! I hear something!' he hissed. They both froze. From close by came the faint sound of movement, drawing nearer. Sam clutched Rory's hand and they held their breath. Closer it came. Closer. And closer ...

Then Nina burst in on them from behind.

'There you are!' Nina whispered in relief. Rory and Sam let of whooshes of trapped breath.

'You almost gave us heart failure!' Sam snapped at her. 'What are you doing here?'

'I saw you slipping off together,' Nina explained, with an edge on her voice. 'I just wondered what you were up to.' In the gloom, she and Sam exchanged a challenging stare.

Rory told her what he had discovered. He had just finished when Jenny's head appeared abruptly in their midst.

'Waaah!' she grinned, imitating a ghost.

The others jerked in fright, then rounded on her. 'You little idiot! Be quiet! There are terrorists round here!' Sam spat.

Jenny's gleeful grin turned to open-mouthed fear.

'There were,' said Rory, looking around. 'If they were still here they'd've heard us by now. Come on.'

He stood up and broke out of the bushes, heading for the container. The girls followed nervously.

Rory scuttled to the rear door, checked around, then hopped up the ramp and operated the door levers. The door swung open.

'Steady lad, it's only me again!' Rory said softly before he disappeared inside.

The girls waited at the foot of the ramp, sniffing the awful smell. From inside the container came the sound of heavy movement, then Rory reappeared leading the stumbling racehorse by a halter rope. The girls looked up in awe at the huge animal as it picked its way down the moonlit ramp behind Rory.

'He's magnificent!' Sam breathed.

'How could they treat him like this?' Nina asked angrily. 'They must be savages!'

The horse stopped at the foot of the ramp and eyed them all warily. Rory tried to pull him forward.

'He's in bits from being drugged,' Rory told the others. 'But we've got to get him out of here, quick!'

He tugged again, but his full strength made no impression on the dazed horse. Then Jenny stepped out of the shadows, an apple in her outstretched hand.

'Good horsey. Nice horsey,' she coaxed gently. 'Come with us. We'll look after you.'

Sir Gert sniffed the apple, then crunched it slowly between his long teeth. Jenny stroked his mucky head, then took the halter rope from Rory and pulled gently on it. The racehorse stumbled into motion and followed her towards the bushes, while the others looked on open-mouthed.

'Right!' Rory said decisively. 'Let's get this door closed and get out of here!'

Sam and Nina helped him lock the container door, then all three hurried after Jenny and Sir Gert.

They pressed along in silence in the weak moonlight till they were almost at the barn. Then Sam spoke.

'What do we do now? We have to tell the police.'

Rory shook his head vigorously, horrified.

'No way! I told you – they'll take Shera off me again!'

'Well, what then?' Nina demanded, exasperated.

Rory shrugged. 'I'll think of something.'

Shera looked round as the barn door creaked open and Jenny led in the shadowy bulk of Sir Gert. The others followed and went to get their handlamps before closing the door again.

Shera lifted her muzzle and made snuffling noises at the racehorse, and Jenny watched fascinated as he replied the same way. Then Sir Gert tried to go towards Shera. Jenny dropped the rope to let him. He plodded over to stand beside Shera, head drooping, while the old mare sniffed at him and rubbed her muzzle over his stained coat.

'Look!' Jenny said, delighted. 'They like each other!'

'That's great,' Sam agreed. 'But we can't keep him here too. As soon as those terrorists discover he's gone, they'll come poking around here in no time.'

'They probably won't go back to the container till the morning,' Rory said, thinking out loud. 'That'll give me a good start.'

He went over to his things in the corner and started packing his bags, putting the leftover food in his pockets.

'What are you doing?' Nina asked him.

'I'm going to take him a few miles away and tie him up near a farm or a house. Then we can make an anonymous call to the cops and tell them where he is. That way, they won't come near here. Not till I'm well gone with Shera anyway.'

Sam and Nina exchanged another tense glance. Jenny was engrossed in stroking the two horses.

'But the racehorse is sick,' said Sam. 'Look at him.'

Rory put the bags beside Shera and picked up Sir Gert's halter rope. 'Ah, he's a tough fellah, this one. Won more races than any horse alive, my Da says. He'll survive.'

He pulled the rope and turned Sir Gert back to the barn door. Shera shook her head in protest. Sir Gert looked back.

'He wants to stay with her!' sad Jenny.

But Rory pulled firmly on the rope. 'Sorry pal, you can chat her up some other time. We have to get you to safety.'

Sir Gert obediently trudged behind him through the door.

'What are we supposed to do?' Nina called after Rory.

'Go home and go back to bed!' he advised in a low voice.

'But what if those men come to the house?' Sam worried.

'They won't! Fellahs like that never show themselves. They're too sneaky!'

Rory and Sir Gert were swallowed up by the shadows. The girls looked at each other. 'Is this really happening? To us?' Nina asked nobody in particular.

'We'd better do as he says,' Sam said. They closed the barn door on Shera and silently hurried back towards the house.

In the middle of the night, there was something of a commotion at the container.

Several cars had arrived, with Hanley and Myler and four or five other men. One of them was a thickset middle-aged man with spiky grey hair, dressed a bit like a small-time businessman. He spoke in clipped, hard sentences, and the other men addressed him respectfully as Boss.

The new men were gathered round the Boss at the foot of the container ramp, looking up at Myler and Hanley, who were shining handlamps into the empty interior, and looking very shocked.

'He was lying right there when we left!' Myler mumbled. 'Doped!'

'How long ago?' the Boss asked with cold patience.

Hanley looked at his watch. His arm shook. 'Two hours. Nearly three.'

'Three hours,' the Boss repeated flatly. He rolled his lips for a moment. 'Your orders were that one of you was to stay here at all times.'

Hanley walked down the ramp, and Myler followed.

'But Boss,' Hanley tried to smile, 'we only nipped away for –'

'Shut up!' the Boss snarled, and grabbed Hanley by the shirt when he got close enough. There was a moment's tense expectancy, then the Boss let go and regained his composure. 'I'll deal with you two later. First we have to find who's got the horse, and get it back.'

'But what's the point?' Myler protested. 'If we're not getting the ransom?'

'We are,' the Boss told him flatly. 'They changed their minds. But first they want us to let somebody see it's still alive.'

Hanley groaned and slapped his forehead. 'Damn!'

'Exactly,' agreed the Boss, and turned to the men beside him. 'It'll be light in a few hours. Whoever they are, they can't have got very far. Find that horse, and whoever has him. And when you do ...' He patted the bulge of a pistol inside his jacket. The other men nodded and turned silently back to the cars.

'Mangan, wait,' the Boss ordered. The man called Mangan, a tall thin type with a neat black beard, turned back in military fashion. The Boss swung round to Myler and Hanley. 'You two. Torch that container. You probably left your prints all over it.'

Myler pulled a large can of petrol from under the container, and

Mangan and the Boss watched as the two men piled up straw in the container and soaked it with petrol.

'What're you going to do with them, Boss?' Mangan asked softly with a malicious little smirk.

'Use them as bloodhounds,' the Boss breathed back at him, still looking ahead.

Myler scuttled down the ramp. Hanley struck a match and threw it into the container. There was a whoosh of flame which almost engulfed Hanley as Sir Gert's former prison turned into a fireball.

The men watched for a moment, then followed the Boss back to the cars, and drove off.

Jenny was sound asleep, but Sam and Nina were lying wide awake in their sleeping bags, stomachs in knots and talking in tense whispers, when the faint light of the distant flames began dancing on the wall opposite their bedroom window.

They got up quickly, but quietly, to look out. Far away across the scrub wood, a ball of orange flame glowed in the night.

'That's where the container is!' breathed Nina.

'The men must have come back already!' said Sam.

Nina clutched Sam's arm as they looked out, the distant flames dancing in their wide dark eyes. 'I'm scared! I think we really have to tell Garry and Monica!'

'No!' Sam hissed back. 'Remember what Rory said about losing his own horse. We have to keep our promise and wait till he comes back!'

They stared at the distant glow.

'If he ever does!' Nina whispered.

Several miles away, by the cloud-straggled moonlight, Rory was strenuously tugging Sir Gert up a sloping field. He paused to catch his breath and wipe the sweat from his face, and caught sight of the fire in the distance. He stared in dismay.

'It's them!' He was sure of it. 'They know you're gone! They're burning the container!'

Rory tried to set off again in haste, but Sir Gert shook himself and snorted, and seemed to want to lie down. Rory looked at him pleadingly, then back towards the fire. Thin beams from car headlamps were weaving and dipping away from it. Rory hauled desperately at Sir Gert's halter rope.

'Look! They're coming now! I know you feel bad, but if they catch up with us, you'll be too dead to feel anything!'

Sir Gert pricked up his ears. He seemed to understand the urgency in Rory's voice. With huge effort, he lifted his graceful legs and stumbled after Rory towards the dark tall shapes of trees at the top of the slope.

10
Running For Cover

THE TWO POLICEMEN watched patiently as Scrapper, surly-faced, finished doing up his buttons and tying his boot laces.

Ma sat at the other side of the table from the policemen, her face tense and anxious. Anto, his back to the kitchen sink, stood munching toast and drinking tea, his furtive eyes glancing at the sombre dark-blue uniforms.

The elder policeman, steely-haired and with an I've-seen-it-all manner about it him, had his pencil poised over an open notebook on the table.

'And he's gone nearly three days now?' he addressed Ma quietly. 'Why did you wait so long before calling us?'

Ma glanced guiltily at Scrapper, and prepared to answer. But Scrapper gave her a glare and cut in. 'It's not a police matter.'

'Any missing person's a police matter,' the second officer, a much younger man, informed him.

'He's not missing,' Scrapper said through his teeth. 'He's just gone off.'

'You're being a bit casual about it,' the older officer commented drily. 'What if he's had an accident. Or maybe even been abducted?'

Ma stiffened at this. Scrapper involuntarily put his hand on hers, then quickly drew it back. 'He's not a racehorse. He's a kid.'

'Precisely,' said the older officer. 'That's why we take a serious view of the matter.' He turned to Ma. 'You've no idea where he might've gone? Any relatives or friends?'

Ma shook her head.

'We checked 'em all,' Scrapper said for her.

'Any idea why he took off?' the younger policeman asked, looking round at all three.

'That horse of his –' Ma began to blurt out, but a fierce glare from Scrapper cut her short. Observing this, the two policemen exchanged a glance.

'Does the young fellah have a horse?' the older officer pursued.

'Did,' Scrapper told him as he poured and drank some tea. 'We had to get rid of it. Too old.'

'Ah. And he got upset.'

'Something like that,' Scrapper agreed. He was radiating hostility.

The policemen exchanged another glance. 'Listen, Scrapper,' said the older one with measured patience. 'If you want us to find this boy of yours, you'll have to be a bit more co-operative.'

'I don't want ye to find him. I'll do it on my own.' Scrapper grabbed some biscuits and stuffed them angrily into his mouth.

'So you *do* have an idea where he could be?' said the younger officer.

Scrapper ignored him and pulled on his jacket. The older policeman closed his notebook, and stood up to put it away.

'Well. All we can do is circulate his description and hope you do find him in the meantime.'

'We will,' Scrapper said without looking at him.

'I hope you're right,' said the older officer seriously. 'We'll be in touch.'

The two policemen said goodbye and left. Ma got up to refill the teapot with trembling hands. Scrapper came up behind her, fighting down his anger, and put his hands on her hunched shoulders.

'You shouldn't have done it,' he told her quietly. 'But I understand why you did.'

Ma's head drooped and tears formed at the corners of her tightly-closed eyes. Scrapper breathed deeply. 'We'll find him. Soon. Today.'

He turned away, suddenly boiling with energy. 'Come on, you!' he snapped at Anto as he headed for the door. 'You can do some of the legwork today!'

Without protest, Anto gulped the last of his tea, grabbed his jacket, and hurried after Scrapper. Ma turned to watch them go, wiping her eyes with her apron.

'Dear Lord, give him back to us safe and sound,' she whispered. 'It'll be different from now on. I promise.'

Outside on the street, the policemen sat in their car watching a grim-faced Scrapper and Anto hurry off in the direction of the yard.

'They're hiding something,' the younger officer commented.

''Course they are,' agreed the older man as he started the engine. 'I know that fellah twenty years. A bit of a tearaway in his time, but under all the hard man stuff, he's more of a family man than most. There has to be a reason he's playing this down to us.'

'Pass it on to the Special Branch?'

'Nothing else we can do.'

The police car moved off as Scrapper and Anto swung into the lane.

Hoppy was sitting grinning in the lorry cab when the yard gates swung open. 'What kept ye?' he greeted them.

'How'd you get in there?' Scrapper demanded.

Hoppy held up a wire coathanger bent into a long hook.

Scrapper pulled a wry face. 'You little ...'

But he hadn't time to be bothered, and hopped up into the driver's seat to start the lorry. Once the lorry was out in the lane, Anto closed the gates and clambered into the cab beside Hoppy.

Hoppy eyed him none too warmly. 'He coming with us?'

'He'll save you having to do all the hopping around,' Scrapper told him tersely.

'You might get your nice clothes dirty,' Hoppy smirked at Anto.

Anto prepared to give Hoppy a sharp dig in the ribs, but Scrapper threw him a cold glance.

'No messing. We've a lot of ground to cover today. We have to get Rory before the cops do. Or somebody else.'

The lorry bumped up the lane to the road, and roared off.

Jenny lay stretched out in the hayloft, munching an apple as she read a horse magazine, trying to keep her mind off the events of the night before. She'd got up while everyone else was still abed, and hurried to the old barn to make sure Shera was all right, and to bring her some morning treats. That done, she was having a few minutes to herself before going back to see if Sam and Nina were up.

She was flicking absently through the pages when she heard the sound of the barn doors opening below. Thinking it must be Rory returning, she crawled quickly to look over the edge. What she saw made her stop breathing. Two men with guns in their hands were padding quietly around the barn floor. Myler and Hanley.

The men scanned around, then walked over to Shera, who eyed them with fearless distaste.

'So that's what made the hoofprints outside,' Myler said with a disappointed snort.

'Would've been a bit too easy if we'd just walked in here and found Sir Gert standing waiting for us, eh?' said Hanley.

'Looked to me like there was more than one set of hoofmarks though,' Myler frowned.

Hanley put his gun away. 'Ah, this one's hoofprints are probably everywhere around here. Eh, old girl?' He gave Shera a smart smack on the rump. She jumped and let out a snort of indignation, and lashed out with her hind leg, just missing him. Hanley reddened with anger as Myler grinned at him.

'You never had the touch with females,' said Myler. 'We'd better go before she does you an injury.'

But just as they turned to leave, Jenny's apple slipped from her fingers and fell softly into a pile of straw below. The men instantly dropped to their knees, guns at the ready. They scanned around, then looked at each other, and stood up again.

'A mouse?' suggested Hanley.

'Probably,' agreed Myler. 'We're getting jumpy from tiredness. Let's push on.'

They went out and closed the door. In the hayloft, Jenny shook for a few seconds, then went limp.

Back at the farmhouse, Sam and Nina sat at the table looking tired and tense, while Monica bustled around serving breakfast.

'Now, once we've finished here,' Monica was telling them, 'you can come upstairs and help me hang some wallpaper. It'll be great to have one part of the place that feels clean and fresh, eh?'

The girls grunted listlessly. Monica gave them a look of curiosity. 'You two look half dead. What's the matter?'

'We couldn't sleep,' Sam told her.

'Any particular reason?' Monica wondered.

The girls exchanged a quick glance before shaking their heads. They avoided her eyes as they ate unenthusiastically. Monica's suspicious frown intensified. 'Where's Jenny?'

'Gone out,' Nina mumbled.

Monica stood in front of them, hands on hips, arms akimbo.

'Really, girls, you've all been acting very odd the last day or two. We can understand that you still feel very strange here. We all do. But I think it's time to buckle down a bit. Agreed?'

Sam and Nina nodded lifelessly.

'Good,' said Monica and started clearing the table as she continued talking. She didn't notice Jenny's agitated face at the kitchen window, signalling urgently to the other two inside.

'Garry and I had a discussion last night. I finally got him to agree we all need a bit of a break from this place now and then.' She turned away to carry some plates to the sink. 'So if we get through the next couple of days, we'll probably be going to Dublin for the weekend. How does that sound to you?'

There was no reply, so she looked around. The girls were gone.

'That does it!' Monica screeched in a tantrum, and smashed a plate on the floor.

Jenny was very agitated when the the other two scuttled up to her in the fringe of the scrub wood. They squatted beside her.

'What is it?' Sam demanded. 'Is it Rory?'

Jenny shook her head. 'It's the men! The ones that wanted to kill the racehorse. They were in the barn. They touched Shera.'

The others gasped.

'Did they see you?' hissed Nina.

'No. I was up in the hayloft.'

'Did you hear what they said?' Sam asked. 'Did they know the racehorse was there last night?'

Jenny shook her head. 'They followed the hoofmarks, but they thought they were made by Shera.'

They gave each other frightened, helpless looks.

'They must be searching everywhere,' Nina breathed. 'They'll probably come to the house next!'

Nearby, among the interlaced branches, a twig snapped. The girls froze. Leaves rustled. Then the foliage beside them parted.

'There ye are!' Rory hissed at them. 'I thought I could hear ye!'

The girls almost collapsed with relief.

'You nearly killed us with fright!' Sam spat at him.

'We thought it was the terrorists!' said Nina. 'Don't do that again!'

'They've been to the barn!' Jenny told him, hugging his arm. 'They're hunting for you everywhere!'

'I know,' Rory said matter-of-factly. 'I had to slip past a few hard-looking types on the way back here. How's Shera? She okay?'

Jenny nodded. 'I went to her as soon as I got up.'

'Great. Thanks.' Rory patted her arm.

'What about the racehorse?' Sam wanted to know. But Nina gave her a scathing look before asking Rory: 'How are *you*?'

'Sir Gert's tied up in a bit of a wood a couple of miles away. He's a lot better now that he's out in the open and moving around. And I'm starving. Anything to eat?'

'We'll go and get something for you,' Sam offered and started to move off. But Nina grabbed her arm.

'If we go back to the house, Garry and Monica will make us stay and work.'

'Right,' agreed Sam. 'What'll we do?'

'We can go down to the village and buy some things,' Jenny suggested brightly. 'Then we can all have a picnic!'

'Picnic!' Nina sneered. 'With all those terrorists running around the place?'

'She's right about the village, though,' Rory said. 'You lot can go and buy the stuff for me while I sneak Shera up to where Sir Gert is.'

He pulled money from his pockets and gave it to Sam.

'But how will we find you again?' Nina asked.

'I'll show you where the place is. You can see it from just back there. Come on. I want to get Shera away from here.'

'But those men are still around,' Sam warned.

'Just keep low and keep quiet,' Rory advised the girls. 'Like in the movies.'

He turned and led them off into the undergrowth.

On the far side of the farmhouse, Garry was hammering stakes into the ground when he saw Monica coming towards him through the thick weeds, a mug of coffee in her hand. He straightened up and wiped his sweaty brow, and gulped the coffee down when she handed it to him.

'Thanks. I needed that.'

He swept an arm across the area around him. 'This'll be the main vegetable area. The soil's great underneath. Over there we can plant soft fruit. Raspberries, and a big strawberry bed. We might even get into mushrooms eventually.'

'Eventually,' Monica echoed, arms folded. Garry sensed her tension.

'How are the girls getting on?'

'They're not,' she replied flatly. 'They ran out on me.'

Garry sighed wearily and drained the mug.

'I've had just about enough of being patient and understanding with them,' Monica told him seriously. 'I think it's time for action. Even if it means being a bit hard.'

'Okay,' Garry agreed. 'Just let me finish this and we'll go and look for them.'

Monica took the mug again. 'I'm serious. If we let them go on running wild, they'll only end up getting into trouble.'

She turned and walked away. Garry watched her for a moment, then lifted the sledge hammer and started thumping the stake again with mighty blows. He was so intent on the task and his thoughts he didn't notice a slight movement among the bushes far away. Two half-hidden faces were peering out at him. Myler and Hanley.

'They're not locals,' Myler whispered.

Hanley shrugged. 'Sounds like English accents.'

Myler let the branch go and turned away. 'Come on. There's nothing there.'

Hanley followed him back into the deep shadows under the leaves.

A mile or so away, Rory led Shera and the girls along a sheeptrack on a hillside field. The top of the hill was cloaked by the edge of an oak wood. Below and much further away, a large country house nestled by the side of a narrow hedged road.

Rory stopped. 'See that house way over there?'

The girls squinted in the direction he was indicating.

'That looks like the kind of place horsey people live in. We'll take Sir Gert over there and let him off in a field where he'll be found. By the time they've checked with the Guards and figured out who he is, me and Shera'll be long gone.'

Nina was unconvinced. 'But what if the men go looking for him there?'

Rory smiled a cocky little smile. 'Sure, they don't know where to start looking for him. We've been too smart for them. I'd say they'll give up pretty quick and blow while they can.'

'I wouldn't be too sure,' said Nina.

'Where's Sir Gert now?' Sam asked him.

Rory nodded up towards the oak wood. 'In there. I'll take Shera up to him while you go down to the village for the supplies.'

'Okay. Let's go,' said Sam, and pushed Nina ahead of her.

But Jenny hung back. 'Can I stay with you and Shera?'

'Sure,' Rory told her. They set off again up the path towards the hilltop wood.

Sam and Nina arrived at the village about twenty minutes later, breathless and hot from having jogged most of the way.

They hung around the side of a house for a few minutes, checking anxiously for anybody suspicious coming along. But the place was dead quiet. So they took a deep breath, and hurried along the long straight street to the little shop with the ugly sign saying 'supermarket' over the door.

The woman at the cash register squinted at them when they hurried in, and grunted a greeting. Nina and Sam nodded briefly, then quickly began choosing their purchases, whispering occasionally.

So intent on the task were they, they didn't notice a lorry with a hydraulic hoist on the back, pulling up outside.

In the cab, Scrapper let out a breath as he looked around.

'Here we are again. Every road in the world seems to lead back to this place.'

'Deadsville,' Hoppy pronounced.

Scrapper leaned forward to peer into the shop. 'Hey. There's a couple of kids in there. Girls.' He turned to Anto. 'Come on, lover boy. Get in there and sweet talk them. Maybe they've seen something.'

Anto moved reluctantly to obey.

'And get us a bottle of Coke while you're at it,' Scrapper added. Anto held out a hand for the money, but Scrapper gave him a look. 'You owe me a tenner. Remember?'

'That was ages ago, Da,' Anto objected. 'I'm broke.'

Scrapper made a resigned face as he pulled out a bundle of notes and gave him one. Anto took it and jumped out. Hoppy and Scrapper exchanged little grins as they watched him furtively run a comb through his gelled hair before he pushed open the shop door. They saw him pretend to look round the untidy shelves inside as he flicked assessing glances at the unnoticing girls.

'Bet he goes for the big one!' Hoppy chuckled.

'No problem to him,' Scrapper commented, still smiling. 'He's a good-looking lad all right. Bit like meself when I was that age.'

Hoppy gave him a surprised frown, then looked back at the scene inside the shop with lowered eyebrows.

Sam and Nina had paid for their bag of provisions, and were heading for the door, when Anto blocked their path, clutching a bottle of Coke and smiling a big white-toothed smile.

'Hi there.'

The girls stopped, nervous.

'I'm Anto,' he went on. 'Maybe you can help me. I'm looking for my brother.'

The girls exchanged a quick nervous glance. Sam put on her cold aloof expression. 'I'm sorry, we don't know anyone around here. We're strangers.'

'Well, he's not from around here,' Anto continued, trying to be ultra-cool and sweet. 'He's from Dublin, and he's run away from home. His name's Rory, about thirteen, cheeky looking. And he's probably riding a scruffy little brown and white horse. Seen anybody like that recently?'

The girls stiffened in shock. Nina pushed brusquely past him.

'Sorry. We're in a hurry. Ask the lady there.'

The owl-eyed lady watched as Sam and Nina tumbled through the door and set off along the street at a run, carrier bags flapping at their sides.

In the lorry cab, Hoppy and Scrapper were highly entertained by the look on Anto's face. 'Looks like I'll have to give him a few hints on chat-up technique,' Scrapper grinned.

In the shop, Anto gave a disgusted snort and went to pay for the Coke, pink-faced.

'English,' Owl-eyes told him confidentially and sympathetically. 'They're all quare.'

Anto went out and got into the lorry.

'What did you say that made them take off like that?' Scrapper asked him as they drove away.

'Nothing,' Anto replied, still miffed. 'I just asked them about Rory and the horse.'

'What did they say to that?' Hoppy asked.

'Nothing. Just shoved me aside and ran. They looked jumpy about something. They're English, the woman says. You know what they're like.'

'English?' Scrapper echoed with a frown. Something in his mind was trying hard to connect with something else. 'Now where did I see an English number plate around here?'

The lorry picked up speed.

Garry and Monica emerged from the thick greenery and stood looking at the barn.

'Does this belong to us?' Monica asked him.

'Yes. The girls are using it as a hideout.'

They crossed to the barn door, opened it, and wandered inside.

'Sam! Jenny!' Garry called out in a stern voice.

'Nina! Come out here this instant!' Monica added in the same tone.

They stood looking around the dim, silent interior of the barn for a moment, then Garry crossed to the ladder and climbed halfway up to the hayloft. His eyes narrowed at the sight of the empty drink cans and food debris.

'Garry, look here,' Monica called from the stall. He climbed down to join her. She was pointing at a pile of dull green stuff on the floor.

'Horse manure?' Garry said, puzzled.

'It's fresh too.'

They looked at each other, baffled.

'But how ...' Garry began. Then, over Monica's shoulder, he caught sight of something half-hidden in the straw. Quickly, he went to pick it up. A teeshirt.

'That doesn't belong to any of the girls,' said Monica.

'Then who does it belong to?'

They looked blankly into each other's eyes.

'This is getting very mysterious,' Monica muttered.

'Let's hope it's not serious,' said Garry.

They turned together and hurried out.

In a layby screened from the road by a line of low trees, the Boss pored over a map spread out on a car bonnet. Other cars stood nearby, and seven or eight men – some of them with walkie-talkies – stood around watching as the Boss drew on the map with a big black marker pen.

'Byrne, you and Jennings take the north road,' the Boss instructed without looking up. 'Corky. Walsh. This area here. Mangan and Laffer, check out these two bits of forest.'

Mangan twisted round for a better look at the map.

'Bits? They cover half the county. That's a needle in a haystack job, that is.'

'Check the entrance roads for hoofprints. There's a million in cash riding on that horse, don't forget. We'll find it because we have to. He's still around this area. Somewhere.'

'Maybe he's been taken out by road,' Mangan persisted.

The Boss shook his head. 'There's only three roads in and out of this area, and our boys've seen nothing that could carry a horse in the last two days.'

The growling sound of an engine approached along the road. They turned to look as Scrapper's lorry sped past, barely visible, on the other side of the low trees.

'There it is again,' said Myler.

'There's what?' the Boss asked.

'That lorry,' Hanley told him. 'It's been cruising round the place for the last few days with a fellah and a little kid in it.'

Myler shrugged. 'Probably nothing.'

The Boss narrowed his eyes in the direction of the fading noise of the lorry. 'Check it out,' he ordered and turned back to the map.

Hanley and Myler hurried to their car and drove off. The Boss turned to the others.

'Right. Let's get on with it. Keep a low profile. Check in every fifteen minutes on the radios, in rotation. Go!'

The men split up and scrambled into their cars.

11
Closing In

IN THE HILLTOP oak wood, Sir Gert and Shera stood close together under the tree where they were tied, nuzzling each other.

Jenny and Rory sat at the base of a nearby tree, watching. Rory was bleary-eyed and weary, but Jenny was as bright as ever.

'They really like each other, don't they?' she remarked happily, hugging her knees.

'Yeah,' he replied after a yawn. 'But he's a bit out of her class.'

Jenny looked at him quizzically, not understanding.

'They're too different,' he explained, a bit irritably.

Jenny frowned. 'What does being different matter if they like each other?'

She turned her gaze back to the horses. Rory leaned back to get comfortable against the tree trunk, yawning again. Jenny flicked glances at him from the corner of her eyes. What is it about boys, she wondered to herself, that makes Sam and Nina go all funny when they're around?

Rory's eyelids drooped.

'Who do you fancy the most?' Jenny suddenly asked him. 'My sister Sam, or Nina?'

Rory's eyelids jerked open and he gave her an annoyed look.

'Who said I fancy either of them?'

Jenny glared back. 'Of course you do. I can feel it when the three of you get near each other. You're all jumpy, and you keep looking each other up and down when you think nobody's watching.'

'Rubbish!' Rory snorted. 'We're just uptight because of the situation we're in!' He slid right down the tree trunk and rolled over on the moss. 'I'm wrecked. I'm gonna have a quick sleep. Wake me up when the others get back.'

He closed his eyes. Jenny's gaze switched back and forward between him and the nuzzling horses. Boys! she thought scornfully. I'd rather have a horse any day.

Garry and Monica hurried out of the scrubwood and across the farmyard.

'You don't really think they stole a horse!' Monica was saying with deep concern. 'That's unbelievable!'

'We won't know what to think till we find them,' Garry replied grimly.

They were almost at the front door when Scrapper's lorry came growling into the yard and stopped right behind them. Garry and Monica turned in surprise to watch Scrapper, Anto and Hoppy tumble out of the cab and stride towards them.

''Morning,' Scrapper greeted them.

'Good morning,' Garry replied, a bit stiffly.

Scrapper nodded towards the house and the various signs of toil. 'Doing the place up, eh? Big job.'

'Yes,' Garry agreed. 'Excuse me. Are you one of our neighbours?'

'Ah no. We're from Dublin. We just stopped by to ask you something.'

Look, I'm sorry, we've got a bit of a crisis on our hands at the moment,' Garry said, and started to turn away.

'This won't take a second,' Scrapper assured him. 'We just wondered if you might've seen a young lad on an old brown and white horse around here in the last day or two?'

Garry and Monica stopped and turned back.

'It's my young fellah,' Scrapper went on. 'My son Rory. He's run off with his horse.'

Anto suddenly darted forward and grabbed the teeshirt from Monica's hand. 'Where'd you get this?'

'I ... we found it.'

Anto held it up to Scrapper, excited and angry. 'It's mine.' He stretched it out to reveal the word 'Superstud' printed on the front. 'I got it done last month. He must've robbed it out of my drawer when he took off!'

Scrapper looked at Garry and Monica. 'Where'd you say you found it?'

'In our barn. Over there,' Garry said, pointing.

'And there were fresh horse droppings too!' Monica added.

'The girls must have been hiding the boy and his horse,' Garry figured out loud. 'That's why they were so jumpy and strange.'

'Girls?' Scrapper echoed.

'Our daughters,' Monica explained. 'They disappeared this morning, and we found the tee-shirt in the barn when we went looking for them.'

'Is one of them blonde, about fourteen?'

Garry frowned and nodded. 'Sounds like Sam? Have you seen her?'

'Could be. Back at the village. There was a dark-haired one with her.'

'Nina!' Monica said. 'What were they doing?'

'Buying stuff,' Anto chipped in. 'Bags of it. And they were in a big hurry to go somewhere.'

'They must be hiding Rory somewhere around here so!' said Scrapper, looking around. 'Any idea where they might be? You know the area.'

Garry shook his head. 'We've only just moved in here.'

Scrapper thought tensely. 'We'll follow the hoofprints. Where's this barn?'

Garry and Monica led them all quickly into the greenery.

They had only been gone a few moments when Myler and Hanley's car slowed to a halt across the yard entrance. The two men stared suspiciously at the deserted lorry in the yard.

'What d'you think?' Myler asked.

'Dunno. The container's less than a mile away. Then there's that barn with the old horse. And all them hoofprints.'

They stared for another second or two, then Myler engaged the gears again. 'We'll put the car out of sight and take a look, eh?'

Sam and Nina had sprinted out of the village, but eventually had to slow to a trot because of the bags. They hurried along the hedgelined road, hardly talking, till they rounded a bend that brought them to a little crossroads. On one corner stood a shiny, brand-new telephone booth, looking very out-of-place.

'Wait! I think we should call Monica and Garry,' Nina burst out when she saw it.

'But we can't!' Sam argued. 'We promised Rory not to tell!'

'We don't have to tell!' Nina assured her. 'I just want to say we're all right. They'll be wondering what has happened to us by now.'

Sam frowned. 'Okay then. But just say we'll be back in a few hours.'

They trotted over to the phone box and dropped the bags outside before going in. Sam looked around anxiously through the glass as Nina inserted the money and dialled the number, which she already had off by heart. The calling tone sounded, once, twice, three times. Then the receiver at the other end was lifted.

'Monica? Garry? This is Nina!' she blurted out.

There was no reply.

'Hallo? Hallo? Monica? Can you hear me?'

'We can hear you,' came a man's voice.

Nina was startled. 'Who's that?!' she demanded.

'A neighbour, you could say.'

'What are you doing in our house?'

'Looking for a lost horse.'

Nina gasped and covered the mouthpiece with her hand. She looked at Sam, face white. 'It's the terrorists! They're in the house! They must have taken Garry and Monica prisoner!'

Sam's mouth fell open. Then she suddenly grabbed the phone from Nina's hand.

'Listen, you can have your stupid horse back!' she shouted into it, trembling. 'Just don't harm Garry and Monica!'

'Ah,' said the voice coolly. 'So you do have the horse? Where is it?'

Sam caught her breath. 'Let us speak to Garry and Monica first!'

'You tell us where the horse is first,' came the menacing reply.

Sam hesitated. Then: 'It's in a wood on top of a hill, two or three kilometres from the farmhouse. Now let me speak to Garry and Monica!'

There was a chuckle from the other end. 'I'm afraid they're not at home right now. But I'll take a message for them if you like ...'

The truth dawned on Sam. 'Not there? You mean, you haven't got them –'

The phone clicked dead. Sam and Nina stared at each other.

'It was a trick!' breathed Nina. 'They tricked us!'

'Garry and Monica must be out looking for us, and the men sneaked into the house!' Sam said.

'And you told them where Jenny and Rory and the horses are!'

Sam dropped the phone and shoved the door open.

'Come on! Hurry!'

In the farmhouse, Hanley stood by the old-fashioned phone, smiling at Myler.

'Well. That's a handy bit of luck all right. It was kids that took the nag. He's in a wood on a hill somewhere near here.'

'Right,' said Myler. 'Let's get on the radio to the Boss. This should clean our slate with him a bit!'

They hurried out of the house and across the yard.

Garry and Monica, led by Scrapper, and followed by Anto and a struggling Hoppy, were also hot on the trail.

Once Scrapper had a quick look around the hideaway barn, he picked up the hoofprints in the bare earth outside, and had no problem following them through green shadows of the scrub wood.

After he had been following the prints intently for about ten minutes, and everybody else had been intently following him, he stopped and knelt down. Nobody asked him why – they were all just glad of the chance to catch their breath – so he told them: 'There's more than one horse making them tracks.'

Monica looked. 'How can you tell?'

'The way they're spaced, for a start. Then look at the difference between this one and that. That's a different shape, and deeper.'

They all crowded around to look. Hoppy had to elbow his way in.

'You're right,' Garry agreed. 'How did you spot that? Are you a hunter?'

Scrapper stood up and grinned at him. 'Na. I just watched a lot of cowboy movies when I was a kid.'

'But how can there be a second horse?' Monica asked, baffled.

'Maybe Rory's got to like this horse rustling business,' Anto suggested with a little smirk.

'We'll find out as soon as we catch up with them,' said Scrapper. 'Let's go.'

Off he went again, with the others in tow. But Hoppy was wilting at the rear. 'Hey! Wait for me will ye!'

In the hilltop wood, Rory was fast asleep at the foot of the tree trunk. Jenny stood by the horses, stroking them.

'Don't wake him up,' she whispered to them. 'I'm just going to check if Sam and Nina are coming yet.'

She tiptoed off through the trees, watched by the two horses. Once she was out of Rory's earshot, she speeded up, weaving through the trees till she reached the edge of the wood, where it opened onto the long, downsloping field. Far to the right, the close-cropped grass gave way to a straggly maze of low furze bushes, some of them still with yellow flowers on their prickly branches. She strained her eyes to the road beyond and waited.

After a while, two tiny figures came into view on the road. They were carrying plastic bags, and seemed in a great hurry. 'Sam and Nina!' Jenny told herself triumphantly. She jumped up and down with excitement, and waved to the two girls below, even though they couldn't see her among the trees.

Then a movement off to the left caught her eye. Hidden from the sight of Sam and Nina by the curve of the hillside, several cars sped up and halted at the gate at the bottom corner of the field. Men jumped out, pointed up to the wood, and started talking among themselves.

Jenny sank down out of sight, horrified. She switched her gaze back to Sam and Nina, who were hurrying towards the slight bend in the road that hid them from the men. Jenny's hands made small helpless signs at them, and she whispered pleadingly: 'Stop, dummies! They're waiting to catch you!'

Down on the road, Sam came to an abrupt halt. Nina, running head down from weariness, crashed into her back and almost fell over.

'What is it?' Nina demanded, half-angry, half-fearful.

Sam stood head up as if listening for something. 'I don't know ... I just suddenly got this feeling.'

'What feeling?'

'A queer feeling. Like a warning. Stop. Danger ahead.'

They both stared towards the bend, which just looked like any other bend on an innocent country road. Then, from behind them, came the sound of a fast-approaching car. Without a word, the two girls jumped in unison into the dry ditch under the overhanging hedgerow, and cowered down. They peeped out just long enough to catch sight of Myler and Hanley's car flash past from the direction the girls had just come.

'They're here already!' Sam hissed.

'What do we do now?'

Sam glanced around. Behind them was a small round gap under the hedge into the field beyond. They nodded to each other, and proceeded to squirm through.

Myler and Hanley were already reporting in person to the Boss, proud of their success.

'You're sure this is the place?' the Boss demanded of Mangan as he took another squint at his map.

Mangan's taut face nodded. The Boss's brows lowered as he peered again at the trees on the skyline above. 'Could be a trick to delay us.'

'There's one way to find out,' said Hanley, and moved to open the field gate. But the Boss grabbed him.

'Hang on! We have to make sure there's no way out for them first.' He addressed all the men. 'Spread out in a circle around the base of the hill. Check in on the radios in five minutes, then close in fast when I give the order. Go!'

In the cover of the trees above, Jenny watched heart-in-mouth as the men pushed open the gate and ran both ways along the bottom of the field. She looked further to the right, near where Jenny and Nina had disappeared from the road. There they were! Still clutching the carrier bags, the two older girls had popped out from under the hedge, and were scuttling up the slope on the far side of the long maze of furze, which kept them hidden from the advancing men.

Jenny turned and raced back into the wood.

Sam and Nina got nearly halfway up the slope before Nina suddenly hissed from behind: 'Hide! Quick!'

They both tumbled sideways into a gap among the furze, and then looked back down the slope. Several of the gang were hurrying along under the hedgerow to take up position on the far side of the hill.

'They'll see us if we go on!' said Sam.

Nina's lips tightened as she thought. She lifted up a handful of dried grass and broken furze twigs, then looked round at the furze bushes. 'I think I have an idea!'

She sat up a bit and rooted in her pockets while Sam kept a fearful eye on the men below. But what Nina finally produced drew Sam's attention even more – a crushed pack of cigarettes and a booklet of matches.

Sam stared in amazement. 'What're you doing with those things?'

Nina quickly heaped up a little pile of dry grass and twigs under a furze bush. 'I just bought them to try it. Once. It was disgusting.'

But even in the midst of their present crisis, Sam still felt obliged to berate Nina. 'Cigarettes are disgusting, filthy, poisonous, dangerous things and –'

'Okay, okay! Quit the preaching!' Nina growled. She had struck a match and lit the little tinder pile. Once it was burning strongly, she stuck the cigarette pack on top of it. 'There! Happy now?' she hissed.

Sam frowned as the flames grew. 'Yes, but ... What's this for?'

Nina wriggled backwards till her foot was at the burning pile. Then she kicked it so it scattered under the furze bushes.

'Just watch,' she advised, and almost smiled.

Rory awoke with a start. Jenny was shaking him like an all-star wrestler and yelling in his ear: 'Rory! Wake up! They're here!'

He jerked upright and stared around. 'Who? The girls?'

'Yes! But the terrorists are here too. Sam and Nina will get caught. We have to do something!'

Rory scrambled to his feet and Jenny dragged him off toward the edge of the wood. The watching horses snorted after them and tugged on their halter ropes.

At the same time, Scrapper and company had emerged from cover on the other side of the road to get their first view of the hilltop wood.

'That looks a likely place,' he muttered over his shoulder to Hoppy, who was by now perched on Scrapper's broad back like an underfed monkey.

Scrapper was about to forge ahead when Garry came from behind and silently pointed out the cars at the field gate. The Boss and one other man were intently watching the wood above.

'Is that the police?' Monica wondered hopefully.

'Don't look like Guards to me,' Scrapper frowned.

Then Hoppy pointed and jiggled up and down on Scrapper's back. 'Hey! Fire!'

From the furze thickets, dense clouds of smoke were streaming across the hillside field.

They all watched for a moment. Then Scrapper let Hoppy slip down off his back. 'You lot stay here. I'll go up to that wood for a look.'

Garry stepped forward. 'I'll come too.'

'No,' Scrapper told him firmly. 'I don't like the look of this. I want to suss it out quiet like. And one of us has less chance of being seen than two.'

Garry nodded reluctantly and Scrapper set off, keeping low and dodging from cover to cover.

But the Boss was too busy to look behind him, anyway. He was yelling into his hand-radio, face red: 'They know we're here. They've started a fire for cover. Close in now. Fast!'

From their positions under the hedgerows, his troops began advancing uphill into the smoke.

On the other side of the smoke screen, Sam and Nina, still clutching the by now battered bags, had at last gasped their way up to the trees. There, waiting to greet them with relief, were Jenny and Rory.

'You made it! You made it!' Jenny squeaked in delight as she hugged each of them in turn.

Rory looked past them at the swirling smoke. 'Come on! We have to get out of here quick!'

He turned and hurried back to the horses ahead of the girls, and had both steeds untied and ready when they caught up with him. 'Jenny and Nina, you get on Shera. Me and Sam can ride on Sir Gert.'

'Can he do it? Is he well enough?' Sam asked dubiously.

''Course he can!' said Rory. 'The fresh air has him nearly cured!'

Rory made sure everyone else was up and ready, before he scrambled up in front of Sam and urged the big racehorse forward in the opposite direction from the smoke-shrouded hillside.

Down at the field gate, the Boss was in a powerless rage, roaring for radio reports from his men, only to be told they could see nothing but smoke and sky.

'If they make a break,' he sprayed into his handset from foaming lips, 'shoot anything that moves! Except the goddam horse!'

Rory found a bit of track through the trees and followed it, holding back the powerful horse's speed to let Shera and the younger girls keep up with them. Sam clutched him tightly from behind, and even in the turmoil of panic and terror, he could sense her close presence causing other feelings to creep through. A curious buzz of excitement, and a surge of determination from the thought that Sam and the others were now depending on him. He forced himself to concentrate on controlling Sir Gert.

The path continued straight for a bit, then began to dip down. Good, thought Rory, we'll be out and away in no time.

But no sooner had the thought formed in his head than a figure materialised among the trees ahead. A man with a gun in his hand.

Sam's clutching arms tightened like steel around Rory and she squealed in his ear. Behind them, Shera pulled up short. Rory tried to pull Sir Gert to a halt, but the horse ignored his tugs of command, and bore down steadily on the man straddling the path.

'Stop!' the man barked, and raised the gun.

Sir Gert looked right over his head and bore straight on.

'Pull up or I'll shoot!' the man barked again. But he had heard the Boss's order about not harming Sir Gert, and was beginning to lose his nerve. Sir Gert advanced till he was right in front of the man, then halted of his own accord. The man seemed relieved. He waved the gun at Rory and Sam. 'Get down!'

Abruptly, Sir Gert rushed at him. The man let out a sharp yell as he fell sideways into some ferns, and his pistol discharged a harmless blast as the soft greenery swallowed him.

The sharp bang acted as a signal to the two horses. In unison, they broke into a fast canter down the tree-lined slope, their riders clinging on desperately. Rory was so intent on trying to get the racehorse under control again that he didn't notice, far away among the trees to one side, a distant figure waving at him.

'Rory!' came the faint echo of Scrapper's voice through the maze of trunks and branches.

Rory heard the tiny sound, but his mind was so busy on other things, it had no time to make sense of it at the moment. And so it was stored away automatically in a dark drawer of memory for later evaluation. If he ever remembered it was there.

Gasping from exertion, Scrapper held onto a tree trunk as he watched the two horses and their four passengers disappear from his view. His dripping forehead was wrinkled in disbelief. Sweat rained from the end of his nose, as he shook his head in horrified amazement, then turned and loped back the way he had come.

At the field gate, the Boss was listening to the latest radio report. 'They got out the other side,' said the voice. 'They're gone.'

The Boss said nothing for several seconds. Then came his cold reply. 'No, they're not. Get back here all of you. Now!'

He rammed the radio set into his pocket and marched back to his car.

12
Hounded

GARRY, MONICA, HOPPY and Anto were anxiously watching the last of the gang's cars sped off from under the smoke-covered hillside, when Scrapper lumbered back into view.

Monica seized him as soon as he was close enough. 'Did you find them? Are they all right?'

Scrapper nodded, gulping for air. 'I saw them, all right,' he wheezed.

'Only saw them?' Garry echoed.

'Rory and Shera?' Anto butted in.

Scrapper began to recover. 'And the three girls,' he informed everyone. 'And a racehorse!'

'A racehorse?!' Hoppy's face crumpled in incredulity.

'But where are they?' Monica persisted.

Scrapper nodded to the trees up beyond the wreaths of smoke. 'They galloped off out of the other side of that wood up there. The mob in the cars are after them, for whatever reason.'

Suddenly Hoppy's face uncrumpled and blazed with a shocking realisation.

'Sir Gert! The racehorse is Sir Gert!'

Scrapper's deep breathing slowed. Anto gaped stupidly.

'It couldn't be,' Scrapper whispered.

'Who's Sir Gert?' Monica demanded impatiently.

'A racehorse that was kidnapped,' Anto told her. 'They want a million before they'll give him back alive.'

'We read about that,' Garry remembered. 'In the newspaper on the ferry. But surely this isn't the same ...?'

They all looked at each other.

'I don't want it to be true any more than you do,' Scrapper agreed.

'We must get the police *now*!' Monica said through her teeth. 'The children's lives are in danger!'

Scrapper's nostrils flared. 'Well you can call them, hang about till they turn up, and then waste more time trying to explain the story to them. Meantime, I'm gonna try getting to the kids before that mob does.'

With that, he turned and set off back the way they had come from the farm. Garry looked to Monica for guidance, and followed without a word when she set quickly off after Scrapper. Anto trotted off too, leaving Hoppy in the rear again.

'Hey!' Hoppy complained. 'I won't be able to keep up with ye!'

Anto turned back and offered Hoppy his back to jump up on. Hoppy was surprised. 'Sure you'll be able for it?'

'Come on! Hurry before I change my mind!' Anto urged him.

Hoppy hopped up and they charged off.

Rory rattled Sir Gert's halter rope to urge him through the close-packed pine trunks into a small clearing. He patted the big horse's sleek neck and praised him, while he and Sam waited for the other girls and Shera to emerge from shadowy forest behind them.

When they did appear, Rory quickly slid off Sir Gert and started to help everyone else off.

'What are you doing?' Sam complained.

'We'll have to walk from here,' he explained. 'Shera's not strong enough to carry anybody for long, and Sir Gert needs a break now and then.'

'But the men!' Nina objected as Rory almost dragged her and Jenny to the ground. 'They'll be coming after us!'

Rory put on a show of nonchalance despite what had almost happened to them only a short while before. 'They'll never find us in here. They'll probably just give up and go home.' But he was expressing a hope rather than a belief.

He reached up to help Sam, but she swung down on her own. 'You said that the last time and look what happened!' she challenged.

Their eyes locked at close range. It looked like becoming a who-out-stares-who match, but Nina decided to intervene. She marched forward with Shera's halter rope, right between the two of them. 'Let's go, then.'

The girls led the two horses the few steps across the clearing to a dark gap in the trees on the other side. The movement disturbed a bird which shot up and away into the blue circle overhead, in turn startling Rory. He stood, head thrown back, staring up the broad tube of light that cut down through the surrounding dense growth. He had suddenly remembered the distant sound of Scrapper's voice.

'Rory!' Sam called back. He hurried to join her. 'What is it? Did you hear something?' she wanted to know.

'Not here,' he mumbled, confused. 'Back in the other place, when that guy tried to stop us. I didn't have the time to figure it out till now. It was like somebody was calling me. My Da's voice.'

Sam's eyes widened slowly as she remembered something too. 'When we were in the village shop, a boy stopped us. He said he was your brother. Anto. And there was a lorry outside. With a man in it.'

'Da!' Rory breathed, hardly daring to believe it. Then Nina and Jenny called to them anxiously from the dark gap. 'We'd better move on,' he said, and grabbed Sir Gert's halter rope.

Scrapper headed straight for his lorry when he arrived at the farmyard ahead of the others.

He had it started and turned to face the gate again, when Garry and Monica turned up.

'The police!' she yelled at him, nearly hysterical.

'You handle that!' Scrapper told her tersely. 'Where's them two lads?'

Anto, with Hoppy still on his back, staggered into the yard, looking fit to collapse. But Scrapper had no time for sympathy.

'Come on, will ye!' he roared, revving the lorry engine.

'But we need the police!' Monica pleaded. 'You can't take on that gang alone!'

Hoppy was already helping Anto into the cab. 'Yeah. Right,' Scrapper agreed with Monica. 'Send them on to us when they're ready!'

Monica turned and ran into the house. Scrapper looked at Garry.

'What about you? They're your kids too.'

Garry nodded, uncertain. 'I'll follow you in a moment.' The lorry roared off.

In the house, Monica had found the number of the local police, dialled, and tugged tensely at the cable of the handset while she waited for the reply.

'Hurry! Please answer! Please!' she breathed.

But it rang and rang, slowly, almost lazily.

Outside, a horn honked. She looked out through the window to see Garry at the wheel of their van, waiting to chase after Scrapper's lorry. Garry signalled urgently at her to know if she was coming. Monica became very agitated. She listened to the lazy ring of the phone again. But when the van's horn hooted once more, she threw aside the handset and rushed back outside.

The phone rang a few more times. Then there was a click, and a man's voice answered through the dangling handset: 'Garda Station. Hello?'

Outside, the van sped out of the yard.

The dangling phone receiver spun slowly on its cord, while the voice continued to probe the silence like an echo-sounder: 'Hello? Hello! This is the Gardai here. Do you need help? Do you need help!'

It was an idyllic day for a picnic, and the elderly couple were thoroughly enjoying it in their quiet, elderly way.

Blue sky above, green trees around, bird song on the gentle breeze. Ah, the glory. The memories.

They had chosen their usual spot to park the old Morris Minor. A little layby at the edge of the pine trees on a half-forgotten side road. The forestry people had set up picnic tables and benches here, but as far as the elderly couple knew, nobody ever visited this place, except them. It was, they were sure, theirs exclusively.

The gentleman – a big bony chap with thick silver hair – puffed contentedly on his pipe and mused over his newspaper, while the lady – plump, muscular, and energetic – laid the table from the basket in the car boot. The spread was just as good as at home – lace-edged tablecloth, second-best china, silver trays for cakes and biscuits, and even a teapot-shaped thermos flask. Perfect.

She was just about to pour the tea when five speeding cars charged into the layby and scraped to a halt near the entrance. The old couple stared in indignant resentment. The cars burst open and disgorged the Boss and his mob, who ignored the staring couple and huddled around a map on a bonnet.

'Are we supposed to find them in there?' protested Myler.

'It'll take us a month,' Hanley agreed.

'Shut up!' snapped the Boss. He tapped his head. 'We only have to use the skull. Look. They went in here, from this direction. They'll most likely keep heading on that line and follow the contours. That means, they'll eventually try to slip out the other side ... here. At that road. And that's where we'll be waiting for him.'

'They might try to double back,' Mangan objected.

'They won't,' the Boss assured him. 'Not when they hear the beaters behind them.'

'Beaters?' Hanley echoed.

'Yeah. The way the game hunters do it,' the Boss almost smiled. 'Send in a bunch of noisy fellahs to scare the animals into the waiting guns.'

The men all smiled as they understood the idea.

'Mangan,' the Boss continued, businesslike again. 'Take two of the lads and move in this direction. Spread out. Make a lot of noise. Let off a shot or two now and then. The rest of us'll be waiting to pounce when they come out. Right? And no foul-ups this time.'

The elderly couple stirred their tea peevishly as they watched the gang split up. The Boss and several others drove off again, while Mangan and his chosen companions came jogging towards the couple's sumptuous table.

''Morning,' Mangan greeted them as they swept past. 'Grand day for it.'

And they were gone. The old couple sipped their tea, staring at the two intruding vehicles by the layby entrance.

'Pleasant young men all the same,' the old fellow ventured with a mannerly smile. His good lady silently lifted a delicate salmon sandwich to her mouth, and beheaded it with one snap of her gleaming dentures.

Deep inside the forest of nodding pines, Rory was leading the band of horses and girls along a soft narrow path.

Jenny began to fall further and further behind. 'Wait!' she called out. 'I'm tired.'

'So am I,' agreed Sam.

'We could all do with a rest,' Nina chimed in. 'Let's take five minutes.'

Rory pulled Sir Gert to halt. They tied the horses loosely to trees and sat down to inspect the contents of the bags Sam and Nina had brought from the village.

'Give us a look. I'm starving too,' Rory demanded.

They divided everything up, and ate and drank in grateful silence for a few minutes. Then Jenny dutifully collected all the rubbish into one bag and tied it on Shera's back.

'What are we going to do now?' Sam asked the others. 'We have to get help.'

'First we have to find the way out of this place,' said Rory.

'Then what?' Nina prompted.

'When we come to a road, you lot can stay out of sight with the horses, while I go and hunt for a house with a phone, or stop a car, or something.'

Jenny got up to give the horses some chocolate and the last two apples.

'You mean, we have to stay in this forest with those men hunting for us?' Nina protested.

'Ah come on!' scoffed Rory. 'They're not mad enough to keep looking for us in this jungle.'

'How can you be so sure?' Sam insisted angrily.

''Cos it's logical,' Rory argued back defiantly. 'You're just letting fear get a grip on you. Panicking.'

The crack of a distant shot rang through the trees around them. Rory jumped to his feet, spilling the last of his crisps, his face shocked. The girls gasped, and the horses started in fright, almost knocking Jenny over.

'It's them!' Nina moaned. 'They're coming again!'

'Maybe it's someone hunting deer!' Sam whispered hopefully.

Another shot echoed. It definitely came from back where they had entered the forest.

'It *is* them!' said Nina. 'Let's go!'

Rory hurried to the horses.

'It is them, isn't it?' Sam pursued him.

'No point hanging around to see,' he muttered, but his bravado was deflated as he helped her and the others clamber once again onto the horses' backs. Then Sam pulled him up, and with a light kick, he urged Sir Gert on deeper into the gloom.

A bit less than three miles in a straight line ahead of them, the boss car and the two others spun off a road onto a forest work track, and slewed to a halt. The passengers all jumped out.

'Right!' the Boss ordered with a smirk of expectation. 'Spread out wide and move in slow. They'll come running right into our arms. Like lemmings.'

The men moved off into the trees, guns ready.

Anto and Hoppy had to hang on as Scrapper swung the heavy lorry through the tight bends of the roads. He sat forward over the wheel, his head as stationary as a robot's. Only the eyes moved behind the thick lenses of the spectacles, scanning the terrain ahead.

'What's your plan, Da?' Anto asked on a straight stretch of road.

'Haven't got one,' Scrapper replied bluntly.

'But we can't just charge baldheaded at that mob,' Hoppy protested. There was some kind of budding unity between him and Anto now, just a bit. 'They've got guns.'

'The Lord's always on the side of the righteous,' Scrapper responded drily. 'We'll be given some way to trip them up. All we have to do is keep looking for it. Ah. There it is!'

He slowed the lorry as they approached the picnic layby.

'That's two of their cars there.'

'You sure?' queried Anto.

'Cars is my business, son. Specially scrapping them. No sign of the men. They must have gone in on foot. Let's do it, Anto.'

The elderly couple, who had by now reached the cake stage of their picnic, watched with distaste as Scrapper's lorry drove alongside one of the gang's two parked cars, and stopped. Scrapper jumped out and hopped onto the flat back of the lorry, nodding and smiling curtly towards the couple as he did so. He handed long metal bars to Anto and Hoppy, who hurried to the car and gleefully proceeded to smash in all its windows.

The elderly couple exchanged a slow look.

Scrapper meantime activated the big hydraulic grab arm behind the cab. He slung lengths of strong chain onto its big hook, then operated controls to extend the main arm and swing it over the car the boys had just eagerly vandalised. Anto jumped up on the car to let down some of the chain. He and Hoppy passed it through the broken windows, under the roof, out again, and back up to the hook.

Then the boys stood back to watch as Scrapper operated the hoist to lift the car into the air, swing it high over the other one, and then let it drop. The second car flattened with a grinding smash.

Anto scrambled up to undo the chain, and the grab arm was docked again. They all got back in the lorry, and waved cheerfully to the couple as it reversed out of the layby.

On the road, Garry and Monica finally caught up in their van.

'That's one lot that won't get away so quick!' Scrapper called to them, smiling grimly.

The lorry roared off, and the van followed.

The elderly couple at the picnic table watched them go, then rotated their eyes back to the two piggyback cars.

'Really!' sniffed the woman. 'And there's a sign down there that says No Dumping. Some people just don't care at all!'

Far into the forest, Mangan stepped carefully along a faint deer path through the tightly-packed tree trunks. Something caught his eye. He put away his gun and knelt down. Hoofprints, barely visible in the spongy forest floor of brown pine needles. A few feet further on, he spotted some horse droppings. Fresh, maybe only ten minutes old.

Mangan stood up and looked around. Far away to his left, one of his companions could just be seen advancing slowly through the densely-packed trunks. Mangan whistled. The man signalled back. Mangan indicated the new direction to go in. The man acknowledged and moved off. Then Mangan looked to the right till he spotted the other far-off gang member, and signalled him the new line of sweep. Then all three pressed on after the fleeing band, faster now as they sensed the hunt was nearing its climax.

Further on, Rory and the girls had been finding it hard to squeeze the horses through the ever-denser ranks of trunks. The light was dim and the ground underfoot treacherous with broken branches and hidden loose rocks. Shera and Sir Gert seemed to stumble and scramble to stay upright almost every tenth step.

Eventually, they emerged into an area where the trees had been thinned out. There were long clear lanes a few feet wide between the trunks here, and the horses hurried along these gratefully, on what felt like a very gentle downward-slope.

Suddenly, Rory pulled up Sir Gert and turned his head as if listening.

'Are they still following?' Sam asked from behind him.

'Ssssh!' he hissed, puzzlement on his face.

Shera halted close behind.

'It can't be them!' Nina protested. 'They're on foot. They couldn't have kept up with us. Could they?'

'Listen!' Rory ordered, annoyed.

They all listened, even the horses.

Drifting gently in through the gaps between the trees came the faint music of a flute.

'Fairy music!' Jenny gasped. 'It's the leprechauns!'

'Leprechauns – don't be mad!' said Rory. 'Unless they're into Kylie Minogue!'

They all listened again. Sure enough, the sound took shape into the unmistakable strains of 'The Locomotion'.

'There's somebody up ahead,' said Sam and slid to the ground. 'Come on. But quietly.'

The others slipped off and followed her on tiptoe.

They stepped cautiously forward, noticing that the light ahead was stronger, till they came to a point where the trees halted abruptly in a straight line. They tied the horses to a trunk and crept forward to look out.

In front of them lay a very large clearing, roughly square, about the size of a decent field. In the centre of this stood a low ramshackle hut made from scrap timber and sheets of battered corrugated steel. Nearby, a goat on a long tether munched grass, and some scruffy hens wandered around. The general area was messy and untidy.

Sunning himself on a camp bed in front of the hut lay a man. A long skinny man, with a dull blond beard and similar hair pulled tightly back into a pony tail. He was playing a gleaming silver flute. And he was totally naked.

Rory and the girls exchanged a slow look. Sam smirked. Nina spluttered. Jenny turned her eyes away, her cheeks pink.

The music stopped. The man had put down the flute and picked up a wooden recorder. He began to play again, and this time the light breeze wafted the notes of an intricate classical piece to their ears. It was faultless, and had them mesmerised.

But Rory broke the spell.

'We'll have to take a chance on him,' he decided and stood up. 'We need help. Let's get the horses.'

They untied the horses, then in a group they all stepped out from the trees and marched purposefully towards the hut.

The naked musician was just as astonished to see the band of youngsters and the horses as they were to see him. He stopped playing in mid-phrase, and his jaw slumped open.

'It's supposed to be rats, not horses!' he breathed.

He rose slowly to his feet as the youngsters drew near. The looks on their faces suddenly reminded him that he was wearing nothing, so he hurriedly grabbed his nearby jeans, and rammed them onto his spindly legs.

'Hello, there!' he greeted them with smiling confusion, once they were close enough. He waved his long hands at the jeans. 'Sorry about that. I wasn't expecting anybody to drop by, way out here.'

'You got a phone, mister?' Rory demanded unceremoniously when the troop halted in front of the hut.

The musician let out a little scoff of a laugh. 'A phone? Here?'

But Rory wasn't in humorous mood. 'Yeah, mister. A phone. Rrring-rring? Know what I mean?'

The musician's eyes flashed for a moment. 'Yeah, sonny, I know what you mean, and the answer's still no. And don't call me mister. That's a term of abuse where I come from. The name's Joe.'

Jenny had wandered to look at the goat, but Rory and the other two girls were looking anxiously back at the forest. Joe the musician's brief hostility evaporated as he sensed the youngsters had a problem.

'What d'you need a phone for anyway?'

'We need help,' Sam explained.

'Help?' Joe echoed, brow beginning to furrow. 'What kind of help?' Then his full attention was caught by Sir Gert. He stepped across to the horse and stroked its neck with admiration. 'That's a fine looking creature you have there. Is he the trouble?'

'That's Sir Gert,' Rory told him flatly.

'Sir who?'

'Sir Gert. The racehorse that was kidnapped. We set him free and now they're after us.'

Joe looked, fascinated, at Sir Gert.

'A kidnapped racehorse, eh? That's a good one, all right.'

'It's true!' Nina insisted. 'You've got to help us!'

'You must have seen it on the telly or in the papers,' said Rory. 'Heard it on the radio even?'

'I don't have any of those things up here, by choice,' Joe informed them. 'But come on inside and tell me all about it while I put on some coffee. Sounds like an interesting story.'

He led Sir Gert over to the hut and tied him up to one of the wall posts.

'He's a spacer!' Rory hissed at Sam. 'Let's get out!'

'But he can help us!' Sam whispered back, and pulled Rory towards the sack-covered hut entrance Joe had ducked through.

Inside was like a tramp's residence. A crude bed with a sleeping bag lay along one flimsy wall, and an old door on some milk crates served as a kitchen at another. On this stood some tins, items of fruit, cups, plates, and a little camping stove.

In front of the third wall, opposite the door, stood an upright segment of a thick tree trunk, perhaps five feet high. It had been partially carved away to reveal the shape of a giant tin opener, its surface covered in elegant Celtic patterns. Wood shavings and carving tools littered the floor around it.

Joe was in his 'kitchen' reheating a pot of recently boiled water.

'So,' he recapped without turning. 'You've gone and re-kidnapped a kidnapped racehorse, and now the kidnappers want to kidnap it back from you. Is that it?'

Fear made Rory aggressive. 'Look, you have to believe us! There's a gang of them out there hunting us down right now. With guns!'

'Sounds like something you'd see on the telly, all right,' mused Joe as he stirred water and coffee together in a cup. 'In a kids' thriller series or something.'

He turned to see Sam and Nina eyeing the strange sculpture. 'Unusual, isn't it?' Joe commented with satisfaction. 'Can't wait to see what it's like when it's finished.'

'Are you a sculptor?' Sam asked.

'Wish I was. But I'm afraid it's just recreation. Like the music, and this primitive lifestyle. All holiday amusements.'

'Holiday?' Nina echoed.

'We haven't got time for this!' Rory began. But Joe talked right over him, obviously determined not to be put off his favourite subject: himself.

'Yes. Believe it or not, in real life I'm a freelance computer programmer. Software artist, I prefer to call it, actually. Ten months of the year I drive myself mad writing control software for industrial robots. The other two months I spend up here in my hideaway, messing around and getting back to nature. Like the old-style hippies. It's the only way I can stay sane.'

He raised his cup to his lips. Rory, bursting with fury at this time-wasting self-indulgence, was about to roar something at him, when the sharp sound of three distant, evenly-spaced shots penetrated from outside.

They all froze. Joe's coffee dripped past his limp lips and dribbled down his bare chest.

'Now d'you believe us!' Rory spat at him and rushed out.

'Over there! They're coming!' Jenny screamed as she rushed back from the goat to snatch Shera's trailing halter rope.

Sir Gert snorted and tugged at his rope. The wall of the hut swayed. The others tumbled out of the hut just as another shot rang out, closer.

'You were serious right enough,' breathed Joe, his tanned face a lot paler now as he quickly pulled on a faded shirt.

'Hurry!' Rory shouted. 'Away!'

He helped Jenny and Nina up onto Shera's back, and slapped the old mare's rump. She galloped off towards the other side of the clearing, knowing herself the best way out of danger.

Rory turned to Sir Gert and started trying to untie him. But Joe had tied some kind of a double knot in the rope, and Sir Gert's tugging had made it pull tight. Rory swore as he picked at it.

'Come on, Rory!' Sam pleaded, hopping up and down as she kept her eyes on the shadows behind the forest edge.

Joe suddenly grabbed Rory's arm. 'Listen, son, if there really are men with guns looking for that horse, my advice is let them have him. As long as you have him, they'll keep coming after you.'

Rory and Sam were horrified at this idea. Sir Gert snorted.

'But they're gonna shoot him!' Rory snarled back, nearly in tears.

'They won't shoot anything that valuable. But they might shoot you and me and all your friends here to get him back.'

'Gimme a knife!' Rory pleaded desperately. 'I'll cut it.'

Another shot rang out, closer again. Sam turned and ran after Shera and the others.

'Leave him, son!' Joe intoned seriously, staring Rory right in the eyes. 'They'll be happy and turn back. Then we can get to the road and get the cops onto them. Right?'

Rory went limp as his will gave way. Another shot, and voices, came to them. Rory looked up at Sir Gert, who gave him a wild look and snorted in protest again. But Rory let go of the rope and allowed Joe to drag him away.

'Come on, hurry!' Joe urged. He and Rory broke into a sprint in pursuit of Sam, and crashed into the cover of the trees, hot on her heels.

The square clearing lay quiet in the sunshine for a few long moments. The goat munched, the hut rattled slightly in the breeze, and Sir Gert waited, head low and nostrils flaring.

Suddenly, Mangan and his companions emerged from the forest, and surveyed the scene with the brashness of men who carry arms. They stared down at Sir Gert tethered and apparently docile, and exchanged a look of jubilation. Then they ran down towards him.

'So there y'are, my old friend,' Mangan grinned up at the racehorse. But the big sleek head pulled back when Mangan's hand reached out to touch him. Mangan gave him a hostile glare.

'Aha. The fresh air's made you cocky again, eh? Well, we'll put that right again shortly.'

The other two men returned from scouting around. 'Anything?' Mangan demanded. They shook their heads.

Mangan nodded to the door of the hut, and they sauntered up to it. They listened for a moment, then barged in through the sack door, guns at the ready. What they found inside both intrigued and amused them, especially the sculpture.

'What kind of a can does that thing open?' one of them scoffed.

Another of them found the coffee. 'Hey, look. There's even something to toast our success with!'

Grinning at each other, they started brewing up.

Rory meanwhile was lying at the edge of the trees, looking back at Sir Gert and the hut. Joe crawled up beside him.

'Leave it, lad! Let's go and get the cops!'

He put a hand on Rory's arm, but Rory shook it off.

'How strong is that hut?' Rory asked him.

'Not very,' Joe asked, frowning in puzzlement. He looked from Rory to Sir Gert and the hut. 'Are they inside?'

Rory nodded and looked at him. Joe's face slowly lit up.

'How well does that horse know you?'

'Let's find out,' Rory answered. He rose to his knees and let out a long piercing whistle.

At the hut, Sir Gert's ears shot up. Then his nostrils widened as he sucked in a mighty breath to fuel an all-out effort on the rope.

Inside the hut, Mangan and his mates were just raising the coffee cups to their grinning lips, when the whole structure around them began to groan and sway. They stood gaping in astonishment as it suddenly folded inwards and collapsed on top of them with a crash.

Outside, Sir Gert gave the rope one last heroic jerk and snapped it. With a cry of triumph, he turned and galloped towards the spot where Joe and Rory stood waiting, delighted and amazed.

'Whew!' Joe breathed to Rory. 'I didn't realise that place was such a death trap. You just saved my life!'

Rory ran to grab and hug Sir Gert as he cantered up to them. 'Good man yourself, Sir Gert! That's them gone for an early bath!'

Sir Gert made a sound that was uncannily like agreement.

Joe joined them and they looked across at the motionless wreckage of the hut. 'Any more of them fellahs?'

Rory nodded grimly.

'Right,' said Joe, and grabbed the remains of Sir Gert's halter rope. 'Let's go and find ourselves some nice fat policemen to hide behind!'

Back at the farmhouse meantime, a fat redfaced policemen was mopping sweat from his balding head as he prodded listlessly around the yard. A police car with blue lights rotating stood at the front door, while inside, another officer, hat tucked politely under his arm, was looking for the phone.

He found it, dangling from a dresser in the kitchen.

'Hello, Liam?' he said into it after he had hauled it up to his face. 'Des here. No, there's nobody around the house. No signs of trouble either. Yeah, it's them new English people right enough. We'll have another look around. They might've gone down the fields or something. Probably nothing serious. Call you back.'

He replaced the receiver, and went outside. The fat officer was perched on the car bonnet, loosening his collar.

'Come on, Johnjo,' Officer Des told him. 'We're going sightseeing.'

Officer Johnjo slid off the bonnet like a hippo off a mud bank, and waddled off to the scrubwood behind his colleague.

Scrapper jammed on the brakes so fast when he spotted the other cars of the gang that Garry's van almost crashed into the back of the lorry. Garry swore. 'Idiot! What's he doing?'

Monica pointed at the cars lying off the road. 'Look!'

In the lorry, Scrapper, Anto and Hoppy were also looking.

'That's them all right,' Scrapper muttered, eyes screwed up with hostility.

'Will we do a job on them too?' Hoppy asked.

Scrapper looked around and thought. 'They must be trying to cut off Rory and the other kids if they try to get out this way.'

'An ambush,' Anto nodded sagely.

Scrapper made a decision. 'We'll drive down the road a bit, then go in on foot. See what we can see.'

The lorry moved off again. Garry and Monica, looking confused, followed in the van.

A few hundred yards further on, the lorry turned into a loggers' road on the right. Here there was a cleared area screened from the main road by the trees, probably a parking place for forestry machines. Scrapper's lorry, followed by the van, drove in a circle, and stopped facing the way they had come in. Everyone tumbled out.

'What are we going to do?' Garry demanded.

'Work our way backwards to head the kids off from where that mob's waiting for them,' Scrapper explained. 'Anto, Hoppy. You stay here.'

Anto began to protest.

'It's too dangerous,' Scrapper intervened forcefully. 'Stay here. That goes for you too, missus,' he told Monica.

Monica shook her head. 'No. I'm coming.' Her voice was firm.

Scrapper looked at Garry, who jiggled his eyebrows as if to warn him there was no point arguing with her.

'Suit yourself,' Scrapper shrugged at her. 'But if it gets rough, you look after yourself. I have to watch out for the kids. Right?'

Monica nodded briefly. Scrapper turned and hurried off into the trees, and Garry and Monica followed after him.

Hoppy and Anto watched till the adults disappeared. Anto looked resigned and disappointed. Despite all the danger, he'd actually been enjoying the involvement with Scrapper.

Suddenly Hoppy nudged him in the side and turned to move off.

'Where are you going?' Anto whined. 'You heard Scrapper.'

'Just taking a look.' Hoppy grinned slyly at him. 'Coming? Or are you chicken?''

Hoppy hobbled away at an angle to the direction the adults had taken. Anto hesitated, chewing his lip, then trotted after him.

13
Recaptured!

DEEP INSIDE THE FOREST, Rory, the girls, and Joe were making good their escape, hurrying on foot through the dense trees with the horses in tow.

Bit by bit, Joe got out of breath. 'Hold on, hold on,' he told the others eventually. 'I'm not as fit as I used to be!'

The youngsters stopped and looked around anxiously.

'Can you hear them coming?' Nina asked him.

'Ah no,' puffed Joe, resting against a tree. 'That lot back there'll still be trying to crawl out of the debris.' He sniggered at the thought. 'If they can!'

'What's on your mind then?' Rory persisted.

'I just think maybe you should – we should – apply some logic to the situation, instead of rushing about like terrified rabbits. We don't know what we might be heading into, after all.'

Rory frowned. 'What d'you mean?' He looked a bit resentful, but inside, he was glad to have somebody take over the decision-making.

'Listen,' Joe lectured them seriously. 'Them fellahs back there were letting off shots to let you know they were coming after you. They wanted you to run scared.'

'Why?' Sam encouraged him to go on.

'Because more than likely the rest of them are up ahead, waiting for you to run into their open arms.'

The youngsters were visibly startled by this idea.

'What'll we do, then?' Jenny chimed in. 'Go back?'

Joe shook his head and looked round. 'No. Sideways.'

He ushered the girls and the two horses off the narrow path they had been following, and through the needle-covered lower branches of the trees. 'Just keep going in that direction,' he urged them. 'You don't have to hurry.'

'Where are we going to?' asked Nina.

'You'll see soon enough.' Joe turned to Rory. 'Gimme a hand.'

He broke off two branches and handed one to Rory. Then he began walking backwards after the girls and the mounts, brushing the pine-needled earth to remove the signs of their passage.

'I get it!' Rory grinned. 'Cover our tracks!'

He began doing the same, and they all disappeared into the gloom under the nodding conifers.

Not too far away, further along the path the youngsters and Joe had just turned off, the Boss and his underlings were waiting tensely in hiding. Every now and then, the Boss would raise his handheld radio to his ear to listen for news. But none came. He frowned and gnawed his knuckles. The other men occasionally bobbed their heads up for instructions, but he waved them down impatiently with his gun hand.

'Wait!' he hissed to himself. 'We'll have them. Soon!'

After a period of slow progress through the trackless section of forest, the youngsters and Joe found themselves at the edge of the tree cover. Joe and Rory came forward to stand beside the girls and look out at what lay ahead.

'That's what we're looking for!' Joe smiled.

In front of them lay a heavily overgrown meadow. Beyond that, in the midst of an army of ornamental trees and shrubs gone wild, stood the desolate ruins of a once grand stately home.

'The old manor house,' Joe explained. 'All the land for miles around here used to belong to it in the olden days, long before this forest was planted. The house got burned out in the civil war.'

'There was a war here?' Nina asked wonderingly.

'A long time ago,' said Joe. 'Let's go.'

He took Sir Gert's halter rope from Sam and led them all out onto the wild meadow.

It was a relief not to feel hemmed in by trees any more, and the little band quickly found themselves at the crumbling outbuildings and stables of the gaunt, ruined house. Joe found a gap in a wall where a dead bush had been jammed in. He pulled it away and looked inside. It was the roofless shell of a large barn or stable, and the mucky earth showed signs of animals having been kept there.

'Leave the horses in here,' Joe suggested. 'I think they've had enough for a while.'

'But the men will find them!' Jenny protested.

'It's pretty hard to find this place even when you know where it is. I've a suspicion some local sheep smugglers use it as a staging post. If it's safe enough for them, I'd say it's pretty safe for these two.'

The others nodded agreement.

'Then what?' Rory asked.

Joe pointed past the ruined house to a low hill with a mixed wood on it, oaks and spruces and pines. 'We'll be able to move faster without having to cover the horses' tracks all the time. There's a house about a mile the other side of that wood there. I know the man. He'll help us.'

Everyone agreed except Jenny. 'I'm too tired to walk any more. I'm staying with the horses,' she announced.

'Jenny you can't!' Sam snapped at her.

'Yes I can!' Jenny retorted. 'You heard him – it's okay here.'

The others looked to Joe, who shrugged. 'She'll be safe enough till we get back.' He smacked the two horses on the rump to urge them through the gap into the roofless shell, then hauled the dead bush back into place.

'Right. Stay out of sight,' he warned Jenny. 'We'll be back in about an hour at most. Okay?'

Jenny nodded and watched as everyone else hurried away.

'Do what he says!' Sam hissed back at her. 'Out of sight!'

When the others had disappeared among the tangled shrubbery, Jenny turned and pulled herself up to an empty window frame in a nearby wall. Inside the roofless shell, Sir Gert and Shera were trotting slowly round in a wide circle, side by side, nuzzling each other. Jenny grinned.

'Hey!' she called to them. 'Would you like some fresh hay? I'll go and gather some from the field, if you want.'

The two horses ignored her and went on circling, so she dropped down and headed off to the wild meadow anyway.

Back in the forest, the Boss was getting more and more tense and uncomfortable, crouched in his hiding place beside the empty trail. He listened, he peered out, and finally he pulled the walkie-talkie from his jacket and spoke into it with a low but harsh voice.

'Mangan! Mangan! Answer, damn you!'

Far away, in the square clearing, the munching goat watched with curiosity as the tangled remains of Joe's hut rose slightly, then collapsed back again. Faint groans came from under the debris.

In his hiding place, the Boss glared furiously at the silent walkie-talkie. Suddenly, he stood up and lobbed it far away through the trees, where it thudded against a trunk before falling out of sight. Then he signalled to the other men, who emerged cautiously. The boss strode forward into the forest, and the others followed, guns ready and heads low between their shoulders.

Hoppy and Anto had crawled along under the low branches of the pines till they found themselves looking out at the gang's cars parked on the other logging track.

'What now?' Anto whispered.

Hoppy flicked his head, and they wormed their way carefully towards the cars. Once there, Hoppy scuttled to one of the front wheels, picked up a twig, and stuck it in the valve of the tyre. He grinned at Anto as air hissed sharply out. Anto's face lit up with comprehension, and he turned to do the same to the next car.

'Two tyres on each!' Hoppy advised him. 'They've got spares, remember!'

Events were beginning to move elsewhere too. At the burnt-out container where Sir Gert had been imprisoned, the fat policeman was puffing and struggling to catch up with his fitter colleague. He mopped the cascade of sweat from his forehead as they surveyed the blackened shell.

'What's this then?' wondered the leaner officer.

'Whatever it was, it's a quare place for it to be,' muttered the fat one.

'Who owns this land?' the lean officer asked as he looked around.

The fat one shrugged. Suddenly, something on the ground caught his eye. 'Look!'

They stared at the hoofprints in the earth, then exchanged a serious glance.

'Are you thinking what I think you're thinking?' the lean officer said.

The fat one swatted a fly off his forehead. 'I think you're thinking the same thing, but you just don't want to be the first to say it.'

They both looked down again.

'Sir Gert? On our patch?' the lean officer muttered. 'Surely not?'

'Surely not, right enough,' the fat one agreed. 'But it could be. We'd better call in Special Branch straight off.'

'And where do these disappearing English characters come into it?' the other asked the sky.

'Dunno,' said the fat one. 'But we'd better find out. Quick.'

They turned and hurried back down to the flat valley.

Joe and Rory and Sam and Nina ran through the mixed wood.

'How much further?' Nina whinged. 'I'm exhausted!'

'Not far,' Joe assured her, holding her by the arm. 'I hope.'

The trees ended abruptly at the edge of a narrow rocky gorge. A thin stream splashed along the bottom of it, and the forest resumed on the other side, fifty feet or so away. Joe looked down for a safe way to cross.

'This way,' he ordered and started to clamber down. Sam followed him, then Rory, picking their way down the mossy sharp boulders. Nina came last, awkward, nervous, and genuinely tired. She had nearly caught up with the others on the gorge floor when her toe caught on a crack of rock, and she pitched forward, head first, towards the jagged stones round which the stream foamed. Her scream of terror echoed loudly against the gorge walls.

Without thinking, Rory jumped up, arms outstretched, and caught her in midflight. He fell back heavily on a level boulder, almost flattened by her. Sam and Joe leapt forward to help them.

'Well caught, lad!' Joe congratulated Rory. 'That was a close one!'

Nina lay quivering in Rory's arms. 'You all right?' he asked her, trying to sit up.

When she realised she was lying on top of him, she gave him an embarrassed little glance, but made no attempt to move. 'I think so.'

Sam stood back and pursed her lips. 'Come on, we're wasting time,' she said unsympathetically. 'There's nothing wrong with her.'

Rory and Nina got up and followed the others across the stream and up the other side of the gorge, which was less steep. Near the top, Joe looked back anxiously.

'Just hope the wind didn't carry that scream too far.'

In the pine forest, Scrapper suddenly stood stock still, listening. Garry emerged from the trees behind him and listened too.

'What is it?'

'Dunno,' Scrapper said softly. 'Thought I heard something on the breeze. Something from far away.'

'A car? A gun?' Garry probed.

Scrapper shook his head. 'Like a yell. A scream.'

Garry tensed up. 'A scream?'

Scrapper shook himself. 'Ah, probably just a bird. Come on.'

They moved forward, but had only gone a few steps when Monica came running after them, excited. 'This way, quickly!'

They followed her back through the trees till they reached a narrow path. Monica pointed to the ground. 'Look!'

There was a mash of hoofmarks and footprints in a bare patch of black soil.

'It's them! It must be!' she said.

Scrapper knelt down to inspect the prints. 'They're fresh right enough. And they're going that way.'

They hurried along the path following the marks for a while, then Scrapper came to a sudden halt. 'They're gone!' he announced.

Garry stared ahead at the unblemished path. 'But how?'

'They turned off, that's how,' Scrapper decided, and began prodding around among the branches beside the path, looking for the tell-tale prints on the ground. Monica and Garry joined in, but they found nothing. 'They can't have just disappeared!' Monica groaned.

Scrapper went to where the prints ended and peered around. His eye fell on the freshly broken stumps of branches on a nearby tree. Then he looked at the prints again, and began smiling.

'Now I get it!' he muttered. Garry came to see what it was he had got. 'See that?' Scrapper told him, pointing down to one of the footprints, which was much larger than the others. Garry and Monica looked. 'They've got somebody else with them,' Scrapper went on, 'and he's using the head. Come on!'

He dived through the stiff branches with Garry and Monica in pursuit.

At the same time, Rory, Joe and the two girls had just emerged from the branches of the mixed wood, to find themselves standing before a low white cottage with a slate roof. The area around it was cluttered with the various equipment and bits of junk used by a smallholder. Hens clucked and picked everywhere. Two ducks scurried away squawking when the group appeared, and from beyond a fenced-off vegetable garden, there was a loud low buzz from where several beehives stood.

'This is it!' Joe breathed with relief.

They rushed forward, scattering the curious hens. Suddenly Nina spotted a large grey hairy object lying on the grass nearby. 'What's that?'

It stirred. The girls backed away, ready to run.

'Don't worry,' grinned Joe. 'It's only Finbarr, the guard dog. Hiya Finbarr.'

Finbarr raised his massive head and regarded them all coolly through his tangled mass of hair. Then he slumped down again and went back to sleep.

'Guard dog?' Sam and Nina asked each other.

Joe ran to the cottage door and opened it. 'Michael? Michael, are you there?'

Inside, the cottage kitchen was neat, tidy, but deserted. The youngsters looked in through the door, tense with expectancy.

'Nobody here!' Joe informed them, irritated. 'Hunt around. Find him.'

Rory and the girls scattered in all directions around the cottage, while Joe walked about with his hands cupped to his mouth, yelling, 'Michael! Michael!' But there was no answer.

The girls and Rory came back, looking grim.

'It's true,' Sam said. 'There isn't anyone here.'

Joe swore.

'But we can still call the police, can't we?' Nina said hopefully. 'Where's the phone?'

'There isn't one,' Joe said wrily. 'Mike's a purist, like myself.'

They stood around looking helpless. Then Rory spotted something in a far corner of the yard. 'Hey! Over there!'

They all looked. Half-hidden beside an old horse-box was a car. They sprinted towards it, and Rory got there first. It was a huge black Mercedes, very old and tattered-looking. They flocked round it, excited. Rory glanced in through the driver's window and his face blazed with delight. 'We're in luck! The key's in the ignition!'

Joe jerked the door open. Rory was right. The keys were there.

'Great! Everybody aboard!'

They hauled the heavy doors open and scrambled in. Joe tried the steering wheel and let off the handbrake. 'Pray it's got petrol in it!' He stomped on the clutch, pumped the gas pedal, and turned the ignition switch. Nothing. He tried again. Nothing.

'Maybe the battery isn't connected!' Rory suggested. 'Open the bonnet and I'll look!'

Joe pulled something under the dashboard while Rory jumped out and wrestled to get the massive bonnet open. Joe joined him and helped him swing it up. The girls hung out of the windows, watching tensely. The bonnet went right up, and Joe and Rory stared into the engine compartment.

There was no engine there.

Rory's mouth fell open. Joe tapped him on the shoulder and pointed to something nearby. A large rusty car engine lay in a clump of thick grass. Two hens perched on it, watching them.

'Oh no!' Rory moaned and closed his eyes.

Joe slammed the bonnet shut and sat on it, arms folded. Rory looked round wildly, desperate.

'If there was even a bike ...!'

'It's gone,' Joe said flatly. 'I checked. He must be gone down to the village to get something.'

The girls scrambled out of the car, agitated.

'What about Jenny and the horses?' Sam wanted to know. 'We left them all alone. The longer we leave them, the bigger the risk they'll be found.'

Joe made a decision. 'Right. We've no choice. Rory and me'll have to go back and get them. You two girls stay here and alert Michael when he gets back.'

The girls didn't like this plan.

'Stay here?' Nina protested. 'On our own?'

'No. We're coming too!' Sam insisted.

Joe was getting angry. 'You can't! The more of us go back, the slower we are, and the bigger the risk. You two stay put, that's an order. Right? Tell Michael to fetch the Guards immediately. Let's go, Rory.'

He stood up and turned back the way they had come. Rory gave the girls a look of tired resignation and followed after him.

Back in the pine forest, Scrapper, Garry and Monica were rooting under the pine branches, trying to pick up the trail Rory and Joe had covered so well.

'We have lost them again!' Monica complained angrily.

'I know that, missus!' Scrapper spat back at her.

Garry grabbed them both by the arms. 'Listen!'

They all froze. The sound of dry twigs snapping drifted through the cool forest air.

'It's them!' Monica hissed and turned back to run in the direction of the sounds. But Scrapper held her fast.

'Wait!' he hissed. 'We just came from back there!'

They listened again. More twigs cracked. Then came a low whistle, and another in answer.

'Quick!' Scrapper whispered. 'Out of sight!'

All three fell to the ground and crawled beneath the canopy of underbranches. They lay there holding their breath as the sounds drew closer and closer. Then, through the web of branches and pine needles, Scrapper saw a pair of legs walking slowly along the path. They stopped right in front of his hiding place. A low whistle sounded, and then another pair of legs appeared.

'There's footprints around here, all right.' It was the gruff voice of the Boss. 'Might be theirs.'

'Well I'm no Indian scout,' a second voice complained.

'We'll keep trying in this direction,' the Boss said.

The legs moved off. Scrapper stayed motionless till the sounds had long died away, then crawled out and got to his feet.

Garry and Monica re-emerged, shaken.

'Did you see the guns?' Garry said, awed.

Scrapper nodded.

'What are we going to do?' Monica demanded of him. He got the feeling she thought it was all his fault.

'Dunno,' he glared back at her. 'I just don't know.'

Anto and Hoppy had successfully completed their sabotage operation on the gang's cars, and arrived safely back at the lorry and van. They were a bit out of breath, but thoroughly delighted with themselves.

'That's put a spoke in their wheels, eh?' Hoppy grinned.

They both spluttered out a giggle, blowing off the tension.

'D'you think Da's found Rory yet?' Anto wondered, serious again, looking around at the silent trees.

'We could go and have a look,' Hoppy suggested.

Anto shook his head, frowning. 'No way. We've been lucky once. We mightn't get away with it a second time.'

'Well, I don't fancy just hanging around getting nervous waiting for them,' Hoppy announced. 'Ah come on! We'll just go in a little way. Stay under cover. We might hear something.'

Anto shook his head with nervous fervour.

'Right so,' said Hoppy. 'I'll go on my own.'

He turned and set off for the trees again. But not so fast that Anto wouldn't have time to reconsider, and catch up with him.

Which is just what Anto did. He took a deep breath and ran after Hoppy, and they disappeared together into the maze of trees.

Jenny had managed to assemble a proper little haystack at the edge of the wild meadow. Mixed in with the tufts of lush, long grass that she had torn up with her green-stained hands were several different kinds of wild flowers she had found growing in nooks and corners. She knew Shera would like the flowers, and she felt sure Sir Gert would, too.

'Horse salad!' she told herself proudly as she stood back to look at her handiwork.

Trouble was, it was too much to carry back in one armful. She pressed the little stack tightly together, then grabbed as much of it as she could hold in her two arms. Then she set off back to the ruins, hardly able to see her way.

She had only gone about ten paces when an arm grabbed her roughly from behind. A hand clamped over her mouth to stifle the scream of shock and fear. The hay fell from her grasp as she found herself struggling in the rough grip of one of the gang members. The face of the Boss leered down at her.

'So this is one of our little horse thieves, eh?' he gloated into her terrified eyes. 'And what have you done with our horse, I wonder?'

Other men appeared and they stood grinning maliciously at the ruins.

'Right!' said the Boss. 'Let's go get him – and get out of here!'

Jenny struggled desperately in the harsh grasp of her captor, as the group moved off towards the ruined house and the horses.

14
Showdown

THE BOSS and his gang approached the ruins warily, guns held at the ready.

Jenny gave up struggling, and limply allowed herself to be half-carried, half-dragged through the overgrown meadow. The man's hand stayed tightly over her mouth.

Once among the derelict outhouses, the Boss signalled to the men to fan out and search. They padded around, checking through empty doorways and shattered windowframes, then came back one by one to shake their heads at him.

They re-grouped in front of the roofless shell where Sir Gert and Shera were penned in. The Boss looked around at the hoofprints on the churned-up ground, then motioned for Jenny to be brought to him. The man holding her took his hand from her mouth, but held tightly to her arms. Gasping, Jenny looked around at the gang.

'Okay, kid,' the Boss addressed her with quiet menace, his teeth hardly parting, 'if you want to live long enough to grow up, you'd better tell me what ye did with that horse.'

The men moved in closer. Then, behind them, a horse suddenly neighed. They all spun around to face the dead bush in the wall.

'In there!' the Boss hissed excitedly.

Jenny was dropped roughly to the ground as the men jumped to the bush and started hauling it out. She lay watching for a moment, then rolled quietly onto her side, sneaked to her feet, and sprinted away towards the meadow.

She did not get very far. Her captor saw her from the corner of his eye and came pounding after her. When he brought her struggling back, the Boss was trying to drag Sir Gert through the gap in the wall by his halter rope. The horse was resisting angrily, and the Boss lashed at its head with his pistol.

'Come outta that, you brute!' he snarled at Sir Gert.

In reply, Sir Gert reared and sent him flying backwards. The other men leapt on the horse's neck to hold him down, but his fiery temper had died down a bit, as if honour had been satisfied.

The Boss lay on the ground, glaring up at the proud animal.

'You're lucky your owners've decided to come across with the money,' he growled. 'Otherwise I'd like nothing better than to put a few holes in that dumb brain of yours!'

Hanley came out through the gap. 'There's another horse in there. The one we saw back at that old barn. What'll we do – shoot it?'

Jenny stiffened in her captor's hands and squealed, 'No!'

The Boss glanced at her, then shook his head. 'The noise might give us away. And we need all the time we can get to make it out of here now.'

'We'll need a horsebox for this lad,' said Myler, hanging tight to Sir Gert's halter rope. He seemed almost glad to be reunited with the racehorse.

'Right,' said the Boss. 'So go and get one.'

'But where?' whined Hanley.

The Boss snorted. 'Go find a farm and rob one!'

Myler handed the halter rope to another man, and he and Hanley started to jog away.

'It'll take us a while to drag this nag back to the cars,' the Boss called after them. 'Be there when we arrive!'

Myler and Hanley hurried off. The Boss turned to Jenny and fixed his steely glare on her. She stopped squirming.

'Right then, madam,' he addressed her, toying with his gun. 'Where're the rest of them? Your mates?'

Jenny shook her head slowly, her eye on the dull grey gun.

'Gone for help, eh? For the Guards?'

Jenny shook her head again. 'I don't know! And even if I did, I wouldn't tell you!'

'Damn kids!' the Boss snorted. He looked around, almost relaxed. 'They're probably wandering around lost and scared brainless out there.' He turned back to Jenny. 'Tie her up and shove her on the horse. She might come in handy as insurance.'

Jenny's captor pulled off his leather belt and used it to lash her wrists tightly in front of her. Then he lifted her easily into the air, and dumped her on Sir Gert's broad back. The horse jerked at the sudden bump, but Jenny leaned forward and whispered in his ear: 'It's okay. It's only me. Jenny.'

Sir Gert's head went up and down, and he stood calm and still.

'Get that lump of burger meat moving,' the Boss ordered.

The man holding the halter rope pulled, and another slapped Sir Gert's rump. But the racehorse resisted for a moment before moving forward at his own pace, carrying Jenny carefully. They moved through the shrubbery and out onto the meadow on their way back to the pine forest.

After they had been gone a few minutes, Shera's head and shoulders appeared from the gap in the wall. She looked around, sniffed, then made some low strange noises. Like a call.

Rory and Joe ran towards the edge of the mixed wood and stopped, breathless. Ahead lay the ruined house and the meadow. Two-thirds of the way to the pine forest, they could see the gang, and Sir Gert with a tiny figure on his back.

'They found them!' Rory burst out. 'And they've got Jenny! What'll we do?'

Joe leaned his back against a tree. 'First thing we do is we don't panic.'

He turned to stare at the distant figures in the meadow again.

'Wait till they're in the trees again, then we'll follow.'

'Then what?' Rory demanded.

Joe shook his head. 'We'll think of something when we're there.'

Rory kicked a tree-trunk in frustration and anguish.

'Wish Da was here! He'd know what to do!'

Anto and Hoppy were picking their way cautiously through the pine forest when they heard a commotion up ahead. They immediately dropped out of sight, and peered through the needly branches to see what it was.

Up ahead, Hanley and Myler were jogging along the path towards them.

'They're in some hurry!' Hoppy whispered. 'Something must have happened!'

'Look!' hissed Anto.

Scrapper and Garry had suddenly erupted from cover beside the path and thrown themselves on Hanley and Myler. The four men crashed around among the branches, flailing and grunting and roaring at each other. Scrapper had gone for Hanley, and got him in a necklock that had Hanley gasping for breath and turning blue in the face. Garry was getting the better of Myler, too. But before he could totally overpower him, Myler whipped out his gun and jammed it in Garry's ribs.

'Stand back with your hands up!' Myler hissed.

Garry obeyed, slowly. Myler struggled to his feet and motioned Scrapper to let go of Hanley. Scrapper did so reluctantly. Hanley immediately produced his gun and trained it angrily on Scrapper, coughing and gasping for breath. He rammed the point of the pistol into Scrapper's belly.

'Who the hell are you? Talk!'

'Not the Guards, if that's what you're thinking,' Scrapper told him without any evidence of fear. 'We just want the kids back.'

Hanley and Myler exchanged a look.

'Concerned parents!' Hanley spat. 'That's all we need!'

'Now what?' Myler asked him.

Hanley grabbed Scrapper by the shoulder and turned him around with some effort. Then he stuck the muzzle of the gun into the small of Scrapper's back. 'Move it. Run!'

He had to give Scrapper a mighty shove to get him going along the path. Myler waved his gun at Garry to indicate that he should follow. The four of them moved into the maze of tree trunks.

In their hiding place, Anto and Hoppy exchanged a look of horror. Then another noise on the path nearby made them jerk their heads around. Monica had emerged from the underbranches, her face white with anger and fright, and stood staring after the departing men. She bit her lip, then picked up a dead branch and started to run after them. But she had only gone a few paces when somebody grabbed her from behind and pulled her back out of sight under the branches.

Monica struggled briefly till she realised it was Anto and Hoppy who had grabbed her. They both held fingers to their lips to warn her to be quiet.

Further back down the path, the Boss and the other men were trying to hurry Sir Gert through the trees. But the racehorse was stubbornly refusing to move as fast as they wanted him to go.

'Move, damn you! Move!' the Boss cursed at him as he tugged viciously at the halter rope.

As if to prove a point, Sir Gert came to a dead halt in response. The Boss raised his pistol to lash the animal on the head.

'No!' Jenny shouted. 'Don't hit him!'

The Boss waited, arm raised. Jenny leaned forward to Sir Gert's ear. 'Please do as he says. Please go!' She squeezed his flanks with her legs.

The horse snorted reluctantly and began moving forward at a sharper pace.

Rory and Joe had reached the ruined house and found Shera standing quietly among the shrubbery. Rory ran straight up to her and threw his arms round her neck.

'Shera! You're safe!'

Shera snorted and waved her head, pleased to see him too.

Joe checked quickly around and then came back. 'You mount up,' he told Rory. 'We'll have to get after them pronto. Let's just pray Michael gets back to the girls soon.'

Rory scrambled onto Shera's back, and they set off into the meadow in the direction of the pine forest.

'For the first time in my life, I think I'll actually be glad to see the Guards!' Rory muttered.

'*When* we see them,' Joe added. 'It's the same old problem with the guardians of the law. They're never around when you need them.'

But this time they were. Or at least, nearly.

At the burnt-out container a whole crowd of police cars were parked on the hillside. Plain-clothes detectives and uniformed officers were intently probing and poking into every nook and cranny in the surrounding area.

Another car arrived, larger than the others, and a middle-aged man stepped briskly out to survey the scene. He wore a light raincoat and a small felt hat, and in some way, looked and behaved a bit like the Boss. He walked towards the container, and a knot of policemen parted respectfully for him.

'Well?' he demanded, looking around at them.

A big detective with cropped blond hair answered him. 'This container seems to have been here since about ten days after Sir Gert was taken, Chief.'

The Chief flashed him a little look, and the detective corrected himself. 'Sir.'

'Anything else?' the Chief went on curtly.

'Well, the blaze burned off any clues there might've been in the container. But there are hoofprints and tyre marks all around the place,' the detective added.

'And an entire English family's gone missing from a house just over there,' chimed in the uniformed officer who had found the container.

The Chief frowned. 'Any unusual activity on the roads?'

'There's been a few strange cars all right,' said the fat officer. 'But then it's the tourist season ...'

'There was that scrap lorry,' his colleague butted in. 'The one with the big grab on the back.'

The chief turned to survey the surrounding countryside, hands behind his back. 'This'd be just the kind of place they'd choose all right,' he said, mostly to himself. Then, after a pause: 'Activate a full search operation.'

He turned and got back into his car, and the driver reversed it away. The blond detective lifted his hand transmitter to his mouth.

'Control?' It squawked in reply.

'This is Delta Nine. The Chief wants the army up here. Now.'

Hanley and Myler were considerably slowed down by having to herd Scrapper and Garry along the path. And they were so intent on the job that they didn't notice Anto, Hoppy and Monica following them at a safe distance, dodging low from cover to cover.

Eventually, the four men emerged at the logging road where they had left their cars. But the relief on their faces changed to dismay when they saw the flat tyres. Garry and Scrapper exchanged a grin.

'Ah no!' Myler swore. 'How did that happen!'

'Never mind that!' said Hanley. 'What do we do about it?'

He left Myler covering Garry and Scrapper while he went to inspect the cars.

'There's still two okay tyres on each car,' he announced. 'All we have to do is swap them onto one car.'

'We?' said Myler. 'You mean our friends here.'

He waved his gun to motion Scrapper and Garry forward. Hanley opened a car boot and threw a jack and a wheelbrace at Scrapper's feet. Scrapper and Garry exchanged a look.

'Come on, do it!' Myler snapped.

Scrapper bent down and picked up the wheelbrace. As he came up slowly, Hanley clicked the safety catch off his gun.

'Don't even think about it!' Hanley hissed at him.

Scrapper and Garry went to the cars and began removing the wheels as the two gang members instructed.

In the trees, Anto, Hoppy and Monica watched from under the branches. 'We'll never get the girls back!' Monica whispered. 'I feel so helpless!'

'Hang in there, missus!' Hoppy advised her, with more optimism than he really felt. 'We'll get our chance.'

Scrapper and Garry finished putting the inflated tyres on one car, and stood back. Hanley opened the boots of the other two.

'Get in,' he ordered.

Scrapper and Garry were in no hurry to obey. Myler gave them both a push towards the open boots. 'Do it!' he snarled at them.

Slowly, Scrapper and Garry climbed in and lay down. Hanley slammed the boot lids shut and locked them.

'The Boss can pass sentence on them later,' Myler smirked.

The two gang members hurried over to the driveable car, climbed in, and sped away in an explosion of scraping tyres and roaring exhaust.

As soon as the car was gone, Monica, Anto and Hoppy burst from cover and ran to the wheelless vehicles. Monica got there first and bent over the boot Garry was locked in.

'Garry! It's me! Monica!' she shouted. 'Are you okay?'

'I will be as soon as I get out of here!' Garry's muffled voice came back.

Monica looked around. The boys were at the other car. Hoppy darted an arm through the open driver's window. 'Hey! They left the keys in this one!'

He hopped round to Anto and together they tried to open the boot.

'Anto? Hoppy? Is that you?' Scrapper bellowed from inside.

'Yeah! Hang on! We're trying to get you out!' Anto yelled.

'I thought I told you two to stay with the lorry!' Scrapper shouted back.

Anto and Hoppy exchanged a look of disgust and shook their heads.

'That's grown-ups for you – all gratitude!' Hoppy muttered. Then he yelled at the boot lid. 'D'you want us to go back then?'

'Cut the wisecracks!' came Scrapper's subdued response. 'Just get this damn boot open!'

Hoppy tried several keys in the lock.

'Hurry please!' Monica urged.

'I'm doing my best!' Hoppy told her. 'None of them seems to fit!'

'Gimme them!' said Anto, and grabbed the keys. He tried them all again, with the same lack of results.

'You're right! It must be a different lock from the doors. Probably the car was in a smash and they put on a different boot lid.'

'How'd they open it then?' Hoppy frowned.

'They must have another key,' Anto suggested.

'Try these keys in the other one!' Monica urged.

They went to try them on Garry's boot, but none worked there either. Monica was on the verge of losing control.

'They'll suffocate in there! And the children will be killed! We must get help somewhere!'

She ran off frantically in the direction of the main road. Anto and Hoppy, helpless, watched her go.

'Monica! Monica!' Garry called from inside the locked boot.

'She's gone, mister,' Anto said flatly.

Scrapper gave a muffled shout from inside the other boot. 'Hey! What's going on!'

Hoppy and Anto hurried back to him.

'The keys don't work on any car, Da. Yer woman's run off to get help. What'll we do?'

'See can you find anything to prise the lid open with,' he instructed them. 'A lever or a bar or something!'

The boys scurried around the place, looking. In the boot, Scrapper squirmed about and braced himself to give a mighty push upwards against the boot lid. He felt it bend a bit, but the lock held fast. He cursed and slumped down again, wiping the sweat from his face.

In his boot, Garry was also moving around, but more carefully. With one hand, he groped deep into the back of the boot, feeling the various objects that lay there, trying to work out what they were. He pulled one large long metal object towards him and ran his hands up and down it. An automatic assault rifle, he decided. He laid it carefully down and went on groping. A hammer came forth next, then pliers, screwdrivers, and other tools. Having made a mental list of everything that was there, he lay back and thought.

The boys found a rusty metal bar in one of the cars, and ran back to Scrapper's boot. They tried all ways to jam it under the lip of the boot and prise it up, but it just wouldn't fit. Anto threw it away in anger. 'It's no use, Da! We can't do it!'

In the boot, Scrapper lay on his back, bathed in sweat. The seriousness of the situation was making him unusually calm and clear-headed.

'Listen, lads!' he instructed them. 'Them two fellahs were in a big hurry to go somewhere. Could be the rest of the gang've caught up with Rory and the other kids. Maybe they need help with the horse or something. I want you two to go back in the forest and see can ye see anything. If ye do, one of ye can stay with it while the other one comes back here. If the English woman's quick getting help, we can still catch them. Okay?'

'Right,' said Anto.

'But keep out of sight, hear?' Scrapper added needlessly.

'Yeah. Right!' Hoppy assured him.

The two boys looked unhappily at the locked boots before hurrying away to the trees again.

In the hot darkness, Scrapper wiped the gathering sweat from his face. 'Just hope she makes it before we run out of air.'

In the other boot, Garry was whistling almost inaudibly to himself as he fiddled around in the dark.

Monica ran all the way to the van and threw herself into the cab. She groped frantically around the dashboard and the steering column. 'Keys! Where are the keys!'

When she realised there were none there, she almost sobbed. Then she delved into her pockets and produced a bunch on a key ring. She counted quickly through them till she came to the one she was looking for. 'The spare! Thank God!'

She put the key in the ignition lock. The engine roared to life.

'Now please let me find help quickly!'

The van stuttered forward, turned onto the main road, and raced away.

The elderly couple at the forest picnic area had finished their elaborate feast, and were sitting gratefully back, she to knit, he to read his paper and puff his pipe.

But they had only just settled into their tranquillity, when a convoy of military vehicles roared into view. The lead jeep braked to a sudden halt at the sight of the gang's cars sandwiched by Scrapper earlier. The convoy immediately turned into the picnic area, and disgorged a large band of armed soldiers and detectives. They looked over the mating wrecks, then ran quickly up to the awed couple.

'Those cars!' demanded the blond detective who had been at the container. 'What happened to them?'

'Well, I'm glad somebody reported it,' the woman began righteously. 'First of all these men came along and parked their cars and went off for a walk in the forest. Nice young men they were too. Then along came these vandals on a lorry, with a big crane thing on the back. They just backed up to the cars, and you can see for yourself what they did to them. Absolutely disgraceful. I hope you catch them and punish them for it. There's far too much of that kind of thing around these days.'

The detective listened impatiently to her. 'How long? Since the men went into the forest?'

The elderly man shrugged through a cloud of pipe smoke.

'Oh, an hour or two,' said the woman. 'Perhaps more.'

A senior-looking soldier standing beside the detective turned and barked an order at the others. The whole group streamed quickly around the picnic table and disappeared into the forest.

Once they were gone, the old woman stood up and began hurriedly packing away the picnic things. The man looked at her quizzically. 'We're going home, dear,' she explained. 'We'll get more peace in our own back garden!'

At the deserted cottage, Nina sat disconsolate on the wheel arch of the horse box, as Sam paced up and down in agitation.

'I wish this Michael man would hurry up!' Sam hissed. 'The waiting is driving me mad!'

'I hope Jenny's all right,' said Nina.

'And the horses too,' Sam added.

'And Rory,' Nina tagged on in a small voice.

They exchanged a quick glance. Nina looked away. Sam frowned.

'He's too old for you, Nina!' Sam pronounced suddenly.

'No he isn't!' Nina spat back. She fidgeted uncomfortably, realising she had exposed herself.

'Aha!' Sam pursued. 'I thought you weren't interested in boys?'

'I'm not!' Nina defended herself. 'Not any more than you anyway. I just hope he's all right, that's all!'

Sam's face became pinched. 'I'm not stupid you know. I've seen the way you keep watching him. The way you go all dewy-eyed when you're talking to him. Little miss innocence. Ha! It sticks out a mile!'

Nina's face reddened with anger. 'And what about you? Think I didn't notice the way you clutched onto him when you were on the horse together?'

Sam reddened too. 'I wasn't doing it for fun. How else was I supposed to stay on?'

'Don't give us that rubbish!' Nina sneered. 'You were loving every minute of it!'

The argument was cut short by the sound of a car engine approaching along the dirt road to the cottage. Sam spun around, and Nina jumped up, their faces radiating excitement and relief.

'It's him! It's Michael!' Nina shouted.

The car drove into view. They ran towards it as it came to a slow halt at the entrance to the cottage yard.

'Hey! Joe sent us! We need help!' the girls shouted.

The car doors opened.

'There's a gang of terrorists after us. They kidnapped a racehorse, and we stole it back from them, and now they're trying to ...'

Sam's voice trailed off and they both froze on the spot. The joy on their faces drained away and was replaced by horror.

Myler and Hanley were standing grinning at them.

The Boss jerked angrily at Sir Gert's halter rope, trying to make the racehorse follow faster through the tightly-packed trees. But every time he jerked, the horse snorted and jerked back in turn, glaring angrily at him with his big wild eyes.

Jenny could see the violence growing in the Boss's face, so she leaned down to Sir Gert's ear again. 'Just do what he wants. Then he won't harm us.'

But the horse seemed more and more reluctant to believe this, and stood stone still, glaring.

Then Walsh, the man who had captured Jenny, stepped forward.

'Listen, Boss, I think we'd better slow up anyway.'

'Slow up! Are you crazy?!'

'No, but listen,' Walsh went on in a soothing tone, 'It might take Hanley and Myler a while to find a horse box or a trailer. If we get back to the cars and they're not there, we'll have to stand around waiting. In full view. We'd be better off keeping out of sight in here.'

The Boss considered this, then nodded once. 'Right. Give it ten minutes. Then you go ahead and look.'

Walsh turned to the others. 'At ease, lads. Take ten.'

The other men exchanged puzzled glances, shrugged, and took out cigarettes. Walsh turned back to the Boss, who was squinting suspiciously around at the silent trees.

'Check around,' the Boss ordered. 'Just in case.'

Walsh nodded and slipped off into the coniferous gloom. The Boss accepted a cigarette from one of the other men, lit it, and blew out a long thin stream of pale smoke. Sir Gert watched him, pawing the soft earth almost inaudibly.

Joe, Rory and Shera were sneaking warily through the forest not too far behind, when Joe suddenly stopped and listened.

Rory slipped off Shera's back, and stood beside Joe to listen too. 'What is it?' he whispered.

'Thought I heard something,' he whispered back.

'Voices?'

'Na. Something moving. Ssssh! There!'

Rory concentrated. 'I can't hear anything.'

Joe shook his head. 'Probably just birds. Come on. But real quiet now.'

They were about to move off again when Rory grabbed Joe's arm.

'What!?' Joe hissed. 'D'you hear it now?'

'Na,' Rory replied, puzzled. 'I thought I smelled something.'

'Smelled something?' Joe echoed, puzzled. 'What?'

'Cigarette smoke,' Rory told him.

They both stood sniffing the secret forest air. Shera sniffed too. Then, very close by, a twig snapped. They stood as still as rocks. Only their eyes swivelled to the dark mass of underbranches from where the noise had come. There was some faint rustling, then another snapping sound. They could see the branches moving. Their hearts pounded as the curtain of pine needles suddenly parted in two.

'Hiya!' Hoppy's blond head popped out and he grinned out at them.

Rory held onto Shera and sagged with sheer relief. Hoppy stepped out onto the path, followed by Anto. On an impulse, Rory grabbed them both and hugged them with delight. For the first time he could remember, he was actually glad to see his brother. Joe stared at the three of them, uncomprehending.

'Lads!' Rory addressed them. 'Ye put the heart crossways in us! What're ye doing here, for godsake?!'

'Looking for you,' Anto told him. 'You've no idea the ructions you've been causing. Ma's in bits about you. Off the head.'

Something inside Rory jumped when he heard this. 'Yeah? Where's Da?'

'Back there,' Hoppy told him, not sure if he should explain Scrapper's plight right now.

'Hey,' Joe intervened. 'Any chance of an introduction?'

'Sorry,' said Rory. 'That's Anto, my brother. This is my mate Hoppy. Lads, this is Joe. He helped us escape from the gang.'

They all nodded to each other.

'Where *is* Da?' Rory demanded eagerly.

'Back there,' Anto repeated. 'In a car boot.'

'What?!' said Rory.

'No time to explain,' said Hoppy. 'The mob's just up the path, with the racehorse and a kid girl on it.'

Joe jumped. 'Are they headed this way?'

Anto shook his head. 'Not right now. They're smoking fags and taking it easy.'

'I knew I smelt it,' said Rory. 'How many?'

'Four,' said Hoppy. 'There's another two gone off in a car. It was them that locked up Da and the English guy in the boots.'

'They must be looking for a horse trailer,' said Joe. 'That's why the main mob's hanging around waiting. We have to do something now. It's our last chance.'

He sneaked off into the trees. Anto and Hoppy waited while Rory led Shera off the path and tied her to a branch.

'Wait here and stay quiet!' Rory told her.

The three boys hurried off after Joe. Shera lifted her head and sniffed the air delicately.

Further along the path, Sir Gert's nostrils flared as he too sniffed the air. He made a small noise and turned to look back. The Boss gave him a glare, and was about to do something else when Walsh re-emerged from the trees.

'All okay?' asked the Boss.

Walsh nodded. The Boss looked impatiently at his watch.

'Them two'd better find something fast!'

Monica drove the pick-up at top speed along the road. She had absolutely no idea where she was going. She was simply hoping desperately that she would come across a house or a farm as she went.

She was going so fast that she shot past a track opening in the hedges without noticing it. Nor did she notice the car waiting there to turn onto the main road. Myler and Hanley's car.

She was completely gone out of sight when the car roared out, towing a horsebox, and turned to travel back the way she had just come. Looking out over the top of the locked tailboard were the heads of Sam and Nina.

Joe half-crawled along under the trees, followed in single file by the three boys. He stopped and raised his head to peep over a low feathery branch.

Some way ahead, partially obscured, he could see Jenny sitting on Sir Gert's back. Nearby were the heads of Walsh and the Boss.

Joe dropped down and turned to whisper to Rory. 'Listen. D'you think he'd come to you again if you whistled him?'

Rory nodded. 'I'd say so.'

Joe scanned round. 'We need some kind of diversion.'

They all looked round. Nearby, they saw a tree which had half-fallen against another one. Only a split branch was preventing it from crashing to the ground.

'If we had a rope,' said Joe, 'we could pull that down. The noise'd panic them long enough to give us a chance.'

'But we've no rope,' Anto objected flatly.

'I can get up to it no bother!' Hoppy boasted brightly.

'No way!' said Joe. 'You'd be a sitting target up there.'

'I could circle around them and call him from the other direction once Hoppy brings the tree down,' Rory suggested. 'The noise'd make them go the other way, and they wouldn't see Sir Gert coming to me.'

'But then you'd be the target,' Anto objected.

'Once I'm up on Sir Gert's back, they'd never catch me,' Rory promised.

Joe thought. 'Okay. We'll have to give it a crack. There's nothing else we can do.'

Rory crawled off one way, and the others made for the half-fallen tree.

Sir Gert's nostrils flared busily and his ears pricked up and down, as information undetected by the humans around him wafted to him on the cool forest air. Only Jenny sensed something. She leaned forward again. 'What is it?' she whispered.

Sir Gert's head turned and his wild brown gaze rested on the half-fallen tree just visible in the trunk-screened distance.

Joe, Hoppy and Anto had by then reached the base of the same tree on their hands and knees. Joe and Anto gave Hoppy a push up into the tree against which the broken one was leaning. Hoppy began climbing carefully but confidently, his bad leg no impediment in this kind of exercise. Every few feet he rose, glancing over in the direction of the gang to make sure he was unnoticed.

The gang were unaware that anything was going on, but Sir Gert grew steadily more agitated as he sensed the distant presences.

The Boss twitched sharply at the halter rope. 'What's spooking the brute?' he frowned at Jenny.

Jenny looked round. Out of the corner of her eye, she caught a tiny movement in the tree next to the half-fallen one. Then, for a moment, she made out the shape of Hoppy's blond head among the branches. She had no idea who he was, but she sensed instinctively he was on her side. She quickly averted her eyes so her startled gaze wouldn't give him away.

Under the tree, Joe and Anto looked up anxiously at Hoppy, who had now reached the broken branch on which the fallen tree was resting. He wriggled to the next branch above, then started to push the broken branch with his foot. At first it would not give, but then he threw caution to the wind and gave it a sharp kick with his good leg. The last strands of the branch snapped, it sheared away, and the heavy tree that had been leaning on it continued its halted journey to the ground, with loud crashing and crunching sounds.

The gang was startled. They all dropped their cigarettes and pulled out their guns.

'What was that!' hissed Walsh, staring and seeing nothing.

'Go find out!' the Boss ordered.

The gang members all began advancing nervously into the trees, guns at the ready. The Boss watched them, still holding Sir Gert's halter rope. Then, some way behind Jenny and the racehorse, Rory's head half-rose from cover. He put his fingers to his lips and let out a shrill whistle.

Instantly, Sir Gert let out a powerful answering call. He spun around and charged off towards Rory, pulling the halter from the Boss's grasp and toppling him over.

The gang members turned around to see the Boss struggling to his feet. 'The horse!' he yelled at them. 'Get the damn horse!'

The men turned back to chase after Sir Gert. Rory stood his ground as the racehorse, with Jenny clinging to his mane and bouncing madly on his back, weaved through the tree-trunks towards him. The movement almost threw Jenny off, and in her terror, she let out a piercing squeal.

Back where she was tied up and hidden, Shera heard this sound and let out an anxious whinny. When Sir Gert heard her call echoing through the trees, he pulled up short. Another whinny came quickly, and he turned around towards its source. Then he began charging back the way he come, right into the oncoming armed men.

Seeing this, the men halted in confusion. As the horse bore steadily down on them, Walsh began to raise his gun. But before he could pull the trigger, Sir Gert charged through the men, knocking them aside like dolls. He thundered past the gaping Boss, and on to where he knew Shera was waiting for him.

Rory stood up full height to watch all this, aghast, then ducked out of sight again.

Hoppy had watched some of this from up in the tree, but when he saw Sir Gert coming in his direction, he started scrambling down. He was still about ten feet off the ground when he looked again and saw Sir Gert with the terrified Jenny on his back coming straight towards the fallen tree. Hoppy stopped. Sir Gert picked a wide gap between the trees and sailed over the fallen trunk. But the force of his leap sent Jenny toppling off into the dense underbranches. Immediately, Hoppy scrambled down the rest of his tree with the agility of a monkey, and dived into the spot where he had seen Jenny fall. He found her lying on the carpet of pine needles, dazed, scratched and bruised, but otherwise in one piece. She stared at him and opened her mouth to ask him who he was, but Hoppy raised a finger to his lips to tell her to be quiet.

The gang members came gasping along in pursuit of the racehorse, and stumbled past their hiding place without even a glance. Hoppy and Jenny clasped each other with silent relief.

Shera called again. Sir Gert slewed to a halt, front legs splayed wide, to get his bearings. He swung his head in the direction of the sound, but as he did, a knot in the end of the halter rope slid into the tight fork of a nearby branch. He pulled powerfully to free himself, but the effort only wedged the rope tighter. He was caught fast.

The gang caught up with him, panting. Sir Gert tried to rear up threateningly, but the wedged rope prevented him from getting high enough. The Boss came forward and quietly showed his gun to the horse. 'Is this what you want, then?'

Sir Gert glared at him, snorted, then calmed down. The Boss moved forward carefully to take the halter rope from the forked branch.

'That beast can nearly talk!' Walsh muttered with grudging admiration.

The Boss led Sir Gert back towards the path, both watching each other warily. Walsh spun round.

'The girl! Where's the girl?!'

'Damn the girl!' the Boss called back. 'Let's go!'

Sir Gert and the gang disappeared quickly into the trees.

In their hiding place under the branches, Hoppy and Jenny listened to the sounds fading away.

'You okay?' Hoppy whispered to her.

Jenny nodded and struggled up, wincing. 'I'm just a bit sore.'

Joe and Anto appeared beside them. 'They've gone! Let's move!' Joe urged. Hoppy untied Jenny's strapped wrists before they all scuttled off through the trees.

Rory was already waiting for them beside Shera. 'What about Sir Gert?' he demanded. 'They've still got him!'

'Can't be helped,' said Joe curtly. 'Too risky now. We'll just have to hope for help arriving quick.'

Monica threw the van around the snaking bends at a dangerous speed, her face a mixture of fear and determination. Suddenly her eyes opened wide in shock. Straight ahead were two army vehicles blocking the road. Soldiers lay across the bonnets of the vehicles, rifles raised, while one stood out in front, arm held up in a halt order.

Monica hit the brakes hard. The van skidded towards the soldiers, causing the one out front to jump for his life. At the last moment, the van slewed to one side and came to rest half-buried in the hedgerow. The soldiers ran forward to help as Monica half-climbed, half-fell, out of the driver's door.

'Are you all right?' asked the corporal who had jumped out of the way.

'Yes, yes!' Monica replied impatiently, clutching a bruise on her head. 'But the children! The terrorists have them! Back there!'

The soldiers helped Monica to get into one of the army vehicles, and they drove off at speed.

The Boss led Sir Gert onto the logging road where the de-wheeled cars lay. He and the other men gaped at the sight. Then the Boss looked to the main road. 'Where the hell are they!'

Inside his boot prison, Scrapper listened, sweating profusely.

On the main road, Hanley and Myler's car appeared with the horse-box, and bounced onto the logging road. The gang hurried forward to greet them as Hanley and Myler jumped out.

'Get this brute into the trailer!' the Boss ordered. 'We've got to get out of here fast!'

Walsh and the others pulled Sir Gert to the back of the horsebox, and one of them let down the tailgate. Inside stood Nina and Sam, frightened but defiant. Ropes had been wound around them to pin their arms to their sides.

'What the ...!' the Boss gaped.

'Two more of the kids that took the horse from us,' Myler explained. 'They were at the place where we found the trailer.'

'And what in God's name did ye bring them here for!' the Boss exploded. 'We've enough problems as it is!' He grabbed the girls. 'Come on – out!'

Nina and Sam tumbled out into the hands of the gang.

'Tie them to a tree over there!' the Boss ordered. 'Get that horse in!' The men did as he ordered.

Walsh was looking at the deflated tyres and missing wheels on the other cars. 'Hey, Boss!' he called. 'What'll we do about this? One car isn't enough to get us all away.'

Hanley hurried up with a foot pump.

'Here! I found this where we got the trailer.'

'Right,' said the Boss. 'Get one car mobile and torch the other one!'

He turned to go. Abruptly, the boot of the car they had been standing at sprang open. Garry jumped up with the assault rifle at the ready, trembling with anger and nerves.

'Stop!' Garry ordered. 'One move and I shoot!'

The Boss and the gang all turned to look, astonished. At the tree where they had been tied, Sam and Nina let out little yells of triumph.

Hanley looked annoyed and guilty. 'Hell,' he muttered. 'I forgot about them two!'

Garry stepped carefully out of the boot, keeping an eye on all the men. 'Very kind of you gentlemen to leave a toolkit in there,' he smirked, and threw a screwdriver and the dismantled lock mechanism on the ground. 'Now throw down your weapons and get over there all of you!' he barked. 'Do it! Fast!'

Inside his boot, Scrapper listened and grinned. 'Good man yourself, Garry!' he called out.

The gang stood immobile, staring. Garry waved the rifle at them. 'You heard what I said! Move!'

Walsh began walking slowly towards him. Garry swung the rifle around. 'That's far enough!' But Walsh kept on coming, licking his lips. Garry began to back away. 'Halt or I'll shoot! I mean it!' he yelled at him, beginning to feel horribly scared that he might have to.

Walsh walked right up to him. Garry shut his eyes and pulled the trigger. Nothing happened. He opened his eyes again. Walsh was grinning at him, holding up the black box of a rifle magazine. 'It doesn't work without the bullets!' Walsh sneered.

Walsh grabbed the rifle and two men leapt on Garry from behind.

'Tie him up with the kids!' the Boss barked.

'There's another one in that –' Hanley began.

'No time!' snarled the Boss and stalked away to the horsebox. Sir Gert had been forced inside, and the tailgate was swung up and locked. The Boss climbed into the driver's seat, and signalled Myler, Hanley and Walsh to come with him. Once they were in, he slammed the car into gear, pulled the horsebox around in a wide circle, and drove off onto the main road.

The two men left behind quickly lashed Garry beside the girls, and hurried to finish blowing up the tyres on the car in which Scrapper was imprisoned.

'Where's Jenny?' Garry whispered urgently to Sam and Nina.

'We don't know!' said Sam, almost in tears.

'What's going to happen now!' Nina wailed in a low voice.

The men finished work on the tyres, threw the tools aside, and jumped into the car. The engine roared to life, and it turned to speed off after the others and the horsebox.

But before it reached the road, two soldiers suddenly jumped from the trees behind the tied-up trio, threw themselves flat on the ground, and left off a volley of shots that blew the car's back tyres to ribbons.

More soldiers and policemen, including the blond detective, flooded out of the pine forest and surrounded the disabled car.

'Throw out your weapons, and come out slowly with your hands up!' one of the army officers bellowed.

Guns fell out of the car windows, and the men emerged with their arms raised high, visibly shaking. Soldiers ran forward to seize them, while others untied Garry and the girls.

'There's someone in the boot of the car!' Garry told them. 'One of us!'

The blond detective hurried forward and took a large bunch of car keys from his pocket. He looked at the car, selected a key, and opened the boot. Scrapper sat up, gulping for air and wiping sheets of sweat from his reddened face.

'Thanks!' he gasped at the detective. His face wrinkled as he breathed in through his nose. 'Remind me to start using a deodorant!'

Garry and the girls ran up to him. 'You okay?' asked Garry.

Scrapper nodded and gave him a friendly pat on the shoulder.

'Where's the horse?' the detective asked them quickly.

'They took him away in a trailer,' Garry told him. 'That way.'

A police car and an army vehicle squealed to a halt on the road outside. The detective turned to the soldier next to him. 'Get onto HQ and alert the helicopter. We'll get after them by road.'

He ran towards the vehicles, signalling Scrapper, Garry and the girls to follow.

While all this had been going on, Joe, Rory, Anto, and Hoppy, with Jenny on Shera, had arrived back at Scrapper's lorry.

Joe checked the ignition lock and looked around. 'Who's got the key?'

'Da has,' said Anto.

Joe slammed the door shut in annoyance. 'And he's locked in the boot of a car. Great!'

'We could hot-wire it,' Rory suggested. 'Easy. I often saw Da do it on old cars.'

'Worth a try,' Joe agreed. He and the boys got into the cab and pulled off the engine cover, while Jenny waited outside, stroking Shera and talking softly to her.

It didn't take them long. With a loud roar and a blast of black smoke from the exhaust, the lorry engine burst into life. The boys let out a whoop and started to clamber into the cab. But a sound from the road attracted their attention. Through the trees, they saw Myler and Hanley's car flash past with the horsebox in tow.

'It's them!' Rory yelled. 'We've got to stop them!'

'Everybody in! Quick!' urged Joe.

Jenny quickly pulled Shera to a nearby tree and tied her up. She ran back to the lorry and clambered in just as Joe clanged the gearstick forward and the lorry jolted off down the road. Shera neighed loudly and anxiously after them as the lorry disappeared.

It took them several minutes of break-neck pursuit before the horsebox came into view again. It was being towed so fast that it swayed dangerously when it went around the bends on the tight road. Joe hunched over the wheel of the lorry, pressing the accelerator flat to the floor. The youngsters had to hang on tight as the heavy vehicle sailed around the bends.

'What're you gonna do?' Anto asked Joe. 'You can't overtake them. The road's too narrow.'

They all stared ahead at the horsebox blocking the road.

Suddenly Rory had an idea. 'The grab!' He and Hoppy looked at each other with wide eyes, both understanding perfectly.

'Slow down a bit! Then drive as close to the horsebox as you can!' Rory ordered Joe. When Joe hit the brakes, Rory opened the cab door, and he and Hoppy monkeyed their way out onto the flat back of the lorry. Once there, Rory banged on the cab roof to signal Joe it was safe to accelerate again. The lorry vibrated as it roared off in pursuit of the horsebox.

Behind the cab, Rory began manipulating the controls of the big grab arm with easy familiarity. He swung it around so it pointed out over the front of the cab, then operated the hydraulic arm that made it grow slowly longer, till the big hook was almost touching the horsebox roof.

In the speeding car in front of the horsebox, the Boss looked in his wing mirror and frowned. 'Something behind us!'

Hanley, beside him in the front passenger seat, looked in his wing mirror. 'Damn! It's that scrap lorry again! Who are these people?'

'Never mind who they are! Just take them out!' the Boss roared.

Myler and the other man in the back seat turned round, guns ready. 'Can't!' said Myler. 'Trailer's in the way!'

The Boss, trying to watch the road and keep the car under control, angrily elbowed Hanley in the ribs. 'Open the door! Lean out!'

'Yeah. Right!' Hanley nodded. 'Like they do in the movies.'

He opened the door slightly and carefully began to lean out with his gun.

In the lorry cab, they all cried out at the sight of Hanley, gun in his hand, slowly emerging from the car door. Joe immediately jammed on the brakes, and the lorry fell back.

'He's going to shoot!' Jenny squealed.

They watched as Hanley took aim. But then the car and trailer swerved round a sharp bend. The car door swung fully open, Hanley lost his balance, and fell headlong out of the car into the roadside ditch.

On the back of the lorry, Rory and Hoppy looked down and grinned as they flashed past the tumbling figure of Hanley.

'One down!' chirped Hoppy.

In the cab, Joe's mouth set grimly as he drove the lorry back up to the horsebox. Sir Gert gave a great pleading neigh when they got up close.

'Don't worry! We'll save you!' Jenny shouted to him.

When the end of the grab arm was over the horsebox, Rory jiggled the hydraulic levers to lower the hook, trying to get it to catch under the rim of the horsebox roof.

In the car, the Boss and the others were baffled. 'What're they up to?'

'Dunno!' said Myler, hopping up and down in back seat. 'Can't get a decent look!'

After two or three misses, Rory finally got the hook to catch. Quickly, he pushed a lever to tighten the hook's grip, grinned at Hoppy, then banged on the cab roof.

Joe braked slowly. The lorry lost speed gradually, its great weight slowing the horsebox and the gang's car with it.

'What's happening!?' the Boss shouted. He had his foot pressed right down on the accelerator, with absolutely no effect.

Rory and Hoppy watched with tense excitement as the horsebox's speed dribbled away, and the lorry pulled it towards a standstill. But then Joe made the fatal mistake. He rammed the lorry's brakes full on. The resulting jerk tore the grab hook through the light metal of the horsebox roof, and sent it springing back to smash the windscreen of the lorry. Jenny screamed, and Joe and Anto ducked as they were showered with shattered glass.

In the gang's car, the Boss suddenly felt the power return.

'We lost 'em!' Myler yelled triumphantly.

The car and horsebox surged forward, leaving the lorry halted in the middle of the road.

'Right!' smirked the Boss. 'We're out of here!'

He rocketed the car and trailer round a bend, and let out a yell of shock at what he saw ahead of them. A military helicopter was flying directly towards them only feet above a long straight stretch of road. He panicked. Just as the helicopter began to lift to scream over the car, the Boss swung the wheel wildly to one side. The car and horsebox crashed through the hedge and toppled down a slope into a grassy gulley.

The lorry arrived on the scene seconds later. Rory and the others stared down in horror at the wreckage in the gulley. The helicopter landed nearby, and soldiers and policemen jumped out. Then, from both directions, army and police vehicles sped to a halt, and more officers swarmed down into the gulley, guns at the ready.

Garry, Monica, Sam and Nina appeared and hugged Jenny with silent relief. Scrapper pushed his way through the crowd to grab Rory with the same feeling.

Down in the gulley, soldiers were pulling the half-conscious Boss and the other men from the car.

'What about the horse!' Rory yelled down at them.

The blond detective went to the back of the overturned horsebox and half-crawled inside. After a moment, he re-emerged, looking grim. He shook his head. 'Neck's broken,' he called up. 'He's dead.'

There was a moment's shocked silence. Then the girls and Rory all burst into tears together.

15
The Final Surprise

ON A BRIGHT SATURDAY MORNING some weeks later, Rory woke at about half past eight, dressed quickly, and hurried downstairs. His insides were bubbling with controlled excitement. The whole family was heading off to Cavan for the day, at the invitation of Garry and Monica. Shera was still up there, living comfortably in the old barn. It had been Jenny's idea, and although Rory had first objected stubbornly to being parted from Shera again, he'd eventually managed to put his own feelings aside and come to see it was the best thing for her. She would live out the remainder of her life in the country, in grass and fields, where she belonged. And she'd never again have to suffer at the hands of Quinlan's mob or their likes.

Besides, as Scrapper had pointed out, it had a plus side for Rory too. He didn't have all the worry of looking after her any more, and he had an open invitation to head on up to Cavan any time he wanted. That was what finally persuaded Rory. Having an excuse to pay regular visits to the farm appealed to him. And though he wouldn't admit it even to himself, it wasn't just to see Shera ...

Scrapper and Anto were finishing breakfast and tidying up the kitchen in preparation for leaving.

''Morning,' Scrapper greeted Rory, and pushed a bowl and the cereal box across the table at him. 'Get that down you quick. We have to be off shortly.'

Anto, dressed in brand new Levi's and a freshly ironed shirt, nodded to Rory and poured a cup of tea for him.

Rory eyed him warily, but said: 'Thanks.'

Things had quietly changed between the two brothers. The full account of Rory's part in the Sir Gert saga had impressed Anto considerably. And every time he went out now, the local kids kept plying him to retell the story. It irked Anto at first to be playing a supporting part in Rory's movie, but the public attention more than made up for that. Besides, with every retelling, Anto's role in the drama was getting more heroic and central, and Rory didn't seem to mind. He's not too bad after all, Anto found himself thinking.

Scrapper stacked the dirty dishes in the sink, then turned around and pulled a folded piece of paper from his shirt pocket.

'Oh, by the way.' He handed the paper to Rory, grinning. 'I'd keep this somewhere safe if I was you.'

Rory took the paper and opened it up. It was a bill of sale for Shera. He looked up sharply at Scrapper.

'I settled up with them dealers that bought her at the auction,' Scrapper explained. 'Pain in the neck having to pay for our own horse, but sure, once we got the reward money off Sir Gert's owners, it just seemed the best thing to do. Clean the slate and be shot of all the bother. Eh?'

'Thanks, Da!' Rory was relieved and delighted. He put the receipt carefully into a pocket, and guzzled his sugar puffs energetically.

'How much did we get anyway?' Anto asked Scrapper, trying to be casual.

'None of your business!' Scrapper snapped automatically, then thought better of it. 'Not the full whack we'd have got if Sir Gert hadn't got killed. But they were fairly generous all the same. It'll see us through for a while. Now what's keeping your ma?'

The kitchen door opened and Ma sailed in. She wore a new dress, her hair had been tinted and styled, and her face was made up for the first time Rory could remember. She looked totally different.

'Well, what're you all gawping at?' she demanded, with a put-on-scowl to cover her self-consciousness.

'Well, well, well!' Scrapper murmured, a smile breaking out on his face. 'If it isn't the stunner I was mad about before I got married. Where've you been all these years?'

'Oh, quit messing!' she ordered him, embarrassed. But Rory could sense she was trying to hide an awkward pleasure at Scrapper's response. 'Are we all ready to go?'

'Just waiting for the hero there to finish his breakfast,' Scrapper said.

'You can leave that if you want,' Ma told Rory. He was still getting used to the change in her manner towards him. It felt unreal at times, but she was genuinely trying, and he liked it. 'I packed some sandwiches and fruit and things for the journey. We can eat on the way.'

She picked up an enormous bag stuffed with provisions.

'We're driving to Cavan, not Hong Kong, Ma!' Anto told her.

'I'm just trying to look after you properly. Now come on. We'd better get going, or the day'll be finished before we get there.'

She went out with the bag. Rory, Anto and Scrapper shared a smile, shrugged, and followed after her.

Hoppy was supposed to meet them at the yard lane, but he wasn't there. 'Better go and look for him,' Scrapper told Rory as he opened the gates to take out the lorry.

Rory nodded and headed back up the lane.

'Wouldn't it be an idea if we bought ourselves an old car with some of the money we got?' Ma frowned. 'You can hardly call this family transport.'

'Car?' Scrapper scoffed, and clambered jauntily into the lorry cab. 'Then we'd just be part of the crowd. Nobody'd get out of our way any more.'

Rory hurried back to the top of the lane and waited there for a few moments, shuffling around with impatience. He was just about to set off for Hoppy's house, when Hoppy himself came hobbling around the corner. His usual jaunty brightness was dimmed, and there was a flatness in his greeting to Rory.

'What's up?' Rory asked him. 'Worried about the operation?'

Hoppy was due to go into hospital the next week to have his knee fixed. He shook his head half-heartedly. 'Na. Just something the doctor told me yesterday.'

'What?'

Hoppy took in a slow breath. 'Well. I'll need to have more operations as I get bigger. Plastic knees don't grow.'

Rory put a hand on his shoulder. 'That's a bummer all right. But it mightn't be that bad. And think – you'll have two good legs, just like the rest of us.'

Hoppy's mouth twitched into a wry grimace. 'Not that good. I'll be able to walk and run okay, eventually. But no weightlifting. That's banned entirely.'

Rory started leading Hoppy down the lane to the waiting lorry. 'But you can take up something that doesn't need knees,' Rory suggested consolingly. 'Snooker. Or darts.'

Hoppy snorted derisively. 'I'll never get muscles like Arnold Schwarzenegger from throwing darts!'

Before Rory could think of an answer to that, the lorry rumbled out of the yard, and Scrapper honked the horn threateningly to warn them to hurry up.

There was an air of excitement at the farmhouse too. Monica was bustling grumpily around the half-finished kitchen, trying to get things in order for the visitors.

'We can't sit them down to eat in this shambles,' she growled irritably.

Garry sighed and lifted his eyes to the sky outside. 'Stop being so perfectionist, Monica. They're just ordinary folk, not royalty.'

'Even ordinary folk don't like eating in a building site.'

'All right then. I'll move the table outside and we can dine *al fresco*. How about that?'

'What if it rains?'

Garry slapped his forehead and groaned. 'Try thinking positive for once, eh?'

Jenny rushed in from the yard. 'He's here! The vet's arrived!'

'Blast, I forgot about him,' Garry muttered. 'Look, I'll have to go and talk to him and show him where the barn is. I'll be back in ten minutes. Right?'

Jenny started to follow after him, but Monica called her back.

'Run upstairs and tell those other two to get down here and give me a hand.'

'But Monica –!'

'You can catch up with Garry in a minute. Now come on – there's lots still to be done.'

Grudgingly, Jenny clumped up the narrow stairs. The redecoration had been completed, and the girls now had their own rooms. Jenny grabbed the handle of Sam's door, but it was locked. She banged loudly and shouted. 'Sam! Open up!'

'Go away!' Sam shouted back from inside. 'I'm busy!'

'Monica wants you downstairs!'

'I'll go down later! I'm doing something!'

'What?'

'Mind your own business!'

Jenny scowled, puzzled, and turned to thump on Nina's door.

'Nina! Monica says you've to go downstairs and help!'

'Buzz off!' came the reply, above a background of music from a radio. 'I'm busy too!'

Jenny bunched up her mouth and clattered back down the stairs.

'They both said they're busy!' she called to Monica in the kitchen, and shot off in pursuit of Garry and the vet.

Scrapper's lorry bumped into the yard about lunchtime. The boys jumped out quickly, then Scrapper got out and helped Ma down. 'We definitely need a car!' she told him sourly. 'Look at the state of my new dress.'

'Ah, you look terrific,' he told her. 'Here they are.'

Garry and Monica came out of the farmhouse, followed by Joe.

'How're ye!' Scrapper greeted them. 'Looks like a big reunion, eh? Thought you'd gone back to Dublin?' he said to Joe.

'I did,' Joe explained. 'But Garry and Monica invited me up. We were just talking about me putting a caravan on their land. I'll be able to come up here at weekends and give them a hand. I'm getting too old to be a forest hermit anymore. Can't take the excitement.'

They all laughed. Ma coughed pointedly, waiting to be introduced. Scrapper took the hint and did the honours, using her real name, Bernadette, which seemed to embarrass her a bit.

In the background, the boys shuffled and looked around.

'Where's the girls?' Anto wanted to know. He had something in his hand he was trying to keep out of sight.

'The horse okay?' Scrapper asked.

Monica nodded. 'Oh yes. She really seems to like it out here away from the city. And the girls certainly love her. I think it's a good arrangement. If Rory is happy with it.'

'Ah yeah,' said Scrapper. 'She's out of harm's way here. Perfect.'

Finally, Rory could contain himself no longer. 'I'll head off and say hello to Shera.'

Rory and Hoppy turned to go. But just then, the farmhouse door opened and Nina emerged. Gone were her jeans and sweatshirt. She was back in her best miniskirt and tights, and the carefully polished Doc Martens. From her ears and wrists hung earrings and bracelets. Monica recognised some of them as hers.

The adults passed a silent look among themselves as Nina made straight for the boys. But she was only halfway there when Sam came hurrying out of the house, her walk stiff with self-consciousness. For she too had discarded her usual untidy clothes, and now had on almost exactly the same outfit as Nina.

Her face looked different too. Her eyes seemed bigger and the colour of her lips had changed.

Make-up! Monica observed to herself. I'd better lock our room from now on.

Nina glanced over her shoulder, and quickened her pace towards Rory. 'Hiya!' she greeted him brightly, ignoring the others.

'Hi,' said Rory. Sam bore down on them quickly and got on the other side of him. 'Where are you off to?' she asked him, trying to give him a pleasant smile and glare at Nina at the same time.

'Down to the barn, to say hello to Shera.' Rory felt decidedly uncomfortable being the centre of such dazzling attention. Hoppy smirked, and Anto looked as though he wanted to say something. But he didn't.

'I'll come with you,' Sam and Nina both announced to him at the same time, and each grabbed an arm.

'Maybe we should go indoors before the sparks start flying,' Joe suggested quietly to the other adults.

'Wait. Here's Jenny with Shera now,' said Garry.

The shrubs parted and Jenny led Shera into the yard. Rory immediately broke away from the two girls and hurried forward. But he slowed when a middle-aged man with steel-rimmed glasses, and dressed in an old blue suit, appeared behind the horse.

'Who's that?' Rory whispered to Jenny.

'The vet,' she whispered back.

'Vet!' Rory echoed. 'Is Shera sick?' The vet heard this and came forward, smiling.

'You must be the young man who owns Shera?' he said.

Rory nodded, with a slightly hostile frown.

'Well,' the vet went on, 'I'm happy to tell you she isn't sick. Far from it. She's in great shape. Isn't she, Jenny?'

He and Jenny grinned as if they were sharing a big secret.

'I think I'll leave you to tell him the good news,' the vet winked at her. 'I'll be back in a week or so just to keep an eye on her. Bye now.'

He waved as he walked over to his car, which was parked at the side of the yard.

Sam and Nina came over to gather around Shera. 'What's going on?' Sam demanded.

Hoppy, Anto, and the adults moved in to form a circle around Shera and Jenny, waiting for her to speak. Jenny stroked the horse's neck and looked at them all with a dramatic expression.

'Come on!' Rory urged her impatiently. 'Tell us!'

'Shera's going to have a baby!' Jenny announced.

Rory was dumbfounded. 'What? She's in foal!'

The girls were wide-eyed. Rory stared open-mouthed at Shera.

Scrapper was baffled too. 'Pregnant? But how?'

Rory's face slowly lit up. 'Sir Gert! Sir Gert's the father!'

'It must've been when we left them alone at the ruined house,' said Sam.

Rory stared at Shera. 'Shera! You shameless old wagon!'

Shera snorted haughtily.

'We can call the baby horse Sir Gert too!' Jenny enthused. 'That way it'll be like he's come back to life!'

'What makes you so sure it'll be a he?' Nina objected.

'That's a good one, all right!' Scrapper chuckled, and slapped Rory on the back. Then something occurred to him. 'Hang on. If we're gonna have the son – or daughter – of a famous racehorse in the family, we'd better keep it real quiet. We've had enough dramatics just trying to hang onto old Shera there.'

'Don't worry,' Monica promised him. 'It'll be the best kept secret of all time. We don't want any more kidnappings!'

Everybody stroked and patted Shera, chuckling in amazement at this unexpected turn of events. Then Garry suggested the adults should celebrate with a drink, and they began drifting back to the house.

Nina sidled up to Rory. 'Like to come up and have a look at my room? It's all fixed up really nice now. Cosy.'

On the other side of Shera, Sam's face reddened. But in front of Jenny and the other two boys, she hadn't the courage to say anything. Even if she could think of something to say.

Rory glanced across at Sam. Dressed up and made up the way she was, she looked different. An awful lot more grown up. He looked at

Shera, then at Nina. 'I was going to do a bit of grooming on Shera,' he mumbled.

'Jenny can do that,' Nina told him, and took his arm insistently.

Uncertain, Rory resisted her pull and looked at Shera again. The horse snorted and waved her head in the air, almost as if to say, Go on, eejit!

'Okay,' Rory agreed, embarrassed. 'But just for ten minutes.'

Nina gave Sam a smile of victory as she led Rory off towards the house. Sam watched them, tight-faced, and was about to turn away when Anto stepped up to her and held something out.

'Brought you this,' he mumbled to her, holding out a cassette tape. 'It's Guns 'n Roses' latest. Don't suppose you can get them out here.'

Sam looked at him, slightly taken aback, and confused. 'For me? Thanks.' She took the tape and hesitated for a moment, thinking. Then her face changed. 'Why don't we go and listen to it?' she suggested.

Anto gave her an awkward silent nod and followed her to the house, avoiding Hoppy's smirking stare on the way.

The adults, seated around the table near the farmhouse door, suppressed knowing smiles as first Nina and Rory, then Sam and Anto, hurried past them, eyes averted.

'Well,' Garry said. 'That all seems to be working itself out nicely.'

'Hmmph!' Ma commented darkly, and plonked her handbag on her lap. 'Rory's still a bit too young for that sort of thing, if you ask me.'

'At least it's a bit more normal than slobbering over a horse,' Scrapper shot at her.

Monica came out with an open bottle of wine and glasses on a tray. Joe jumped at the opportunity to change the delicate subject.

'Well!' Garry said expansively as he lifted a full glass. 'A toast to the reincarnation of Sir Gert!'

But Jenny and Hoppy, left standing in the yard with Shera, weren't exactly sharing the mood of celebration. Jenny stroked the horse protectively, disgusted at the way the others had walked off.

'What do you think of all this boyfriend-girlfriend stuff?' she asked Hoppy.

Hoppy pulled a face. 'No time for it. Strictly for saps.'

Jenny flashed him a warm look. Here was someone of her own mind. Without noticing it herself, she moved closer to him. 'Will we take Shera back to the barn?'

Hoppy shrugged. 'Sure.'

They turned Shera around and led her back into the scrubwood.

'When's your operation?' Jenny asked him on the way. Hoppy told her. 'Great!' she said. 'Then you'll be all fixed up.'

Hoppy shook his head and explained what the doctor had said. 'No weight training,' he said glumly. 'I'll be an undersized runt for the rest of my life.'

'But you can do something else,' she encouraged him the same way Rory had. 'You just have to find the right thing.'

'What?' he asked, unconvinced.

Jenny looked him up and down. 'Well, you could be a jockey. You've got the perfect build for it.'

'Me? A jockey?' Hoppy was incredulous. But his face slowly brightened as he turned the idea over in his mind.

'Sure? Why not? You could start by getting a job as a stable hand when you leave school. That's what I'm going to do.'

'But I don't know anything about horses,' Hoppy objected.

'I'll teach you,' Jenny offered brightly. 'I've been reading all about it for years.'

Hoppy stared at Shera. Images of him thundering past the winning post on Son of Sir Gert were already taking shape in his mind. He could hear the crowds roaring.

'Okay,' he agreed. 'When do we start?'

'Right now,' said Jenny.

And they hurried Shera on to the barn.